Fran[illegible] a b[illegible] programmes [illegible]tional lieracy. She also co[illegible] [illegible]ontinuing Professional Development [illegible] Course Director of Personal Development Programmes at City University.

INTELLIGENT EMOTION

FRANCES WILKS

Published in the United Kingdom in 1999 by
Arrow Books

1 3 5 7 9 10 8 6 4 2

Arrow Books
The Random House Group Limited
20 Vauxhall Bridge Road, London, SW1V 2SA

Random House Australia (Pty) Limited
20 Alfred Street, Milsons Point, Sydney,
New South Wales 2061, Australia

Random House New Zealand Limited
18 Poland Road, Glenfield
Auckland 10, New Zealand

Random House South Africa (Pty) Limited
Endulini, 5a Jubilee Road, Parktown 2193, South Africa

The Random House Group Limited Reg. No. 954009

www.randomhouse.co.uk

A CIP catalogue record for this book
is available from the British Library

Papers used by Random House are natural,
recyclable products made from wood grown in sustainable forests.
The manufacturing processes conform to the environmental
regulations of the country of origin

Printed and bound in Norway by
AIT Trondheim AS

ISBN 0 09 927153 2

To my nieces, Harriet and Alexandra,
with the hope that their generation will see
the full flowering of an emotionally intelligent world

'But mine were not the wings for such a flight
Yet, as I wished, the truth I wished for came
Cleaving my mind in a great flash of light.

Here my powers rest from their high fantasy,
But already I could feel my being turned –
Instinct and intellect balanced equally

As in a wheel whose motion nothing jars
By the love that moves the sun and the other stars.'

Dante, Paradiso, *Divine Comedy*

Acknowledgements

I would like to acknowledge all the people who have helped me in so many ways in the preparation of this book. Especially Hilary Barnard, Cara Denman, Michèle Deverall, Jessica Duxbury, Jan Edwards-Treloar, Jackie Herald, Clare Mackie, Sue and Charles Marshall, Sarah Matheson, Santo and Allyson Volpe, Lucy Smith, Austen Wilks. I would also like to thank my friend and colleague, Caroline Leigh, for first bringing the subject of emotional intelligence to my notice and for her continued support.

To my other colleagues at City University, I offer my grateful thanks for their encouragement and support. They are: Jennifer Bailey, Maggie Bankart, Anne Brockbank, Julia Carter, Judy Early, Judith Fiennes, Chris Haines, Yvonne Hillier, Jas Kaur, Phil Leahy, Andrew Lewis, Maria Luca-Stolpin, Gabriella Pollard, Denise Stanley, Sylvia Tyler. I would like to acknowledge the contribution my colleagues from the world of psychotherapy have made in discussions over the years: Em Farrell, Heather Formaini, Jenny Goodman, Brett Kahr, Derek Linker, June Roberts, David Smith, Ernesto Spinelli, Emmy van Deurzen. I would also like to thank Neasa Mac Erlane of the *Observer*, the occasional queries for her 'How to deal with . . .' column stimulated my thinking in a different way.

A chance meeting on the Gatwick Express led to my acquisition of that most valuable commodity – a literary agent – and I would like to thank Jane Gregory and Lisanne Radice, of Gregory and Radice, for their insight and input. Through them I met my editor at Heinemann, Maria Rejt, for whose sensitive but incisive editing I am most grateful. And I would like to thank Clare Calder for her help in the final stages of the editing process.

To my patients, clients and students, I am much indebted. Although aspects of some of them, and indeed of myself, are reflected in the case histories, none of them is a specific person. They are all fragments of my imagination but were inspired by the transformations I have been privileged to witness.

Finally, my most profound thanks must go to the psyche, the true author of this book, and perhaps of all books, whose dictation I have only been able to write down in part.

Contents

Introduction: The Power of Emotions 1

Part One: A Right Frame of Mind
Chapter 1: Emotional Literacy 9
Chapter 2: The Relationship Between Reason and Emotion 16
Chapter 3: Ways of Learning from Emotions 23
Chapter 4: Men Think, Women Feel – The Venus and Mars Myth Exposed 31
Chapter 5: Developing the Inner Family 39
Chapter 6: How to be your own Emotional Mentor 47

Part Two: Heart of the Matter
Chapter 7: Aggression 63
Chapter 8: Anger 74
Chapter 9: Anxiety 87
Chapter 10: Boredom 99
Chapter 11: Depression 114
Chapter 12: Envy 127
Chapter 13: Fear 140
Chapter 14: Grief 153
Chapter 15: Guilt 165
Chapter 16: Hate 178
Chapter 17: Hope 191
Chapter 18: Loneliness 202
Chapter 19: Love 214
Chapter 20: Pride 228
Chapter 21: Rejection 241

Epilogue: The Cultivation of Joy 255
Bibliography 263
References for Chapter Quotations 267

INTELLIGENT EMOTION

Introduction

The Power of Emotions

'The road to excess leads to the palace of wisdom.'
William Blake

A DEFINING MOMENT

On one of the last days of summer, 31 August 1997, Diana, Princess of Wales, died in a car crash in a Parisian tunnel. Her death, and the circumstances around it, released a flood of emotions which were truly global. During her sixteen years of life in the public eye, she had become perhaps the most famous person in the world. An ordinary woman, of average ability, had become extraordinary, tragic, archetypal. And her premature death ensured that her image would become frozen in time, her beauty untouched, her youth unchallenged. Who was she and why was she important?

Few of us had personally met her, let alone known her. In many ways, she was a media creation, whose glittering image and unfolding story had entertained, and occasionally infuriated, us. We didn't know who she really was and yet many people said that they had grieved more for her than for a member of their own family. People used the emotions aroused in Diana Week in a variety of ways, both positive and negative. First of all, there was the straightforward expression of mourning. Most bereavements have some edge of ambivalence about them, some guilt or anger, perhaps. We could feel pure grief for Diana because we didn't truly know her. Unhealed sorrows could be expressed, unfinished mourning completed through the transference of individual feelings on to her.

The initial grief and shock started to shift quite noticeably through the week. It became overlaid with an anger towards the Royal Family – who will forget the 'Show Us You Care Ma'am' headline? – and an intense amnesia. People, and journalists in particular, simply forget the more negative aspects of Diana's personality. In death, she was deified and there was a collective hunting for a scapegoat. First it was the photographers who had been pursuing her. Then it was the monarchy. The flowers which had spontaneously piled up outside the royal palaces of London took on more complex messages. Besides expressing grief they became a subversive form of mass protest against the aloof, seemingly isolated, attitude of the House of Windsor. The Queen wilted visibly in the face of the threat.

There was a darker side to Diana Week. Because so many people were suddenly feeling long-suppressed emotions, there was an assumption that everybody was feeling the same way, too. People who hadn't shared the general *Zeitgeist* said later, rather quietly, that they had been frightened to speak out against what they saw as a form of mass hysteria. They made the point that Diana had not been that popular and she was now suddenly and hypocritically elevated to sainthood. During this time everything was seen in black or white, as good or bad. Diana Week was a very total occurrence and some people experienced it as a form of emotional blackmail.

Her life had had many elements of a fairy tale. First the marriage to a crown prince, then the discovery of 'the third person in the marriage', the 'wicked witch', Camilla. Princess Diana was very beautiful and devoted to good causes despite having her heart broken. After much suffering she finally met another prince from a different sort of kingdom who promised to rescue her. Before he could, however, both died and were taken to live in the Land of Eternal Youth. Thirty-six is an interesting age at which to die. It is around the time that we enter into the second half of life. Death and ageing increasingly become realities and the fantasy world of fairy tales has to be left behind. If Diana had survived into old age, she would have had to change emotionally as well as physically. She would have had to let go the projections of youth and beauty – ultimately of soul – onto her. Projections give us so much power that it is very hard to hand them back and there is little doubt that it would have been hard for her to have done so.

There are strong parallels with Marilyn Monroe. They were both thirty-six when they died, vulnerable, beautiful, equally attractive to both men and women, of international superstar fame, adored by millions and yet emotionally intensely needy. They had each tried various forms of therapy and had had a series of failed relationships. Both, perhaps unconsciously, had invited the projections of millions of people onto them. Their sudden night-time deaths, explainable in terms of suicide and accident, have both been seen in terms of conspiracy and murder. In fact the complete truth about either of their deaths are mysteries that may never be revealed.

It may be partly because we cannot let them die. They were both icons, or archetypes, and they reflected the parts of ourselves that we could not see or own. Their stories have to run and run because they still have meaning for us. We both loved and hated them because we don't yet see our own glory or our own weakness. Only by understanding that and acknowledging it in our own lives will they be allowed to really die. Diana's death was a defining moment in our collective consciousness because it showed the powerful nature of emotion. It will not be complete without a withdrawal of our projections onto her. Only then will she rest in peace.

EMOTIONAL TRANSFORMATION

If any event could have underscored the need for emotional literacy, it was this one. Diana Week allowed and encouraged emotion to break through but it also demonstrated the need to understand what lay behind those feelings. Emotional literacy requires a marriage of feeling and reason. It's perhaps one of the most important and exciting projects now facing us. Just as human beings learnt to read and to count, so we can become literate about our emotions. It requires honesty – learning to name our emotions, feel them fully, reflect on what they're telling us, discover the events that have evoked them. In this way we can move flexibly through our surface feelings to find their hidden meanings. One emotion often masks another. For example, a raging man may be denying a fear that he has hidden since childhood. Uncovering that fear and working with it may give him the opportunity to transform the energy of his anger and fear into useful passion.

If we confront what we're feeling, it releases us from being stuck in it. It becomes a visitor who is passing through. As we learn to read our emotions and work with the self-knowledge which is their gift, our feelings transform from autocrats to friends. A space is opened up to feel a wider range of emotions which gives life greater depth and meaning. All our lives are shaped by emotions. We feel them passionately and honestly as children but later, as adults, the early clarity is usually lost. Only on reflection can we see what our emotional patterns really are. This understanding gives us the choice to avoid repeating negative patterns and develop positive ones which will support our growth.

Our emotions are very intelligent – it is up to us to take hold of that intelligence and use it fruitfully. Emotions are the dynamic facilitators of life. Misunderstood, they bring havoc and pain. And, as emotions can 'jump' from one person to another, emotional literacy is perhaps vital for the development of a more advanced and increasingly global society. Emotions are like an internal weather system and emotional literacy is a bit like weather forecasting. Just as it's useful to know there's likely to be a hurricane or a sharp frost in the outer world, so if we know an emotional storm is on the way, we can take preventive measures to lessen the damage caused by it.

The benefits of emotional literacy are considerable in both the private and public spheres. We don't make a knee-jerk response to an explosive situation. We can take a little more time and work out a considered response to it. Things which would have made us unquestioningly angry or sad, for example, can be evaluated without the need for an impulsive reaction. Employers, too, are fast recognising that emotionally intelligent people are a great asset. They can manage both themselves and others more effectively as well as being better team workers. In our personal lives, too, emotional literacy makes possible more satisfying and intimate relationships. This book will help you to:

- understand and distinguish between fifteen major emotional states
- work with the roots and triggers which underlie each emotion
- move beyond the emotion and allow it to bring change into your life
- understand the rational and intelligent basis for emotion
- become your own emotional mentor

What this book will not do is to make you happy. But it will make possible a form of happiness which comes from inside rather than outside. We all fantasise about happiness that comes from outside. At various times these fantasies range from a bar of chocolate to winning the lottery, falling in love, getting a brilliant job, gaining a place at university, or becoming rich and famous. Whatever the event is, we imagine that it will fill our cup with joy and make us very happy. And often it does, but have you noticed how short-lived the pleasure is? One bar of chocolate either leads to guilt or to another bar, we discover that money is important but not everything, new jobs and new relationships go through their honeymoon period and come out the other side into hard work.

Outer events cannot make us content for long. By contrast, inner emotional attitudes can make us profoundly and unshakeably happy. There is a great joy in being able to feel our emotions but not be totally taken over by them. This is a state of grace and we can then walk amid the wonders and dangers of the world, feeling love, anger, depression and all the rest but our thoughts are no longer destructive. Most of the emotions described in this book are the so-called negative ones, such as guilt, anger, anxiety, fear and hate. As we shall see, repressing them is ultimately more miserable than feeling them. They have to be faced but not given the status of gods. Even though they are still uncomfortable, the work of becoming emotionally literate transforms them from monsters into friends.

It is through our emotions that we are able to develop the as yet unseen sides of ourselves. Only by feeling does anything really shift inside us although it may be preceded, and accompanied, by much rational analysis. Learning to value and work with our emotions means that we can ultimately give birth to ourselves as whole (and healed) human beings. This book is intended to be a guide in this process. The first part, A Right Frame of Mind, explores the relationship between reason and emotion, and looks at ways in which we can see them as equally valuable. The second part, Heart of the Matter, looks at each emotion in depth. Read the first part for an overview and then use the second part as and when you are touched by a particular feeling. In this process you are encouraged to be your own mentor rather than your own therapist. It is for this reason that this is less a self-help book and more a *self-cultivation* book. Each emotion is a starting place for personal growth but care is also needed – because this book is emphatically not a substitute for therapy. The third and final part of the book looks at the relationship between inner joy and outer happiness and looks at ways we may cultivate flow.

The time is right for such work. Daniel Goleman's widely acclaimed bestseller, *Emotional Intelligence*, showed us *why* emotional literacy is important and described its role in bringing about happier families, more viable businesses, better careers and the development of a more stable society. This book attempts to show us *how* to be emotionally literate.

Emotions will lead us and light the way. They are the transformational fire of the soul. Emotions throw challenges at us which are often experienced as a form of 'being under fire'. A state of grace is realised when we can live with the fiery heat of these intense passions and not be burnt by them. Emotional literacy will not bring about utopia but it may bring about a situation where there is less fear and more joy. As we find that we no longer react with destructive thoughts to our painful emotions, the prophetic words of the poet, Rainer Maria Rilke, may come true:

> 'Perhaps all the dragons in our lives are but princesses that are waiting to see us act just once with beauty and courage. Perhaps everything terrible is, in its deepest essence, something helpless that needs our help.'

PART ONE

A RIGHT FRAME OF MIND

'Only connect the prose and the passion, and both will be seen at its height. Live in fragments no longer. Only connect, and the beast and the monk, robbed of the isolation that is life to either, will die.' E. M. Forster, *Howard's End*

1

Emotional Literacy

WHY IS EMOTIONAL LITERACY IMPORTANT?

A man comes into his office one morning. He has just had a major fight with his wife who has threatened to leave him if he doesn't 'open up emotionally'. He has reacted to this with extreme fear (which he has immediately suppressed because he can't stand the feeling of vulnerability that fear brings). He has put a bubblingly angry crust over this painful wound and come to work ready to do battle with anyone he encounters. He has already had cross words with another driver (who was so upset at being abused that she may go on to have an accident) and with the carpark attendant before he actually arrives in his office.

He continues the day aggressively finding fault with the people who work for him. He is sarcastic and domineering and they start to feel disempowered and incompetent. Their work suffers as a consequence and so the angry manager doesn't get the most out of the people who work for him. By lunchtime people are ready to kill him – metaphorically if not actually. When he gets home that evening, he finds that his wife has made him a special meal. She became frightened at the thought of losing him because she knows she is as unable to cope alone as he fears he is. The quarrel is patched up over a bottle of champagne and sex.

We can see the knock-on effects of the man's inability to deal with his emotions in making other people around him unhappy, unproductive and possibly dangerous. But the interesting thing is the cause of the incident. The man was upset at the thought of his wife leaving him but couldn't cope with it. He was emotionally illiterate but so was she. In the first place she demanded of him an emotional response when he clearly wasn't able to make one. She was possibly projecting her own need for emotional openness onto him. Because she didn't feel comfortable with her own emotions, she demanded that he produce an emotionally open response. And then she added blackmail to her demand. Blackmail is never part of an emotionally literate person's armoury. Emotional responses have to be genuine, they may be asked for, but they can never be demanded by threats. This is an abuse of power. The reconciliation scene is a fake. Nothing has, in fact, been reconciled. Fear has led both parties in the marriage back to the status quo but nothing has moved on.

The emotionally literate response on the part of the man would have been to say to her that he heard her request for emotional openness but that he was not able to comply at the moment for his own reasons. He heard her desperation but he cannot be blackmailed into talking about his feelings because it suits her. He can take some time to himself on the way to work (after calling to say he will be half an hour late) to work out what has happened and process his own emotions. He will then arrive at work (without having upset any other drivers or the carpark attendant) ready to work with his colleagues, to manage and motivate them successfully. They will probably reward him with some very efficient work.

When he comes home that evening, his wife may have had the opportunity to do her own emotional work. As they talk they will probably find they can speak of quite painful things and receive support rather than coldness in return. They can look at their fear, their anger and their boredom and see that they are not exclusively caused by the other person's behaviour. In fact they have their roots in each person's early life and their attitudes. Realising that we are to some degree responsible for our feelings takes the burden off the partner. Quite spontaneously they may find themselves opening a bottle of wine and going to bed but it will be as a result of the discussion they have had and not as a 'set-piece' attempt at reconciliation. Both will have confronted their fears about the other leaving and have decided that, although they really don't want that to happen, both of them could cope on their own.

Which outcome would you choose? If you want the former, this book is emphatically not for you. If you would like the latter, or something similar, then read on. This is a route to emotional literacy. It means learning to read emotions just as we can read words. Another term for it is emotional intelligence. Emotional literacy is applied emotional intelligence and these terms, although not synonymous, amount to much the same thing in practice. We can learn to be intelligent about our emotions and to apply that intelligence to the situations of our daily life. It requires knowledge and the development of skill through practice to achieve mastery. Like learning a foreign language, this won't happen all at once. Any new skill requires practice and patience. The set-backs on the journey are an essential part of the learning process.

WHAT IS EMOTIONAL INTELLIGENCE?

It has been realised that there's more to success (either in the personal or business sphere) than merely academic intelligence, or IQ as it has been called. Intelligence as a concept has been re-invented to include emotional skills rather than the old categories of linguistic, mathematical and logic abilities that used to previously define it. Daniel Goleman, in his book *Emotional Intelligence*, lists five categories of emotional intelligence. These key areas are:

- *Knowing one's emotions*

This is the ability to recognise feelings when they happen and not put off feelings if they are inconvenient. It's important to be able to say 'I'm feeling envy' even though it may be uncomfortable to admit it. It may not fit my view of myself to be envious. And even when we can't put a precise label immediately on an emotion, we need to know that we are in an emotional state and can make allowances for our decisions and maybe act with a degree of extra caution. For example if a person is angry, it is important that she can learn to say to herself 'I'm angry' rather than suppressing it and taking a painkiller for a headache that's mysteriously appeared.

- *Managing emotions*

This relates to the ability to handle uncomfortable emotions once we've accepted we're feeling them. A lot of this work is about developing an 'inner mothering' mode and learning to soothe ourselves when things seem difficult. A good manager knows when to push her team on to greater heights and when to congratulate them on what they've achieved. For example, when I'm depressed, I manage it by not beating myself up about it but by switching to a caring mode. I might give myself a hot bath, a good book, a nice meal, or arrange a massage or decide to give myself the pleasure of planning my next holiday. Whatever it takes to make me feel I care about myself and value myself.

- *Motivating oneself*

The word emotion and the word motivation come from the same Latin root *movere*, to move. It's no surprise, therefore, to find these two concepts linked. Emotions motivate us but they can also disempower us if they are too strong and we allow them to overwhelm us. If I want to get what I decide I want out of life, I will have to develop some emotional self-control. It may require my delaying gratification or stifling my impulsiveness. I can develop ways of mentoring myself which mean that I can put my immediate emotional needs to one side for a time, confident in the knowledge that I will deal with them later. If I can do this I may be able to get into the 'flow' state or zone which enables outstanding performance.

- *Recognising emotions in others*

As I begin to recognise emotions in myself and realise my own emotional weather systems, so I will be able to sense them in others more accurately. This means I can feel with someone rather than just feel about them. It's different from sympathy and when people know that someone is genuinely empathising with them, they don't feel patronised. Recently, a man sent a card to mark a friend's bereavement. Where it said 'with deepest sympathy', he crossed out sympathy and wrote empathy. He had lost someone close to him and knew how it felt. Later his friend remarked how much this small gesture had meant to her. They were in it together and that made her loss more bearable. Although some people appear to be born more naturally empathetic than others, it's an ability we can all develop.

• *Handling relationships*

Relationships which don't merely depend on power and predefined roles, require emotional intelligence. Understanding other people's emotions gives us the ability to motivate them, be effective leaders and to work in successful teams. We can give and take and be spontaneous as the moment requires. Our old rigidities, which were born of fear and anxiety, can dissolve into acceptance of ourselves and others. In family life, emotional literacy is paramount for raising happy and cohesive families. One-to-one relationships, whatever their format, benefit too. Emotional intelligence gives us the ability to have 'grace under fire' and to act with integrity and courage.

I would add a sixth category of emotional intelligence:

• *Transforming emotions*

There are many pragmatic reasons for learning to be emotionally literate but perhaps one stands out more than the others. That is the personal and life-changing transformation that understanding our emotions can bring us. As you read through the sections on specific emotions, you will realise that each emotion has an opposite (sometimes more than one). If you can grasp that opposite, and its meaning for you, as well as the feeling itself, then it is like being able to balance both sides of a see-saw. You will be out of kilter no longer. Transforming depression into useful anger, despair into attitudinal hope, or loneliness into connection with other living beings, dramatically alters the quality of our lives. The effects are potentially far-reaching, as we realise that everything in life is potentially transformative if we can find the key.

SELF-KNOWLEDGE AND FAMILY PATTERNS

There are two further ingredients in emotional intelligence: self-knowledge and an awareness of family patterns. Self-knowledge includes an understanding of how you function emotionally. Do you go through many emotions in the space of a few hours, swinging from despair to hope and back again like a yo-yo? Or do you hunker down into depression or guilt and stay there for days? Do you tend to project your emotions on to other people and try to fix their lives instead of your own? At times we all do all these things but most of us have a basic emotional pattern.

Just as we can have financial capital or intellectual capital, so we can have emotional capital. It constitutes the emotional reserves we have to draw on. We may lock it away in a long-yield deposit account or we may spend our emotional capacity to the limit and end up exhausted and overdrawn. Some of us are more naturally volatile and extravagant than others. What is important is that we find the right mode of expression for ourselves. As we become emotionally literate, we can learn to spend our emotional capital more wisely.

As with other forms of capital, we can inherit emotional capital. Emotional patterns are often passed down through the generations. Some families encourage expression of feelings, some do not. Many families allow their members to express one emotion but not another. A common example of this is when children are permitted to feel depression, for instance, but not anger. Girls and boys may be expected to feel and act differently. Some families carry an inordinate amount of self-destructive rage, for example, which can manifest itself as repeated suicides down the generations. Many families are co-dependent which means that everybody wordlessly accepts the situation, although individually they may find it very painful. Fear of leaving this difficult situation keeps many people emotionally 'at home' long after they've physically left. Television comedies are full of stories in which, for example, middle-aged, successful, married men are terrified of what their mothers think. We find it funny because it's so close to our own experience.

Positive emotional patterns can also be handed down. A capacity for quiet reflection, an ability to relate harmoniously with others, a feeling of faith in the future can be inherited. We don't start equal in this respect. However, if your emotional inheritance was less favourable (as mine was), the work of developing your emotional literacy can lead you eventually to surpass those with more favourable starts. Often those people who haven't had the best parenting go on to develop an excellent inner family which is a source of strength to them long after their original parents have died. If a broken leg is treated in the right way, it will go on to heal so that it's stronger than before. In the same way our emotional brokenness can be integrated into a stronger and deeper personality. The trick is to allow our feelings to transform us.

In the husband and wife story quoted at the beginning of this chapter, their work of emotional transformation could lead them both to have a happier marriage but also to become more developed and creative individuals. Because most of our culture is built on emotional co-dependence, it is often very hard for us to strike out on our own. Usually it's not until we have to that we do. Being born into an emotionally difficult or fractured family can then be seen as an advantage because it can set us on the road of emotional literacy all the sooner.

2

The Relationship Between Reason and Emotion

IN THE LIGHT OF REASON ALONE – AN IDEA WHOSE TIME HAS GONE?

This chapter looks at the crucial relationship between emotion and reason. Up to now it has been a struggle for supremacy with one or the other attempting to rule. In the Western world reason has been elevated and emotion downgraded. But recent biological discoveries point to the need to integrate reason and emotion. Could this relationship now become one of equals celebrating their differences and working together?

Science fiction often illuminates contemporary concerns. Perhaps we can see things in sharper definition if they are projected into the future or onto another world. The television series, *Star Trek*, which has run over thirty years in various formats, is a case in point. Mr Spock, in the original series, acted only on logical principles, never allowing feeling a role in his deliberations. In *Star Trek: The Next Generation*, this idea is taken up by another character, the sentient computer, Data. Data is an android who longs to have feelings. He spends a lot of time asking his fellow crew mates what emotions feel like. He can calculate and act with incredible speed and logic but, in a sense, this is not enough for him. A computer chip which will give him emotions has been developed. The first time it is inserted into his positronic circuitry it causes him to behave so uncontrollably that it has to be removed. Much later on Data comes to believe that he has developed enough to be able to handle the complexities of both logic and passion for the chip to be re-implanted. Although the emotion chip floods Data with powerful and uncomfortable emotions, it cannot be removed this time because it has fused with his own circuits. An integration between reason and emotion cannot now be avoided.

In a way this is a little parable illustrating the importance of self-development for the wise handling of emotion. Interestingly the rational system is seen here as the more primitive and mechanical, the emotional system, more complex and mature. This is, of course, a reversal of our normal viewpoint. Emotions are usually downgraded and seen as inferior to reason and thought. 'You're so emotional' and 'it isn't rational' are often said dismissively. This is primarily a Western and European stance and one that has held sway since the eighteenth century. It was allied to the development of a science which thought that logic alone was the basis for understanding the laws of the universe. Emotion simply got in the way and was a distracting nuisance. But this view hasn't always prevailed, even in cultures which have cherished reason.

Ancient Greek civilisation saw human beings as having two minds. They noticed a dichotomy between the head and the heart, the mind and the soul, but saw neither as superior to the other. Although they praised reason, logic and empirical understanding, they also revered the intuitive, aesthetic and imaginative forms of intelligence. The civilisation of Greece is remembered today not only for its outstanding contribution to science and philosophy but also for its development of drama, art and mythology. They believed that the study of natural phenomena (the basis of science as we know it) satisfied not only the intellect but also the soul and the heart.

IN TWO MINDS

The notion of two minds has continued as an important theme in the history of the relationship between reason and emotion. Both the great depth psychologists, Freud and Jung, made contributions to the ongoing debate. And the insights of modern biology deepen our understanding of the way the two minds work.

The French philosopher René Descartes's famous dictum, 'I think, therefore, I am', displays a valuation of the rational faculty above any other form of intelligence. The eighteenth century in France was called the age of enlightenment, when it was thought that man could and should live in the light of pure reason alone. Until recently, culture has generally reflected this view.

The founder of psychoanalysis, Sigmund Freud, continued the excessive valuation of reason while describing some other less controlled mental and emotional processes which human beings are subject to. Freud saw unconscious desires and repressed wishes as breaking through the ordered fabric of rationality. He thought that there were two mental systems in operation which he called the primary and the secondary process. They had very different characteristics and very different modes of expression. The primary process he saw as irrational, and purely pleasure-seeking. The secondary process was logical, ordered and in contact with reality. The two processes roughly correspond to the ego and the id. He believed that the primary process must give way to the secondary by the time of puberty. Thus Freud perpetuated the idea that emotion, in its broadest sense, must subjugate itself to rational thought. His great contribution, however, was to show that the power of the shadow-side of reason was far greater than anyone had thought.

Freud's primary and secondary processes

Primary process	Secondary process
Infantile, primitive	Mature, adult
Emotional, irrational,	Logical, rational
Timeless, chaotic	Linear, ordered
Concerned with pleasure	Concerned with reality
Corresponding to the id	Corresponding to the ego

Carl Gustav Jung, on the other hand, saw that thought and feeling both had a rational basis. Feelings were perfectly reasonable provided we understood their logic. For him, the greater division was between judgement (thinking and feeling) and perception (intuiting and sensing). Jung defined perception as a way of being able to apprehend the world without prejudice (that is pre-judgement). Both intuition and sensation are naive faculties. Intuition sees the invisible world and sensation the visible world. Jung thought that we usually operated in one of the four functions through preference but that, in order to be whole human beings, we needed to be able to make use of them all. Anyone who has done a Myers-Briggs test will know which their predominant function is. What is usually not so well recognised is the need to develop the other functions so that all four can act in some sort of harmony.

So Jung's contribution is important for two reasons: the elevation of feeling to be on a par with thinking and the recognition of the need for integration of all four functions.

The four functions of the psyche according to Jung

Rational functions:	Irrational functions:
Judgement	Perception
Thinking	Intuition
Feeling	Sensation

THE CONTRIBUTION OF BIOLOGY

Modern science has tended to support and develop the idea of two minds. Fairly recent research reveals that the two halves of the brain operate in very different ways. The left side controls verbal, analytical, rational, conceptual and linear activities. The right side deals with non-verbal, imaginative, spatial, intuitive, perceptive functions. The functions cross over in terms of controlling the sides of the body. The left side controls the right side of the body, which is the dominant side in most people, as most people are right-handed. In teaching people to draw accurately, the dominant left-brained mode has to be sacrificed to the more fluid right-brained way of seeing things.

Further light has been shed on the relationship by research into two specific areas of the brain: the amygdala and the neocortex. The amygdala, or emotional brain, is more primitive whereas the neocortex, or rational brain, is a relative newcomer in evolutionary terms and is only found in mammals. (It is particularly large and well-developed in human beings.) The amygdala seems to act as some sort of psychological sentinel and is responsible for our impulsive and occasionally life-saving actions. When we flare up in anger or run away from a raging bull, the amygdala is working on our behalf. The neocortex, on the other hand, enables us to have feelings about feelings, to be able to sustain relationships and to reflect on what is going on emotionally.

If the amygdala acts without the neocortex then we may end up out of control and, in an extreme case, killing someone. But if the neocortex acts without the amygdala's passion, then life becomes colourless. Moreover, vital emotional memories are stored in the amygdala, and these actually aid the process of decision-making. In a sense, emotional memories enable us to imagine what would happen if such-and-such occurred. The corresponding emotional feeling, be it pleasurable or painful, gives us a foretaste of the proposed activity. Thus, paradoxically, emotions are the basis of rational action.

ONLY CONNECT – A CREATIVE RECONCILIATION OF THE TWO MINDS

The results of this new biological research stress the importance of co-operation and interdependence between reason and emotion. As Daniel Goleman in *Emotional Intelligence* expresses it:

> 'The old paradigm held an ideal of reason freed from the pull of emotion. The new paradigm urges us to harmonise head and heart.'

Artists have always known the importance of this. Creative endeavour has to combine the discipline and mastery of the left brain with the passion and intuition of the right brain. But because our culture has favoured logic over passion, it is hard for those of us who are not artists to fully accept and work with this. But how can we connect the two minds? Obviously, the roulette wheel of genetic inheritance gives some of us better natural connections than others at the cellular level. But there is strong evidence to suggest that these kinds of connections can be learned.

The first thing is to acknowledge that there are two ways of looking at anything, the rational and the emotional. The second thing to hold neither way as superior to the other. When we favour one way above another, the repressed function usually becomes unconscious. As is more fully described in the specific chapters on the emotional states themselves, whatever is repressed usually returns to haunt us in another form. If we repress thought and downgrade it, then our emotions become out of hand, dangerous and chaotic. Our ability to think will be stunted and will be confined to making rationalisations of our actions. If you want to do something badly enough, you will always find a logic for it somewhere. If we repress emotion, then our thoughts become dry and colourless. We will lack motivation and imagination as well as the inspiration to take the next logical steps. Our feelings will go underground, only to come up in another, often disguised, location where they are far harder to deal with.

By now, you probably have a sense of whether you favour thinking or feeling. If you have done a psychometric test, you may well know. The important thing is to try to work with the side of you that you don't normally favour. For example, if you are rationally oriented, try to feel those little flutterings of emotion that you normally overlook. Try to still the chatter of words and be receptive to what your emotional mind and body are telling you. Or, if you are more emotionally oriented, try to think logically about what is going on. Work out why you are feeling the way you do. Thinking about feelings doesn't destroy them, as some people fear it will. In fact, it deepens their range and profundity. As someone remarked to me in surprise, 'I'm finding that my emotions are in fact entirely reasonable, their logic is intelligible provided I understand and respect their language.'

Another way to increase the connections between the two minds is to work with the emotions themselves. They make us feel so much that we have to start thinking. Then we can begin to recognise that feeling and thinking are interactive systems, each feeding the other. In many ways, though not all, emotions are actually created by our thoughts. Working with the emotions themselves reveals the deepest levels of our thoughts and offers us a chance to revise assumptions that are no longer valid or useful. The real problem, as E. M. Forster so accurately perceived, is the isolation of the thinking prose and the feeling passion. Bringing them together offers new avenues of hope and potential.

3

Ways of Learning from Emotions

HOW CAN WE LEARN FROM EMOTIONS?

Emotions are great teachers but their educational methods are not the conventional classroom ones. They teach us primarily through the experiences of suffering and joy. Suffering brings us up short and opens us to the possibility of seeing things differently. When we suffer the depths of emotional distress, it makes us want to do something to end the pain. This desperation often opens the way to actions which we might previously have been too lazy or diffident to have undertaken. Similarly, the promise of joy is the catalyst for many breakthroughs. We seek happiness not only as a cessation of pain but as an end in itself. Both suffering and joy are great motivators for change. Once our emotions have got our attention and we begin a dialogue with them (which is what this book is about) then they can teach us specific things about our life. They give us important information about:

- what we're thinking (both consciously and unconsciously) about the past, present and future
- our deepest goals and values (even those we've hidden from ourselves)

- our purpose in life – and how we will ultimately define our success

We're often not fully aware of what we're thinking. We just let some things gently slip from our consciousness because they don't fit the picture we have of our life. Perhaps I consciously think that my best friend is a very nice person because I believe I'm nice and I want everyone around me to be nice. Unconsciously I may be envious of her, and so our friendship will not be an authentic one. My envy of her good looks and many talents may lead to my making bitchy remarks and trying to outsmart her in subtle ways. If anyone notices me doing this, then they may conclude that I am envious. Worse still, by not recognising the situation, I am denying myself the creative chance to enhance my self-esteem. This might be through improving my self-image and developing my own talents. I may have to revise past messages when I may have been told that I was 'not a pretty child'. Recognising this will give me the power to shed false and outdated views and then I will begin to see that I am an attractive adult with a vibrant future. So, emotions give us the chance to:

- revise the past
- revitalise the present
- redirect the future

Emotions often show us that our goals and values are different from what we had supposed them to be. Although this is not its only cause, the onset of anxiety can reveal to us that we are not living an authentic life. Anxiety often strikes us in the midst of what looks like a successful and happy time. An example of this is Susan who has just achieved a much longed-for promotion. But the problem is she really wants to do something other than be a director of a firm of chartered accountants. Susan's fundamental values do not lie in the business world. She has reached the pinnacle of her conscious ambition and pleased every member of her family but herself. Achieving this mark of success may plunge her into unaccountable anxiety. She has worked desperately hard to reach the top of the ladder only to find that the ladder is against the wrong wall. Emotional discomfort may be the catalyst to make her move to the right wall for her.

It is always surprising when a person who has achieved a great deal feels that he is not a success when someone else who's done far less may consider herself highly successful. Generally speaking, people have a need to self-actualise, that is, to grow into their fullest potential. In a way, a new-born human being is like an acorn. It is tiny but, given the right soil and weather conditions, its code will cause it to grow into a tree. Some people stunt themselves into privet hedges or thorn bushes when they should be majestic oaks. As each tree is individually coded so each human being has a unique purpose. We can't buy or inherit our purpose, we have to develop into it. Achieving this is the only thing that will give us a feeling of success. Emotions, particularly the more negative ones, tell us when we're off course during our journey. Most aeroplanes are off course for ninety per cent of their journeys but they manage to land in the correct place. Emotions are course correctors and will help us to get to our destination.

WAYS OF KNOWING – HEAD AND HEART

There are different ways of knowing things – with the head and with the heart. We can think logically through something or we can intuitively feel it. We may want to analyse a situation rationally or we may prefer to see it in terms of relationships. Things may unfold in a stately succession or everything may appear to happen to us at once. We may find ourselves bathed in the clear light of Apollonian reason or swept off our feet by a Dionysian orgy of emotion.

As we saw in the last chapter, thinking and feeling can operate as an interactive system. This is the optimum situation and requires very hard work. It brings the tremendous benefit of being able to see things from more than one perspective. This gives us a depth and authority which can be gained in no other way. For instance, a senior manager who can make logical judgements but who is also informed by his or her intuition will be highly effective. Their decisions will be rounded and, most importantly, the people they work with will respect them. They will feel the warmth and reality of a marriage between empathy and analysis.

One way we deal with the problem of reconciling the head and the heart is to give men the head side of the equation to carry, and women the heart side. This is discussed more fully in the next chapter. Men think, women feel – a myth exposed.

Perhaps the way forward is to encourage the development of both head and heart within each individual. Emotions help us to do this because our patterns and our pain are repeated until we understand the message. As a man described it, 'I felt so much that I had to start to think.' The emotional learning in this book is about rationally discovering the reasons why you feel as you do. This is not an overnight task but a lifetime's work. However, the results are so exciting and rewarding that once you start you'll probably want to continue.

The parallel ways of knowing

Head	Heart
Reasonable	Emotional
Thinking	Feeling
Left-brained	Right-brained
Logical	Intuitive
Objective	Subjective
Successive	Simultaneous
Convergent	Divergent
Analytic	Relational
Aggressive	Yielding
Yang	Yin
Apollonian	Dionysian
Masculine	Feminine

When you look at this list, it's important not to think that one form of knowing is superior to the other which will mean that the other is inferior. Almost all of us have a bias towards one, but that means that we must embrace the other. The Chinese symbol for yin and yang stresses interdependence, each part intertwining with and relying on the other. Wholeness comes from recognising that both halves are necessary. By contrast the world of inferiority and superiority, of power and submission, seems sterile.

EMOTIONAL LEARNING

We go through a learning cycle when we experience an emotion. Emotion is triggered by an event which may be highly dramatic or so trivial that it is hardly noticed. The response could be an uncontrollable rage, pangs of grief, a bitter feeling of guilt, the numbness of depression. Or it could be the early stirrings of love, the beginning of hope or a fleeting sensation of joy. Whatever the emotional response, it gives us the possibility of looking at life in a new way and examining some of our assumptions, values and life beliefs. When we have done this, we may modify some of the thinking that has led us to this emotional state. This can then result in fresh attitudes and possibly new behaviour. If we learn the lesson emotion may be showing us, then we can jump off the cycle. If we don't, it tends to repeat itself as a negative feedback loop.

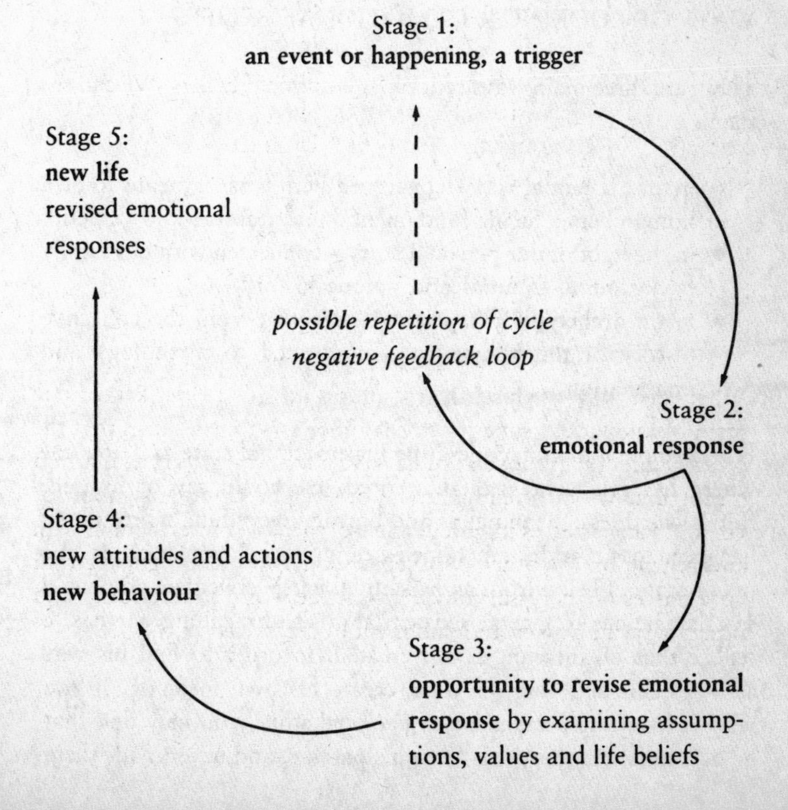

We will always have emotional triggers to contend with and we will always have an emotional response. Stage 3 is really interesting because it's when we have an opportunity to revise our emotional response by looking at our assumptions, values and beliefs about life. If we funk Stage 3 work then we will simply repeat the pattern. But if we do it well, then we will reach Stage 4 which means that we will have new attitudes and actions as a result of our learning. Because our own behaviour is different, then we will call forth different behaviour in others which may make life more delightful. In Stage 5 it can literally seem as if we have been reborn. Life deepens and opens up. Our emotional responses change and those things which would have in the past, perhaps, made us furious or suicidal now only evoke a wry smile. The emotional energy which so consumed our lives can now be put to creative use.

WAYS OF LOOKING AT EMOTIONAL BELIEFS

There are three main ways to look at emotional beliefs. We can see them:

- in an existential way – concerned with what it means to be a human being, facing fundamental uncertainties and anxieties
- in the light of our personal story – connected with our family background, traumas and unique history
- in an archetypal perspective – deriving from the collective history of the human race, connected to mythology and imagination

For example a man may describe his emotional state as being one where he feels depressed and bored. He could say of himself: 'Life's worthless, meaningless and boring. Everything worth doing has been done and I am hopeless anyway.' If you look at this man's state of being from an existential perspective then you could say that he has to face an existential crisis of meaning. He has to realise that all meaning is self-created. In order to find his way through this suffering, he must create his own meaning. If you view it from the perspective of personal story, you may find that he has 'inherited' his goals from his parents, and never made them his own. No wonder he doesn't really want to pursue them! From the archetypal perspective, we might see that this man has never really left home – although he may be living a physically separate life. He may need to go on a symbolic version of the hero's journey and discover the purpose of his life. Only through emotional discomfort will he get out of his armchair and start this work. Going out and finding his true path will most likely lead him to a very exciting and meaningful place.

WHY EMOTIONAL OPPOSITES ARE IMPORTANT

Emotions are a bit like a see-saw, when one side is up, the other side is down. Learning from our emotions gives us a chance to balance the see-saw. The opposite of the emotion felt is usually hidden and it is part of the work of emotional intelligence to find the secret, concealed opposite.

Emotional Opposites

Emotion	**Concealed opposite**
Aggression	Desire for tenderness, intimacy
Anger	Need for power, self-esteem
Anxiety	Longing for meaning, purpose
Boredom	Desire for commitment, real values
Depression	Desire for soul, repressed fear, anger
Envy	Wish for self-improvement, self-esteem
Fear	Suppressed courage and excitement
Grief	Desire for transformation beyond loss
Guilt	Need to shed false image of self
Hate	Need to integrate shadow side
Hope	Wanting to escape despair
Loneliness	Need for intimacy, connection
Love	Wish for self-knowledge and transcendence
Pride	Need for real humility, not humiliation
Rejection	Longing to accept life and become free

Uncovering the opposite makes us bigger and deeper people. As a woman described it: 'I had a dream once where I found my house had many more rooms than I had ever realised. There were rooms for music and rooms for art and just rooms for playing in. In a way it was a metaphor for my emotional journey. I realised that I was on the right track and that emotional intelligence would lead to a larger space to live in – perhaps physically but definitely psychologically.'

The so-called negative emotions aren't truly negative, they contain a hidden positive which is the alchemist's secret gold. Learning to live in the balance between the force of emotion and its opposite means we are no longer one-sided. It opens us to our compassion and our empathy – not only to others, but also to the wounded parts of ourselves.

4

Men Think, Women Feel – The Venus and Mars Myth Exposed

'WHY CAN'T A WOMAN BE MORE LIKE A MAN?'

The question above is posed in one of the songs in the film *My Fair Lady*. The question touches on a raw nerve: if men and women are different, then which is better? Whenever there's a difference, it is very hard to avoid categorising one as superior and the other as inferior. If people passing by in the street were asked 'why can't a woman be more like a man?', then they might reply along these lines:

- because she's different – so why should she be like a man?
- because the more a woman is like a man, the more undermined he will feel, so she has to be feminine to keep him happy.
- she is – but you haven't noticed it because you haven't seen past her obvious sexual characteristics.
- why can't a man be more like a woman?
- some parts of a woman are masculine, some parts of a man are feminine.

- it's a stupid question anyway!

Some people try to deny the differences between the sexes, and some try to minimise their significance. Others see the difference in terms of male/female politics. They challenge the dominance of patriarchal culture which they see as having stressed the differences between men and women in order to control women more effectively. Yet others see that there are differences between the sexes but think that the differences between each individual are more important. They argue against the stereotyped view of men as masculine and women as feminine. There are several different tones of voices in the replies above. The question of gender difference brings up all sorts of emotions such as: love, hate, anger, envy, fear, pride and aggression. How we respond emotionally to this question is just as important as what we rationally think about it.

Until we have reconciled this question to some degree, we will probably feel envious of the other sex for the privileges and benefits we imagine they have. In the past women have tended to envy male freedom and men have tended to envy female reproductive creativity. Of course, the social changes of the last generation have added new twists and considerably complicated our view of the opposite sex. One of the ways we deal with envy is by denigrating the envied person. So if you find a man or woman really speaking disrespectfully and hatefully about the opposite sex as a generality, you may be sure that envy or fear are somewhere in the picture. This might be in the form of 'all men are rapists' or 'all women are sluts'. The fact that some women are sluts and that some men are rapists doesn't mean that they all are. The generalisation is the clue that an emotion is aroused but that the speaker has not yet recognised it consciously.

There may be no cut and dried answer to the question of the existence and importance of gender difference but it nevertheless affects us all. Do the biological and anatomical differences between men and women mean that men and women are fundamentally different in every other way as well? Perhaps nowhere is it more sharply shown than in the rational/emotional split. Men have traditionally been placed on the rational side and women on the emotional side. But is it true or is it a just a convenient way to deal with the tensions between the sexes?

MALE AND FEMALE STEREOTYPES

By stereotyping men as rational and women as emotional, we remove much of the joy which comes out of any encounter between men and women. This doesn't only apply to romantic relationships but also includes friendships, family relationships and business partnerships. To understand a little more about the dynamics of male and female stereotyping, let's eavesdrop on a couple, David and Linda, who are separately talking about their relationship to respective friends. When we first meet them, they are in their twenties and have been together for a year.

Linda is having supper with her close friend, Anna. Linda says, 'I think David's absolutely gorgeous but he has no idea what he's feeling most of the time.' Anna chimes in with 'Well, he's a man, what do you expect? After all men are from Mars.' Linda then replies, 'It is a bit like living with someone from another planet. But at the beginning everything seemed so wonderful – he could read my mind and meet my needs. He was always surprising me with something romantic and always calling me. Now all that's gone. I wonder if he's cooling off. But there doesn't seem to be anyone else. I made a scene the other day because he had forgotten our anniversary. He said – have you got PMT or are you *just* being emotional. Just! I ask you.' Anna then says, 'He's probably wildly out of touch with his real emotions and just projecting them onto you. It's so unreasonable of him to forget an important anniversary and then blame you for making a fuss.' Not really listening to Anna, but musing along on her own thoughts, Linda says, 'But I do love him and when I go to tell him, he seems to shrug it off, and say don't bother me now – I've got enough to worry about with my work right now.'

A few miles away, David is talking to his best friend, Roger, over a pint of beer. Roger is asking about the relationship and how it's going. David says, 'Well, I'm really fond of Linda but there are times when she just can't think straight. The other day I had a really difficult problem to sort out at work. You know the kind of thing?' Roger nods sagely. 'Well, Linda was on at me,' David continues, 'because apparently I'd forgotten some anniversary of our first meeting. She'd had it in mind for weeks. How was I to know? But last month I took her to Paris to show how much she meant to me. Doesn't that count? Do you know I couldn't get it through her head that I did that because I *do* care.' Roger says, in response, 'Women, they're so illogical and manipulative. I don't know how they manage it and, on top of it all, they accuse us of not having emotions. One for the road?'

Probably all of us have had conversations like this at one time or another. The friend's role is to echo and exaggerate what the partners are saying about their experience of the opposite sex. Both Linda and David have got into the pattern of thinking and feeling which stereotypes the behaviour of the other. She says he doesn't care, but he can point to an example of his caring. He says she's illogical but she can think through the development of their relationship. He says she is unreasonable, she says he is not in touch with his emotions. What's the way through? The more they argue about it, the more they will become fixed in these polarised roles. Perhaps the truth is that men and women have the capacity to be both rational and emotional but only if they can see it in themselves as well as in the opposite sex.

THE INNER MALE AND FEMALE

A way of resolving the problem of stereotyping is to see ourselves as having an inner figure, which is the opposite sex to our own. A man then has an inner woman, and a woman, an inner man. The inner woman contains a man's emotional side, the inner man, a woman's rationality. These inner figures are a bit like sub-atomic particles, in that they can't be seen. Their existence can only be inferred from the effect they have on their environment. We may be able to catch a glimpse of our inner figures in the way we behave, particularly in unguarded moments, and in our attitudes and dreams. The outer man and woman are our conscious way of describing ourselves. Linda may say, for example, that she's in touch with her feelings. David prizes the way he can think rationally. But below the level of conscious awareness, Linda's inner man has a tremendous interest in reason and David's inner woman a great deal of feeling. It looks a bit like this:

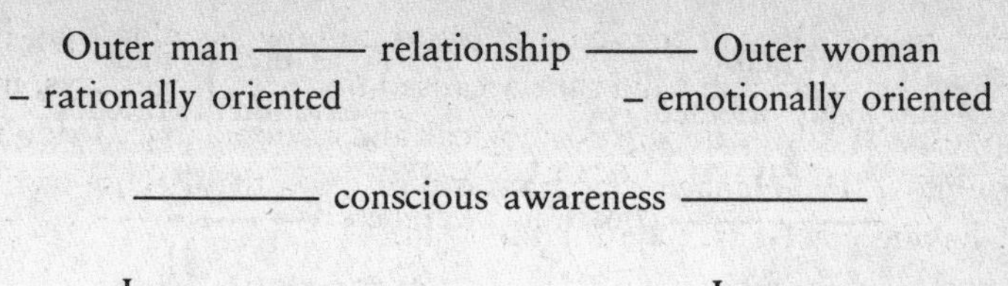

Inner woman – emotionally oriented

Inner man – rationally oriented

A way of seeing conscious awareness is to imagine that it's like the sea. Going underwater makes us realise our limitations; we can no longer walk but must swim, we cannot breathe the water, but must take our own oxygen. Consciousness enables us to do many things which we take for granted. Descending into another element gives us a sharp change of perspective. It's not altogether comfortable which is why we often resist doing it until we are forced to acknowledge there's more going on than we had realised. Often the pain and distress of emotional states can do much to bring this underwater area to our conscious attention.

For much of the time, we experience our inner man or woman much as we would if we had someone living in our house who kept out of sight most of the time. Because we hardly know them, we can't or don't communicate with them and are not aware of them for most of the time. But we can come to resent their presence when we discover that they've used all the hot water, eaten the last croissant, or used the telephone to make unauthorised long-distance calls. If we don't understand our inner man or inner woman's meaning, then we come to resent their presence.

Resented or understood, they are still living under our roof and they influence us in all sorts of different ways. Without really thinking about it, we may pick up their opinions and feelings. Because we don't tell them what is really going on for us, they are not in full possession of the facts. Also, because they haven't been to school, or gone out into the world to have a job, they seem rather less developed than the rest of us.

When a man and a woman get into a relationship, then we can see that it's a lot more complicated than simply the outer man and the outer woman getting together. A number of relationships start taking place, some consciously recognised, some not.

Outer man – rationally oriented		Outer woman – emotionally oriented
	conscious awareness	
Inner woman – emotionally oriented	←----------→	Inner man – rationally oriented

A further complication comes about when the inner woman or man is projected onto our partner. If we haven't recognised our inner male or female, then we tend to confuse them with our outer partner. So David, for example, may not be fully aware that his inner woman is complaining that he doesn't listen to her views or take enough notice of her. She may be feeling jealous that he is spending so much time with Linda. The inner woman may emotionally manipulate David into feeling guilty that he neglects her. Then, in the outer world, Linda, starts to say the same thing! David feels attacked on all sides and says things to Linda that he should really be saying to his inner woman. In fact, they both need his attention. It's the same for her, too. Her inner man has many opinions about other men. He may feel jealous that she is spending so much time with David so he brings all sorts of rational-sounding arguments as to why David fails on the emotional front. She then repeats them word for word to David. If we're not careful, the inner men and women can poison our relationships.

THE ENTIRE MARRIAGE

Jung wrote about these inner male and female figures extensively. He called the inner man, the animus, or spirit, and the inner woman, the anima, or soul. There have been many criticisms of his model as it has been used to justify a continuation of patriarchal ideas. The idea of the anima has been used to justify men's irrational behaviour, while the idea of the animus has been used to degrade women by suggesting that her thinking is opinionated and aggressive. The choice of terminology is probably unfortunate and perhaps rather outdated, and so inner man and woman has been used here.

In fact Jung and later workers in his tradition did progress beyond the idea that we simply contain an opposite figure and came to see that we have a potential couple within us. Understanding and relating to the couple gives us access to the deep feminine and deep masculine at the deeper layers of the psyche. The deeper layers are sometimes called the ground of being because they represent things that are common to all humanity. If a man or a woman is in touch with the deep masculine and feminine then they can modify their behaviour according to the circumstances. If a woman needs masculine penetrative linear energy to solve a problem, then she can call upon it. If a man needs feminine nurturing rounded energy to negotiate a situation, he can call upon it. Neither is dependent on their partner of the opposite sex and neither has to envy or resent their partner's power. This is true equality and brings the gift of harmony.

Outer man	Outer woman

conscious awareness being pushed back

Inner woman and man creating entire marriage	Inner man and woman creating entire marriage

——— ground of being ———

access to deep femininity and deep masculinity

The way we achieve an entire marriage is not only or even through having a marriage in the outer world. It is by creating a marriage within. A few years down the track David and Linda may be able to look at the rational/emotional split from another perspective. Now in her early fifties, Linda says that she can love David more than she ever did because she no longer demands an emotional response from him. She is on good terms with her inner man and this gives her a feeling of being secure and married inside. David no longer patronises his emotional side or projects it on to Linda because he has realised its importance in his life. Without it he can't function and so he has made friends with his inner woman. He, too, feels married inside and can act strongly from either his masculine or his feminine side.

Both acknowledge that many years of hard work on their

emotions have got them to this state. As Linda says, 'In many ways, middle age is a well-kept secret, because life feels much more interesting than it did when we were young. Facing my negative and painful emotions like anger, fear and loneliness led to their transforming me. And then when I stopped trying to change David, he changed anyway. What a bonus!'

This chapter has concentrated on heterosexual relationships but this does not mean that same-sex relationships do not follow something of a similar pattern. In gay relationships, the partners still have to recognise the differing demands of masculine and feminine. One partner will often take the lead in one area and the other in a different area. We have looked at the means of access to the deep feminine and the deep masculine through the lens of male/female relationships. It's much easier to see it in this context but this is a journey that we can all undertake whatever our sexuality or gender.

5

Developing the Inner Family

THE PEOPLE WHO LIVE WITHIN US

We are never alone even though we may feel completely isolated. Our inner space is peopled. In the last chapter we met the inner man and the inner woman but this is only the beginning of getting to know our diverse inner family. Why are we unaware of this? Probably because our culture encourages us to think of ourselves as one person and no more. It's more convenient and practical. Taking account of the other inner people is time consuming and could be a nuisance. Consulting ten people instead of one when you cross a road or fill in a form could take ten times as long. So, in order to act effectively and efficiently, we normally limit ourselves to expressing just one personality. Psychologists have called this main personality the ego, or Latin for I. It can become such a dominant force that all the other inner people are silenced. In some forms of mental illness, the opposite can be true. The ego may not be powerful enough to hold the personality together and the various inner people start to act inharmoniously and destructively. But for most of us, the ego has come to believe that it's the undisputed master of its own house.

In a way, our inner world is like a large rambling mansion. At the top is a smart modern penthouse suite in which the ego lives blindly ignoring the other higgledy-piggledy tenants on the floors beneath. Their flats are rather shabby and neglected and they live in an overcrowded way with washing, children and animals all competing for space. In the morning the ego rises, showers, puts on a business suit and goes out to work. Sometimes it mutters a bit as it passes the doors of the tenants who it disdainfully imagines live on welfare. 'My work puts food on their table but do I get any thanks for it!' it may say to itself in a self-righteous way. But while the ego is otherwise occupied, the other people are working very hard in their own way. Although they are not involved in the hard-nosed, upwardly-mobile, 'yuppie' lifestyle of the ego, the part they play is vital.

These figures determine how we deal with the emotional situations in which we find ourselves every day. As the ego drives aggressively to work (and the driving may represent a driving attitude rather than actually driving a car) it may encounter a beggar. The beggar is homeless and asks for any spare change. 'Haven't got any *spare* change,' the ego snarls back. 'Why don't you get a proper job?' The ego strides on feeling angry. Then the ego feels sorry for the beggar and worried that if it doesn't keep going in this forward-thrusting way, it, too, could be living on the street. At the ego's workplace, it nags and belittles its colleagues and subordinates. 'Can't you get that done better/faster/without so many spelling mistakes? Do I have to do *everything* myself?'

The ego believes a theory it has read in a book – the eighty-five/fifteen rule. It thinks to itself: 'Eighty-five per cent of the world is passive, dependent and hopeless. The other fifteen per cent is active, competent and has to pull along the rest. Why do I have to pull along all this dead wood? It makes me cross.' When the ego arrives home, it finds its neighbours having a spontaneous party with music and dancing. 'Come and join us,' they say warmly, 'we've got food cooking.' The ego snaps back, 'I can smell that – I've had a hard day – I had to do some serious work and don't make that dreadful noise after 10.00 p.m. or I'll get the noise patrol onto you.' With this threat the ego retires to its lofty bower. After a couple of stiff drinks, it starts to feel lonely and long for company but the thought of going down and joining those unwashed neighbours is impossible. So the ego's pride makes it isolated and increasingly sad.

But who are these rough neighbours? The answer does not

please the ego but they are as much part of the whole person as the ego is. The ego is the public front that we have constructed, our showcase. The other parts contain some of the things we don't want to acknowledge, or haven't been able to accept about ourselves. The less we can accept the inner figure within, the more angry we'll be about seeing it in the outside world. The beggar is a good case in point. If we know that inside us there's a part of us which is impoverished, crippled, needy and demanding, then the outer beggar seems less threatening. We may or may not choose to give money. We will decide whether we wish to meet his needs but we won't feel manipulated into giving the money by our own guilt. We will not carry any additional burden because of the people we encounter. Almost any situation that arouses our emotions in a painful way points to an inner figure that needs our healing.

THE ORIGINS OF OUR INNER FIGURES

Where do these inner figures come from? Although each person's inner figures will be slightly different, there are broad human similarities. Basically our inner figures are derived from two sources: our unique experiences and the collective archetypal ground. Both these sources will colour and create our emotional patterns. In a way we create our inner family from a combination of our actual experience and the archetypes we encounter.

Our father and mother, or whoever was responsible for caring for us during our early years, leave an indelible imprint. This is our personal story and is unique to us because, in a sense, even siblings have different experiences of the same parents. The colour of the emotional memories we have of them – whether they were loving, abusive, stupid, generous, or cold – will always be with us. Their contradictions, beliefs, hopes and fears leave their mark. A man may say, 'Mothers are very emotional and always want more than you can give', because his own mother was like that. A woman may expect all fathers to be generous to the point of indulgence because she was a 'Daddy's girl'. Our siblings or other close relations with whom we grow up also become a benchmark for our emotional standards.

Later on we may project our parents onto other authority figures we encounter. This could be a boss or supervisor, a teacher, a psychotherapist or a priest. Some charismatic political or spiritual leaders actually encourage people to project the image of parent onto them. They do this in a variety of ways which can include being very loving and reassuring, or perhaps harsh or punishing. Because the parent has such power over a small child, an adult can be confused into surrendering his will to a parent figure. This is one of the major ways in which dictators get their power and so emotional literacy is important not only for personal development but ultimately in terms of democracy and political freedom.

Beyond the personal realm, at the ground of our being, there are the archetypes. The word archetype means literally first type: they are the master patterns of the psyche. They are inherited but are modifed by our unique experiences. No-one has scientifically proven the existence of the archetypes but they are a useful working model in the absence of any empirical knowledge. The idea of the archetypes goes back to Plato, but Jung developed it when he was studying the mythology of different parts of the world. He realised that many stories seemed to be essentially the same, only names and other details varied.

Many cultures, for example, have creation myths in which the world is born from a coupling of male and female. In the Christian tradition, Adam and Eve are considered to be the father and mother of the human race. The ancient Egyptians believed that the world came about through a mating of the sky goddess, Nut, and the earth god, Geb. Some cultures reverse this and see the world as a result of the union of a sky-father and an earth-mother. And in Greek mythology, the world was created by Cronos and Gaia, who were later overthrown by the Olympic race of gods. These examples show us that there is a possibility of a shared common ground to which all human beings have potential access. In a way the archetypes are like a form of psychic internet: its websites can be entered from anywhere in the world. But the internet is only virtually real whereas the psychic internet contains the possibility of real virtue.

WORKING WITH THE ARCHETYPES

The archetypes influence us in a number of ways. They form the basis for the stories we can enjoy collectively. They come into our dreams, pervade art and also provide much of the hidden power in advertisements. The images that advertising creates lock onto our archetypal longings and imply that, if we buy the product, that deep ache will be filled. Usually material products are not the answer, these profound longings can only really be assuaged by contact with the archetype itself. You may, for example, be seduced by the image of a perfect family eating a meal and begin to think that if you bought a particular stock cube then your family would be healthy, happy and loving. Instead of wishing that your kitchen was as perfect or your family life as harmonious, and rushing out to buy the cube, pause for a moment and review the real situation. You have been gripped by the archetypal longing for perfection and are devaluing what you already have. If you can begin to hold an idea of the archetypal family as an ideal, then you may get the strength to accept your own human and faulty family. But only through consciously recognising the archetype can you be released from its power.

The archetypes also provide a corrective healing presence in the absence of positive experience. For example, a person who has received poor or careless mothering may derive strength and consolation from an image of the 'perfect' mother, which might be the Virgin Mary or the Goddess. Through the contemplation of absolute goodness, a man or woman may derive the strength to forgive their actual parents' shortcomings. As someone expressed it to me: 'I know my mother was stupid, harmful and self-centred. But by getting in touch with the archetypal mother through my dreams, I have a much stronger, more caring mother inside me now. I realise that the woman who took care of me when I was little did her best even though it wasn't good enough. On my better days I forgive her. I now have an inner mother who is strong and nurtures me.' We can modify other family members as well as our parents through connection with these archetypal forms.

But just as the archetypes can heal, they can also destroy. If a person comes to believe that he really is God, for example, then he will overreach himself and some catastrophe will befall him. One thing that is essential is to recognise and deal with our envy of the archetypes. Because the archetypes are pure types of goodness, beauty, divinity, healing, intelligence etc., they have tremendous power. It is understandable that a vulnerable and fragile human being might like some of that power. So sometimes we grab it but find that it overwhelms us.

The paradox is that, as we go deeper into our inner world, we actually find possibility of shared ground. Many religious rituals use the archetypes to bind the participants together in a shared experience which derives its power from the very fact that it is collective. All our lives we will experience the interplay between the archetypes and our personal story. Much of the work of emotional literacy is to bring these two influences into some kind of harmony. Emotional pain and discomfort often cause a revaluation of the balance between the archetypes and our unique experiences. And the archetypes also bring about the possibility of empathy between people because they contain the seeds of potentially communal experience.

ourselves

personal story
mother, father etc.

———— ground of being ————

the inner family of the collective archetypes

c o m m o n   g r o u n d

There is considerable confusion between the personal and the archetypal worlds. Many of the self-help books published in recent years have singled out the theme of the inner child. They have made a valuable contribution in that they have focused attention on the traumas and difficult experiences we may have had in the past. But the inner child is also an archetypal figure which points to the future. The child is an image which contains possibility as well as history. So it's important not only to see the inner child as a figure which needs our loving and support, but as a figure which can lead us to the next stage of our lives.

THE EGO'S PARTY

We left the lonely ego, upstairs in its penthouse suite, hearing the sounds of revelry below. Why can't it join the party? The reason is because it feels ashamed of its inner family and so it disowns them and isolates itself. The inner mother is a rather badly educated and coarse woman (reflecting the ego's own parent). The father likewise is a rough, working man who doesn't match the ego's 'yuppie' aspirations. Then there's garrulous Aunt Mary who can't stop talking about the most irrelevant subjects. Dull, deaf grandpa. Smelly, old Uncle Albert. Insistent, opinionated cousin Valerie. A ghastly brother who works in some dreary job and who has an equally pedestrian wife. And hordes of noisy tiresome children who start to whine at the drop of a hat. And the in-laws about whom the less said the better.

And then there are all the inner family's friends. They seem to have no selectivity but allow all and sundry to come to their party. There's this man whom they call the Trickster, who makes things appear and disappear as if by magic. He upsets all the norms of civilised behaviour. Then there's the incredibly sexy Greek woman called Aphrodite, who goes around seducing people in a totally shameless way. And what about dark Mr Pluto from Hades who casts a gloom over everything he touches?

The ego is shocked and embarrassed by these people and is even more horrified when it realises that these people have as much right to exist as the ego does. Emotions show the ego what it has neglected and discarded and what now needs to be integrated. Emotions make us feel so much that we have to begin to question the ego's solitary viewpoint. In this way they make the ego join the party of the entire self. When the ego can go downstairs and say to itself, *these people are part of me and I am no longer ashamed of them*, then the ego will be emotionally intelligent. It won't necessarily be like these people, it has to be itself, but it will no longer be in denial about them. It can then recognise that there are times when the father's rough strength, or the noisy curiosity of the child are necessary. It may also be able to say to them, 'Now be quiet. I'll handle this one.' When the ego is assailed by strong and painful emotions, it will be able to call upon far greater resources to deal with the emotional crisis. Developing emotional intelligence ultimately means developing a firm but tremendously flexible ego.

6

How to be your own Emotional Mentor

BECOMING YOUR OWN EMOTIONAL MENTOR

A mentor is a wise, but not overpowering friend. Mentoring involves the development of a supportive relationship between an older, experienced person and a youthful, developing person. Sometimes actual age has nothing to do with it; a younger person with the right ability and attitude may well be able to mentor someone who is chronologically older. And in this era of lifelong learning there is no age limit in mastering new skills. But this chapter is really about learning to distinguish the inner, more mature personality from the less developed side within each of us. The wiser, or teaching side is called the mentor, and the receptive, or learning side, the protégé.

Much of this chapter is about the imaginative work of hearing these two voices inside your head and your heart. Another way to do it is to practise these roles with a friend you trust. But if there is no-one available, then do not despair. If you have been able to read this book up to now and respond to it in some way, then you have all the tools inside you that you will need. And, as you start to do this inner work, you will usually find that help in some form comes from the outside, too.

Both sides of the personality play a very important role in

developing emotional intelligence. The mentor brings the knowledge and experience, the protégé responds with energy, feeling and zest to learn. The mentor provides commentary and response to the protégé's experience of the emotional states. To mentor yourself effectively, you have to allow both sides to enjoy a dialogue. The following is a piece of inner dialogue between a mentor and protégé, which was written down by a young man just after he had had an argument with his father. He found his father to be very controlling, domineering and rigid. Disagreements in the past have usually led to the young man losing his temper and falling into a fearful rage. Then his pattern is to fall into a state of guilt and remorse for having said such terrible things to his father. This time he acted differently and the mentor commented on it.

Mentor: I liked the way you handled your anger earlier. You recognised why you were angry with your father and, instead of flying off the handle, you kept your cool without suppressing your feelings.

Protégé: Did you notice how he tried to guilt trip me – how often I've fallen for that one in the past! Why does he do it? It nearly caught me this time but I left the room before it got to me.

Mentor: I think you did the right thing. But I wonder how you're feeling right now?

Protégé: Well, it's interesting you should ask that. I was feeling elated that I'd handled it so well, but now I'm suddenly feeling down and lonely. I haven't got my father any more. I've left him. I feel abandoned – I'm alone and it's terrifying.

Mentor: I'm here for you. I'm listening and I'm trying to feel the pain you are feeling alongside you. Can you describe it?

Protégé: It feels black, black as the jaws of hell. I'm alone in the universe. No-one cares, I'm alone. Alone.

Mentor: I'm here. I support you.

Protégé: Perhaps you do. Just being able to talk about it helps.

(*Ten minutes later*)

Protégé: The worst of the loneliness has passed. I feel better for being able to cry. I don't want to feel like that again.

Mentor: How well you dealt with it. You stood up to your father and broke a pattern. In a sense, you became an adult and

> stopped being a child when you did that. Being an adult does feel lonely until we realise we have far more resources inside us than we ever imagined. Perhaps you don't need to fear feeling like that again – you coped with it very well.

Notice how the mentor supports the protégé every step of the way. The mentor asks the young man to describe how he is feeling and then empathises with it. Notice how the painful emotion starts to change when the young man starts to describe it. At no stage does the mentor impose his will onto his protégé, he just encourages him into self-development. There is a sense that the mentor here is masculine and perhaps represents a form of archetypal father for the young man. His actual father has been damaged by a difficult start in life and negative family patterns and so the inner mentor is the wise father the young man never had. Mentors can be both feminine or masculine or of no sex at all. At different times, we may need the healing of a male voice or the healing of a female voice – or it may not matter. As a woman said: 'When I start to mentor myself, I just wait and see who shows up. Sometimes it's Jack and sometimes it's Jill but they're usually just right for the situation.'

THE SKILLS OF MENTORING

Just as with any other form of mentoring, you will need specific skills to practise self-mentoring. These include:

- knowing your emotional temperament
- practising listening skills and ability to empathise
- understanding projection
- acceptance of your shadow side
- commitment to emotional transformation

Knowing your emotional temperament

Emotional temperaments are partly a gift of nature and partly an inheritance from early life. The good news is that they are not fixed attributes although they can seem that way. Many people who work with emotional literacy will probably find themselves gently shifting the ground of their temperament. The temperaments are presented as opposites because we naturally polarise towards one end of the spectrum or the other. For example, we need both the optimist and the pessimist because both have important insights. We need both sides to work for us in harmony. Beware of being one-sided and allow yourself to move flexibly from one end of the spectrum to the other as the occasion dictates.

Take a moment when you have finished looking at the following pairs to decide where you place yourself in terms of emotional temperament.

- **optimist versus pessimist**
  It is often said that the optimist believes that this is the best of all possible worlds while the pessimist fears that it is. The pessimist will see his glass as half empty while the optimist will think that it only needs the merest top up from the wine bottle to be brimmingly full! Both temperaments have their advantages. At times we need positive optimism if we are to get a job done. But we need the voice of the pessimist to wake us up to reality if we are taking on too much. As the optimist inflates our expectations and abilities, so the pessimist deflates them.

- **brooder versus flarer**
  Brooders sit quietly on the things that have hurt them. They store up the slights and transgressions of other people as well as their own. When it suits them or when they feel deeply provoked, they angrily attack with a list sometimes going back weeks or months of the other's shortcomings. On the other hand, flarers fly off the handle at a moment's notice, they are volatile and speak without thinking. In half an hour's time they have forgotten the entire exchange. Brooders can seem very emotionally constipated but flarers can often regret their hastiness. At times we need both the reflective quality and the ability to wait of the brooder as well as the capacity for emotional discharge and the ability to start afresh which defines the flarer.

- **easy-going versus highly strung**
  The easy-going person chronically under-reacts to emotional stimulus while the highly strung person overreacts to the same stimulus. If you're easy-going, you will probably suffer less but miss a lot of the nuances that others notice. If you're highly

strung you will find that you're much more sensitive than the jovial easy-going person and that this sensitivity is costly in terms of your emotional equilibrium. Most creative people are highly strung but the more successfully they can develop easier-going sides to their nature, the more effective they will be at their work. But don't be fooled by external appearances – many people develop a hearty easy-going or clown-like side to cover up their highly strung sensitivities.

- **introvert versus extrovert**
  For the introvert, what is going on inside herself is always the most important thing, for the extrovert, it is the opposite. An introvert can say 'hell is other people' while for the extrovert being totally alone is hell. Often these categories are confusing because many introverts have developed excellent social skills and can hold their own in any gathering and some extroverts are socially clumsy and awkward. When it comes to feeling, the extrovert will place as much emphasis on other people's feelings as his own, while the introvert will always refer to his own inner world and give less weight to the outer situation.

You can be an optimist in one area of your life but a pessimist in another. Quite often a person copes by being at one emotional pole in their private life, for instance, but the opposite in their professional life. Sometimes we can be one sort of temperament, e.g. easy-going when we're in a relaxed situation and then display very highly strung characteristics when we're under stress. Also in mid-life, we may find ourselves changing from introvert to extrovert or vice versa. It's the ultimate in self-development not to be fixed in one temperament but to be able to allow ourselves the experience of the other side.

The role of the mentor is to comment in the situation when we're going too far towards one pole. For example, our inner mentor may say: 'You're flaring up a lot in situations. Perhaps you could allow your brooding side to come a bit more to the forefront?' It's important for the mentor to understand emotional temperaments because otherwise he or she will tend to compensate and speak from the opposite pole. In those cases the mentor may try, for example, to balance the protégé's pessimism with a false, jovial optimism. They might say something like: 'It'll be all right really – just you wait and see', which will not help the protégé to move forward one inch. There is a great deal of difference in asking the protégé to see things from another point of view and representing that point of view yourself. The mentor must try to maintain the balance.

Practising listening skills and the ability to empathise

Listening skills really mean the art of inner listening. If a mentor is bothered by their own problems, then a flow of inner dialogue will impede their ability to listen accurately. Empathy depends upon hearing what is actually said and responding to it. So the mentor must first of all listen to what he or she is saying before any help can be given. A good way of doing this is to spend ten minutes writing down whatever comes into your mind. Write without regard for spelling, punctuation, logic or grammar. Write without censorship and without judgement. Set a clock timer and keep your hand moving over the pages without pause until the bell rings. Do not necessarily bother to read the results. It's the process and not the outcome which is important.

This technique is often used by creative writers and artists. It is described extensively in Julia Cameron's excellent book *The Artist's Way*. She calls it morning pages, a kind of brain drain which clears the creative channels before work begins. It is also useful for preparing the inner mentor. He or she is now ready to hear what the suffering part of your personality is saying. It's more important that the mentor is emotionally present than that they say something clever.

Some people can mentor very successfully in their own head, but to begin with it's very useful to write it down. It allows you to see the process objectively. Some of the time a little voice will probably pipe up and say, 'This is ridiculous, I've got better things to do with my Sunday afternoon. This is a silly book, why did you buy it?' or words to that effect. If you start to hear something like this, don't take it at face value, but accept instead that doubt and resistance are part of the process.

Empathy is different from sympathy and much more healing to the recipient. To be the object of someone's sympathy is degrading and humiliating. There is a world of difference in saying 'I feel with you' and not 'I feel for you'. Feeling with someone puts them on an equal footing and acknowledges that neither is superior – just that one is suffering at the moment.

When you are listening to yourself with the mentoring side of your personality, ask the other part to describe what they are feeling. Be encouraging and don't make judgements, just allow the process to unfold. With practice you will develop the ability remarkably fast. You have the capacity to draw on depths of human wisdom as deep as the deepest well in the world.

Key tips for active listening include:

- know what's going on for yourself first of all
- avoid asking *why?* questions because it implies a form of judgement
- ask the person to describe what they are feeling
- be empathetic, not sympathetic
- listen to yourself

Understanding projection

When people are blocked emotionally, sometimes they force others around them to feel it instead. This is very common in the world of work where more powerful people may force others to feel their insecurity and inadequacy. It also happens a lot in close personal relationships. It is called emotional projection. It's important to recognise if you are projecting your emotions onto others but even more important to realise when you are being projected upon.

For example, a woman may feel incredibly angry in the presence of a particular man who invites her out from time to time but never takes the relationship any further. She may think that she is angry about this confusing situation, which perhaps she is. But the difference is that when he goes away, she feels fine. As she develops her emotional literacy, and gets into contact with her own repressed anger (which often manifests as depression), she realises the difference between her anger and the man's anger which has been projected onto her. It feels different – like another person's scent. She can then unhook from the projection that she has unconsciously picked up and metaphorically hand his anger back to him.

The man has got into this state because he hasn't been able to come to terms with his own anger. He wants to take the relationship further with the woman but he is held back by invisible tight psychological strings to do with his relationship with his own mother. He is a scientist and believes in logic and reason above all else, so the idea of emotion is very foreign to him. Because he won't or can't own his feelings, he makes other people around him feel angry.

Projection jumps from one person to another almost in the way an infection does. For example, you may find yourself criticising your mate harshly. Thinking back over the day, you remember that your boss has done the same thing to you and you were not able to work through and come to terms with the resulting feelings you had at the time. Instead you have transferred the 'put down' feeling onto another person, who either has to swallow it or pass it onto yet another person. But, if you can recognise the trigger, you can avoid making someone else unhappy and also, most importantly, have the choice of honestly confronting your critic at work.

The inner mentor's role is to sniff out these projections and to tell the protégé what they think is happening. The key indicators of projection are when:

- you feel an emotion which doesn't feel like your own. As you begin to recognise your own envy, for instance, you will realise that someone else's envy has a different flavour.
- you feel an emotion strongly in someone's physical presence but when you move away from their 'force-field' it vanishes.
- you feel almost as if something has been taken away from you without your consent. This is a very subtle feeling which takes much practice to detect. It feels like something you half-know but is frustratingly just out of reach and that reaching for it won't bring it into range.

The important thing with projection is not to accuse the other person of it. This will make them defensive and they will deny it and may be hostile to you. And also, you could be wrong. If you feel an emotion being projected upon you, then it's a wonderful opportunity to work with that emotion within you. If you feel unbearably sad or lonely in someone's company, work on your own feelings of loneliness. Projection always has to have a hook and you cannot be successfully projected upon if you are in a state of balance about the particular feeling concerned.

Acceptance of your shadow side

'Fear is the main source of superstition, and one of the main sources of cruelty. To conquer fear is the beginning of wisdom.'

Bertrand Russell

The development of emotional intelligence makes us look at those things about ourselves that we don't like or don't think will be socially acceptable. This area is often called the shadow – we can't quite see it because we've put it behind ourselves but it clings closely to us, following us wherever we go. We start putting things into the shadow when we are very young. As time goes by we add more and more so that, by the time we get to mid-life, the shadow we cast can be very long indeed. Ego and shadow are in opposition. The ego denies the shadow and projects it onto other people.

Thomas is a man who has put his greediness into his shadow. When Thomas was a child his mother frequently reproved him for being a very greedy little boy. He grew up thinking that to be greedy was the worst thing of all. He put his greedy side into his shadow so that he didn't have see it. Instead he projected it onto other people. He married a woman who was very greedy about both food and material possessions. He could criticise her and feel that he himself was blameless. When she left him, however, he had to stop projecting his greed outwards. When he realised that it was part of him and a necessary part, provided it didn't get out of hand, he ceased being so upset by seeing it in other people.

Not everything in the shadow is negative. Sometimes, people put their best attributes in the shadow. Many of us hide our talents because we fear that other people won't find our splendour acceptable. As we work through the pain of our emotional states, we usually find that repressed attributes come to light. If we can accept our multi-faceted imperfections, then we no longer need to hide things in our shadow.

Shadow projections often go beyond the personal. Families often have communal shadows and whole nations can develop terrifying collective shadows. The psychological background to so-called 'ethnic cleansing' and genocide are shadow projections. The disowned parts are projected onto another racial or ethnic group who are then killed. The evil enemy is expelled outwards which seems, on the surface at least, easier to bear. If the perpetrators of an atrocity could do enough inner work, then they would recognise that what they are really attempting to destroy is the hated part of themselves.

The role of the inner mentor is to try not to accept the ego's point of view at face value. If you persistently find yourself hating someone or something, it is always worth looking at what may be happening in your own shadow. When you are in the mentoring state, always treat yourself as gently and non-judgementally as possible. It's usually fear that has made us put part of ourselves into our shadow. Self-forgiveness and patience can bring about the most healing results. As Dostoevsky expresses it in *The Brothers Karamazov*: 'avoid a feeling of aversion towards others and towards yourself: what seems to you bad in yourself is purified by the very fact that you've noticed it.' By not hating yourself and instead accepting your imperfections, you can break the cycle of shadow projection.

Commitment to emotional transformation

Emotions transform us. That is their function. At the biological level, fear makes us run away from danger, sexual lust inclines us to mate and love encourages us to form affectional bonds. All of these are needed for the survival of the species. At the psychological level, pride forces us to realign our view of ourselves, anxiety calls us to a greater future and loneliness invites us to reconnect with the world once more. At a spiritual level, hope perhaps requires us to find an attitude of hope rather than the expectation of a specific outcome, anger understood purifies us and depression can be a severe mercy which deepens life.

Emotions are created by our thoughts and beliefs as much as by the events that surround us. In turn, emotions can be faced negatively or positively. If they are faced negatively then they produce destructive thoughts. And if they are faced positively, then they produce saving thoughts which have the potential to save not only us but the entire situation we find ourselves in. All emotions have a positive and a negative side. So even the most deeply negative emotion can be transformed into its positive opposite.

An example of this is Sara who is deeply envious of her friend's job. It's well-paid, interesting and has a high status. By comparison her own seems dull, badly rewarded and dreary. Sara's envy poisons their relationship and makes her feel empty and desolate inside. With inner work, she can see that she hasn't realised her own career potential. She has two choices: to accept her job as it is and find other interests, or to look for a new job, possibly taking on the fact that she may need further training. When she decides to progress down the road of one these choices then she is no longer stuck in the emotion. As she processes her envy then her relationship with her friend is also transformed. This is a blessing for the friend as she needs Sara. This is what envious people, and in fact anyone with low self-esteem, often forget, that they are valuable to, as well as needed by, other people. The transformation of Sara's envy not only leads her into her new activity and growth but it also improves her friend's life as well.

The role of the inner mentor is not to agree with the destructive thoughts of the negative emotion but to always work for the transformation of it into a positive state. It's often very hard not be dragged down when you hear a chronically depressed or angry voice, for example. Perhaps a man will go for a drink with a colleague after a hard day at work and spend an hour bitching about what a terrible workplace it is. And the boss, and the incompetent secretaries. The other person may try to say things are not too bad, but in the end will be so cast down by the other's negativity that they will join in. On the way home, they may wonder why they feel so bad. Destructive thoughts always cause destructive feelings. It's just the same on the inner level. But, in your mentor mode, the trick is to hear the emotion for what it is and give it a label. The mentor can say, 'I think you are feeling rejected but I am not rejected by your feelings. On the contrary I want to feel it with you and support you through it.'

In each of the chapters on the specific emotional states in *Heart of the Matter*, each emotion is shown to have a potential transformative side. So the inner should always be aware of this possibility and gently allow the protégé to find this through self-understanding.

THE PRACTICALITIES OF MENTORING

As this is a task you will probably be doing by yourself, you will need three things: pen and paper, a quiet room and some time to yourself. It's a good idea to set aside say three quarters of an hour once a week and to increase it if you find you enjoy the activity. Whatever you do, don't make it onerous, and don't feel that this is something you must do. Rather, think of it as something you are doing out of self-love and commitment to your own development.

It's really useful to be able to write down dialogue between the mentor and the protégé if you can. You will probably feel very silly to begin with but you are not going to show this to anybody else. Many of the exercises in the next section call for writing things down and it's useful to have the practice. Putting the dialogue down in writing is beneficial for other reasons as well because it:

- enables us to separate the voice of the mentor and the protégé. If you don't write it down, then the voices tend to get jumbled up and the process collapses.
- allows us to see what we are thinking and feeling with a certain objectivity. Getting it outside ourselves moves us on and starts the process of emotional transformation.
- gives us the message that we are taking the task of our emotional development seriously. Only by doing this can the work of emotional intelligence really take place.

It's quite a good idea to keep this work to yourself for a bit. If you tell everyone you are starting to do it, they will expect immediate results and will say it's no good if you don't get over your emotional patterns inside a week. Real transformation is going to take time. Let others notice the changes in you and then start to tell them how they came about. It will be far more convincing and you will be under far less pressure.

This work is a bit like a commitment to going to the gym. Self-mentoring is emotional fitness training and needs just as strong a commitment. The pen and paper, quiet room and free time are your emotional gym. If you do the work, you will achieve results. Part of the benefit of this book can be obtained just from reading it but you will get far more from it if you interact with it. You may find that you disagree with parts of it. That's excellent. It's written by me and contains the things I've learnt, and am struggling with. As you do the work of emotional self-mentoring you will find that you have written your own work, hugely satisfying in itself.

PART TWO

HEART OF THE MATTER

'God turns you from one feeling to another and teaches us by means of opposites so that you will have two wings to fly, not one.'

Rumi

7

Aggression

'Mankind must evolve for all human conflict a method which rejects revenge, aggression and retaliation. The foundation of such a method is love.' Martin Luther King

WHAT IS AGGRESSION?

A bully comes up to me in a school playground. She is bigger than me and demands my apple. She menaces me physically and humiliates me verbally until I give her the apple. I am six years old.

Now the interesting thing is what I do next. I have a number of options. I can fight back. I can go and threaten another child who is smaller than me. I can decide to save the painful feelings until I'm grown up and can be aggressive to others in a much more potent way. I can decide that feeling aggressive is too uncomfortable and decide to make other people feel aggressive instead. Or, if I'm very lucky, I might get the chance later in the day to talk to a wise older person who will give me time to talk about the feelings of fear, powerlessness and humiliation that aggression brings up. Being able to speak about these painful feelings means it's less likely that I will respond to subsequent aggression by becoming aggressive myself – either actively or passively.

Everybody knows that the human race is aggressive but very few of us are prepared to admit our personal aggression. Perhaps this is because we are in two minds about aggression. On one hand we deplore it. We may speak pessimistically about the impossibly aggressive human race. We may say, 'You can't change human nature. Human beings are hostile. There have always been wars and therefore there always will be wars.' We may be genuinely shocked by images of war and genocide which appear frequently on our television sets. But on the other hand we reward aggression. Much of modern society is built around the aggressive use of power and success. We speak of *aggressive* marketing and *penetrating* new markets, we want to *attack* problems, we have an *aggressive* new treatment for our illness, and *get our teeth* into things. The imagery is very revealing.

Because we both abhor and revere the same thing we may find it difficult to recognise it in ourselves. It also makes us feel hopeless about trying to mitigate human aggressiveness on a global level. Only people who have faced their own aggression are really able to deal with the aggression of others. All of us at some time have been the victims of some one else's aggression on a personal, national or corporate level. The playground scene described at the beginning of the chapter is probably a pretty universal human experience. The choice for us is how to respond.

AGGRESSION AND POWER

Aggression is intimately concerned with power. If we think that there is only a limited amount of the thing we want (e.g. food, love, money, status, sex) we will fight aggressively to have it for ourselves. If we have suffered in the past because we haven't had enough of whatever it is, we will fight all the harder. If we believe we can only be safe by being powerful then we will seek aggressively to become powerful. If we are afraid of power, we may ally ourselves to another person who is powerful and employ their aggressiveness second-hand.

In some languages (and unfortunately English isn't one of them) there are several words for power. These distinguish between power in the sense of might or force and power in the sense of energy or an enabling factor. Power in the sense of might requires us to arm ourselves with weapons (which may be psychological, economic, political or physical weapons) and adopt an attitude of hostility.

Power in the sense of energy is something we profoundly need to act effectively with ourselves and others. It is the basis of genuine co-operation between individuals. The irony is that power in the sense of might often obstructs the power in the sense of energy from flowing creatively and constructively. If we don't believe we have access to power as energy we will often resort to power as might if we are threatened.

If we believe that there is enough of the thing we want and that we have a good chance of getting it, then we can afford to be less aggressive in the pursuit of it. We can put ourselves assertively in the path of it, making our needs and requests known. A management consultant who does a lot of work with international companies told me that 'you can always tell the insecure managers from the secure ones, they're more aggressive. If someone's insecure I have to ask myself whether they're really up to the job. And also how do they work in a team where aggressiveness is often destructive?' As the world of business is changing and responding to the importance of emotional literacy, it may no longer pay to be aggressive.

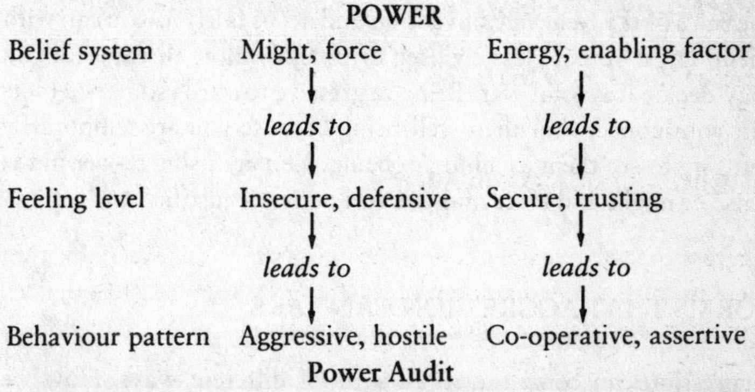

POWER

Belief system	Might, force	Energy, enabling factor
	↓ *leads to* ↓	↓ *leads to* ↓
Feeling level	Insecure, defensive	Secure, trusting
	↓ *leads to* ↓	↓ *leads to* ↓
Behaviour pattern	Aggressive, hostile	Co-operative, assertive

Power Audit

Take a sheet of paper with five columns. Put the name of a person you are in close relationship to in each of the columns. Try to include a variety of people from all the activities you are involved with e.g. family life, work, study, close relationships, friendships etc. Taking each column in turn examine which kind of power (might or energy) predominates. Start by looking at your feelings (ask yourself *do I feel secure or insecure with this person?*) and then examine your behaviour and the behaviour of others towards you. What would you like to change?

WHAT DOES AGGRESSION FEEL LIKE?

One woman expressed it like this: 'It feels like I'm very angry and often I am, but aggression is different. I feel it all over my body as tiny pinpricks of hate. If I see another car overtake me or cut me up in a particular way, I want to get back at them. I want to humiliate them the way I feel they've humiliated me. A few stages further on and I could kill them.'

Aggressiveness is closely related to both anger and fear. Anger is 'cleaner' than aggression. It usually involves the provocation of a specific action or behaviour pattern on the part of the person you are angry with. You can still be in relation to a person you're angry with but aggression involves seeing the other person as the enemy. As George described it, 'When I feel aggressive, I stop seeing May as my wife and friend. She seems to me a monster, she seems like all the most hateful sides of my mother and all the vicious women I have ever known rolled into one.'

For the aggressive person, the person they are aggressive towards is an enormously powerful enemy. You may decide to treat them by the rules of the Geneva Convention and act as fairly as you can with them. Or, if you are less civilised or possibly more threatened, you may decide it is total war. Being aggressive towards someone blots out your concern for their well-being because you are temporarily refusing to see them as a human being. You are using power in the sense of might and force and you feel perfectly justified.

FORMS THAT AGGRESSION CAN TAKE

Aggression can come out in all sorts of different ways. How we express it can depend on the class and culture in which we live. For example, it may be common in some communities to express aggression physically. A man will settle his differences with another man by asking him to step outside. The disadvantages of it are that it can easily go too far and someone can be hurt or killed. But if aggression isn't physical, we are less likely to own up to it. For example, the film *Ridicule* showed extreme aggression on the part of the French aristocracy. As they sat in their salons, elegantly dressed and immaculately coiffeured, they demanded wit from everybody present. The rewards of producing wit were that a person moved up the social pecking order. But if they failed to be witty, they were humiliated and often made outcasts. Beneath the veneer of civilised behaviour the activities of these aristocrats were in fact extremely hostile. No physical blow was struck but people felt annihilated, humiliated and destroyed by the group aggression.

Another form of concealed aggression can take the form of verbal and practical jokes. Not all jokes humiliate people but if they do, then they are aggressive. They are cowardly ways of expressing aggression because the aggressor can jump behind the defence of 'don't take it to heart – haven't you got a sense of humour then' if challenged.

Yet another form of aggression can exist between a man and woman who are sexually attracted to each other. Sexual attraction and romantic love are potent forces. If we want someone very much and we believe that their presence is necessary to our happiness (or even our survival) then we will feel vulnerable. Vulnerability is a key trigger for aggression. Many forms of courtship, e.g. where a man *chases* or *pursues* a woman, are forms of ritualised aggression. He sees himself as the hunter and sees her as the prey. The woman plays a role in it, too. The old saying 'a man chases a woman until she catches him' probably has a fair amount of truth to it. As long as the game is played lightly and generously with respect for the individual, it can be fun. But the danger is that the idea of the woman as prey can get out of hand. It can become literal and dehumanising. In a highly vulnerable and insecure man, it can lead to rape, which is one of the extreme forms of aggression.

The other major form aggression can take is to be passive rather than active. You may remember in the playground example that one of the options a person could take in face of aggression was to decide that the feelings were too scary to feel themselves. The only way to deal with those feelings is to make other people feel aggressive towards you. You start to notice it when people repeatedly tell you that they've been hit or hurt. Now and again this can happen to anybody, it's part of the random pattern of life. But when it happens on a regular basis, it may be because the person is passive-aggressive.

People can catch feelings from each other but more often than not the passive-aggressive person provokes the other person. They know what to say or do which will get them in their weakest point. If, for example, you're fat and feel defensive about that, they'll make demeaning references to your weight, or bring up the fact that you don't earn much money or that you failed your 'A' levels – whatever is the most difficult thing for you to deal with. The goading makes you mad and you start acting very aggressively to them. They've got rid of their aggression and they've made you the aggressor. The pay-off for the passive-aggressive person is that they can be the innocent victim. Nor do they have to feel aggressive. The downside is that they have to cope with the other person's verbal or physical aggression.

You may be reading this because you feel aggressive towards someone. It can take discernment to realise you are aggressive and not angry. If feelings of anger are suppressed over a period of time then you can become aggressive. If you have realised your aggression, you are halfway to dealing with it. You may also be reading this because you feel that everyone around you is aggressive and you are repeatedly being attacked. The rest of the chapter will tell you how to start dealing with these emotions.

A good man provoked – Brian's story

Brian is in his forties and is married. He is developing a comfortable middle-aged spread and has accepted that in his work he will not be a high flier. He is in a middle-management position, lives in a middle-class suburb and prides himself on being a good person. His home is conventional and his taste is safe. In fact everything about him on the surface seems to indicate that he is a respectable, if somewhat staid, pillar of society.

When you ask him about his relationship with his wife he'll say, 'We've been married for twenty-three years now. I adore her. I'd do anything for her. I put her a bit on a pedestal. She's very special. Of course we have our differences from time to time – what married couples don't? It's wonderful to know that she's there and on my side. I'd never leave her. We've got a pact of absolute fidelity. We're all in all for each other, really we are. Are you married yourself, by any chance?'

Now and again Brian beats his wife. He is able to do this because he had come to see her as two people. Mostly he sees her in a kind, if rather sentimental, light. Because he believes she's so good, she can never have faults. But 'when she's bad', in his phrase, he has to beat her. If she provokes him, he responds with physical aggression. 'I'm doing this for your own good, it's to make you better,' he says. Afterwards he cries and apologises to her, swearing his undying love.

Brian himself was beaten as a child. His step-father was jealous of him, tried to love him as a son, but failed. When he had had too much to drink, he would come up to Brian's attic bedroom and thrash him. He told Brian it would make him a better person. As a small, defenceless child, Brian couldn't stand up to a powerful adult, and so he had to accept the abuse. It made him very angry inside and he built a wall around that anger. When he became an adult, he did to his wife exactly what had been done to him. The only way he can justify it is by seeing his wife as being part angel, part devil. He really believes he is beating her to make her a better person, to 'get the devil out of her'. Almost all abusers have been victims in the past.

Victim of a vicious husband – Jo's story

Jo is a very attractive women in her early forties. She has long blonde hair and the figure of a model. She's been married for over twenty years and lives in a comfortable suburb. She doesn't work and is entirely economically supported by her husband. Occasionally, she has a fling with one of the husbands of her women friends. She takes care to swear them to secrecy. At first they are flattered and then dismayed when the sexual relationship turns out to be only a one-night stand. She tells them it's not safe and hints that her husband would be violent if he found out.

She is beaten by her husband. 'It's always when he's had a bit to drink,' she'll say, half apologising for him. 'He'll come up the stairs, and I'll know that tonight's the night. He does it very carefully, mind, never on a part of my body that shows.' If you respond to Jo's revelation by asking her why she doesn't leave her husband, she say that it's more complicated than that. If you press her, she will start to go back on what she said. 'It isn't really like that and I don't want a lot of do-gooding social workers telling me what's normal and what isn't.' Anybody listening to her starts to feel angry with the husband and to believe that Jo is the victim of an aggressive and tyrannical man.

What Jo has not revealed (and she keeps many relevant facts secret) is that she tells her husband when she has slept with another man. She doesn't even need to use words, she can imply by the way she walks and the toss of her long blonde hair, that she has just had the time of her life. As her husband has low self-esteem and feels badly about his own body, it is easy to provoke him. Because she cannot handle her own aggressive feelings, she makes her husband feel them. She will goad him until he responds by beating her. Both get rid of their feelings, until the next time.

Jo is a typical passive-aggressive personality. The roots of Jo's behaviour pattern lie in her childhood when she was severely punished for any assertive behaviour. If she really wanted something, it was usually denied to her on the grounds that she would become spoilt. If she fought her brother, as children do, she was shamed and humiliated by her parents. She got the message that aggression would be punished and that it wasn't safe to show it. She then developed a method that, as an adult, seemed to work effectively – to get her husband to carry her aggression and anger.

THE ROOTS OF AGGRESSION

All aggression starts with a realisation of vulnerability. This is usually loss of self-esteem and accompanying feelings of powerlessness. If we can tolerate these uncomfortable feelings, it is unlikely that we will resort to outright aggression. But if we can't, they will trigger a response in us. In Brian's case, it is when his wife taunts him with his unattractiveness and impotence. In fact she tells him she has had sex with another man. But he hears it as he is not good enough. Once he is in the cycle of low self-esteem and vulnerability, he feels aggressive and becomes physically violent.

Jo, on the other hand, reacts to her feelings of aggressiveness by provoking her husband to be aggressive towards her. Because she feels frightened of her feelings of aggression, she makes her husband feel them for her. She becomes the victim, but she is in control of the situation. Everybody around her falls for it and believes she is the victim of her husband's violence. This is not to say that everybody who is the victim of another person's violence is the passive-aggressor. Many people are recipients of random aggression – and that has nothing to do with them. If, however, the pattern repeats itself, then it's worth looking at.

The attentive reader will perhaps have noticed that Jo and Brian are married to each other. In a way, it's a perfect fit and they both get what they want out of the relationship – although it perhaps satisfies their immediate needs, it doesn't meet the needs of real relationship. Let us imagine they have mutually recognised that the way they have been acting is not what they want in the future. This is a huge step. The task for each of them is to find their own sources of self-esteem which are not dependent on other people.

The potential reward of coming to terms with our aggression is the ability to have a real relationship with another human being. When we are being aggressive to someone else, we are not seeing them as they truly are. If we can see that they are another suffering human being, we may find it in our hearts to love them.

BREAKING THE CYCLE OF AGGRESSION

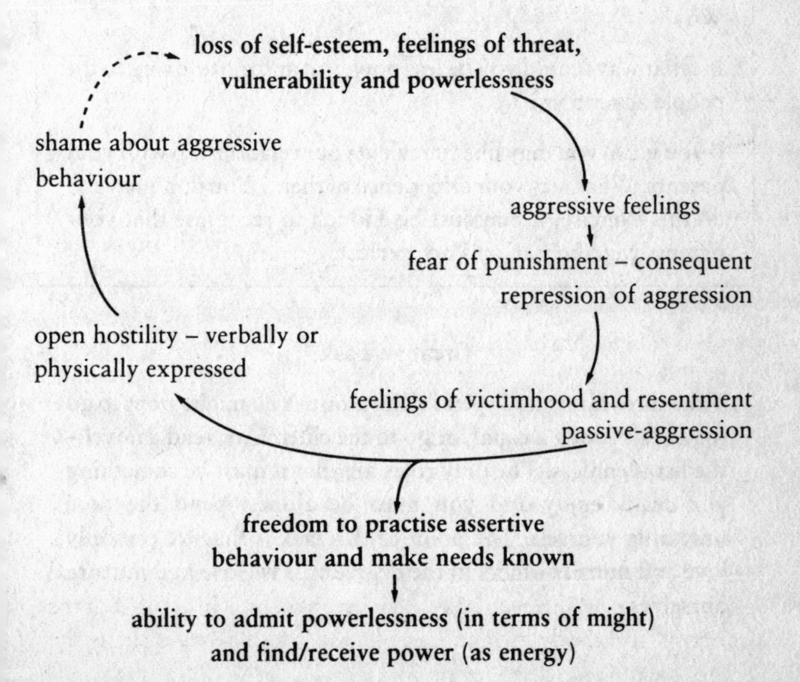

Inner Work

Look at your power audit. What sort of patterns do you see in the close relationships you have?

When are you most likely to be aggressive? When are you mostly likely to be a victim?

Recall an instance from your childhood when you were bullied or hurt in some way. Gently replay the scene in your mind and make a different ending.

What things about yourself are you vulnerable about? (Remember that naming them often takes the sting out of them.) Are there any practical ways you could boost your self-esteem?

Reading Brian's and Jo's stories, did you notice where you felt angry, impatient or pitying, or any other feeling. Is there some message here for you?

Which person did you feel more sympathy with – Brian or Jo? Why?

In what ways could you be less powerful and more loving to the people around you?

If you wish, you may like to review your relationship with your parents. What was your experience of them? You don't have to do this exercise, it may just be enough to recognise that your parents were human and not perfect.

Creative Task

Take three hours and spend them alone. You might want to go for a walk along a canal, or go to the cinema, or read a novel – the list is endless. The only rules are that it must be something you really enjoy and you must be alone. Spend the time nurturing yourself. The point of this task is that we can only love and nurture others to the degree that we love and nurture ourselves.

TRANSFORMATION OF AGGRESSION – POWER AS ENERGY AND LOVE

When Jo and Brian started their inner work, they found that their life together had to change. Jo found her self-esteem was very tied up with her physical image. While acknowledging that it's pleasant to look as attractive as one can, she no longer thought her whole self-worth was dependent on how she looked. She came to see that she was valuable in other ways, too. She decided to get some training so that she could get a job and so would be financially a bit more independent. Mixing with other people in the workplace gave her the chance to make new friendships and to feel that her contribution was important. She also did a lot of work with learning how to be assertive. (Assertiveness techniques are discussed in Chapter 8: Anger page 74). The results of being more assertive were that she could ask for what she wanted in a nonmanipulative way.

Brian's work started around his negative self-image. Like Jo, he came to realise that his whole worth wasn't tied up in the way he looked, or even around the fact that he could or couldn't make love. Reviewing his childhood, he was able to see that he had beaten Jo because he himself had been beaten. While feeling very angry that his step-father had abused him, he also realised that it was probably because he himself had been abused. Brian decided to break the chain of abuse and be the last of that particular line. He decided that the conventional life he had been leading was too restricting and that he could afford to take risks and experiment with new ways of doing things.

Brian didn't know what he felt about his marriage. He asked Jo if she would agree to living apart for three months while they thought about things. She was very frightened at the thought but decided that it could be a good idea. They both noticed that when they were alone they could rediscover some of the loving feelings that they'd originally had for each other. The transformation of aggression often leads to a greater capacity to love. Only passionate people are aggressive and that passion can become love.

Whether they decide to end or renew their marriage is a question for the future. Both are committed to end the cycle of aggressive power. As Jo put it, 'If you see power as energy, you realise that energy is love.'

8

Anger

'To be angry with the right person to the right extent and at the right moment and with the right object and in the right way – that is not easy.' Aristotle

WHAT IS ANGER?

Anger requires very considerable wisdom and yet, anger properly experienced, creates wisdom. It is crucial to emotional literacy because it calls for both restraint and expression – considered, reflective restraint and the creative finding of appropriate expression. Perhaps we're more frightened of anger than any other emotion. We know how destructive it can be in our own lives and we fear the rage of others towards us. Anger can kill, as in murderous rage, but anger suppressed can also kill in other ways. These can include alcoholism and other addictions, depression, loneliness and chronic resentment. In a way, anger is like the genie in the bottle in the *Tales of a Thousand and One Nights*. When it comes out of the bottle, it enlarges to giant size and dwarfs our human scale. It makes us, as people, feel small and its awesome force makes us feel fearful. It can kill and lay waste entire countries. But, if the genie is treated in the right way, it has the power to transform the entire situation and bring about a satisfactory ending to the story. Anger is like this and, if we overcome our fear of it, it can transform our lives, bringing us all the riches of the inner orient.

Let's look at some specific situations which are likely to cause anger:

- A company, full of excuses and promises, again fails to deliver the package for which you have been waiting three weeks and without which your business will fail.
- A car overtakes you aggressively and causes you to brake, missing the green light. You are already late for your meeting and this selfish action on another driver's part will make you even later.
- Your partner says they have had enough of you and announces that they are going to leave you as soon as they can find another place to live.
- The video machine you have kindly lent to a depressed friend to cheer her up is returned broken without comment or apology.

Should you be angry in these circumstances and can you allow yourself be angry? How much of your anger is caused by the actual event itself and how much by all the things that have gone before? In the case of the missing package you may well lose your temper, but you have held onto your frustration with the situation for three weeks. You are also frightened that your business will fail and that your economic stability will be threatened. Your anger has a huge amount of fear mixed in with it.

In the case of the car, not only are you are running late and feeling stressed but you are also very anxious about the meeting you are on your way to. To be prevented from going through the green light is the last straw. You are worried that the meeting will go badly but you are secretly angry with your boss for letting you down at a crucial time. You don't want to admit all these things to yourself yet so you displace your anger onto another person.

When your partner leaves you might say 'good riddance' or you might feel devastated because it reminded you of all the other times you have been abandoned. Perhaps the relationship hasn't been working well for a while. You are probably angry about all the things she or he hasn't done but when they announce their actual departure, you suppress your anger and feel sad and rejected.

In the case of the broken video machine, you have already spent hours trying to cheer up your depressed friend and now would like to watch a film yourself. You feel you can't lose your temper with your friend because they are too depressed to take it. But nevertheless you resent the time they take up and the emotional drain of their constant depression. You swallow your rage, say nothing and smile falsely at them.

All the anger in all these circumstances is provoked by another emotion: fear, anxiety, feelings of abandonment and feelings of resentment. The rest of the chapter explores ways in which we can uncover the roots of the anger – the powerhouse behind its passion – and looks at ways in which we can safely express our anger.

HOW DOES ANGER FEEL?

Anger feels uncomfortable. Many physical changes prepare us for the fight-or-flight response. This hangover from our past enables us to fight an enemy or to run away from one if we need to. (It is more fully described in the Chapter 13: Fear, page 140.) Rage can make us feel as though we're literally swelling up. 'You feel as if your heart is too big for your body,' as one man said. 'It feels as though you have been taken over,' said another person. People's complexions change colour going red, purple and occasionally white with rage. Physical symptoms of anger can include:

- thumping heart
- tightening of throat or chest
- indigestion and/or hunger
- some of the symptoms of irritable bowel syndrome
- prickling at back of head
- feeling of pain in chest/heart area
- headache
- weary feeling in the body

Although the physical symptoms are uncomfortable, they become less so if the anger is recognised for what it is and not suppressed. Anger is visceral and feels primitive. What is even more frightening is the fear of loss of control which can go with rage. Anything could happen. Our rational faculties seem suspended. People are *out of their mind*, *beyond reason* or *beside themselves*. Revealingly in America the word 'mad' means angry, but in Britain, 'mad' means insane. This shows the link between anger and temporary forms of insanity.

It is unlikely that you are reading this now in a state of rage because you wouldn't remember that this book was of any use to you. But you may be reading this now in a moment of relative calm because you have repeated angry outbursts and want to learn how to deal with them more effectively. Or you may be reading this because you have many of the physical symptoms of anger but never express the emotion itself. Instead you short-circuit it and feel fear, depression or resentment instead. Or, you may be reading this because you have a friend or family member who is chronically angry and you want to find out more about the way they feel.

TWO MYTHS ABOUT ANGER

There are two major myths about anger and both are false. One is that you can express your anger whenever and however you wish and the other is that you can repress your anger and never have to feel it yourself. Families often perpetuate such mythology. For example, I may have grown up in a family where I was encouraged to act on my feelings, whatever they were. It was OK to let it all hang out. In later life, if I'm angry, I just shout at the person I believe has made me angry. In schools and in workplaces such behaviour is not usually tolerated and I may find these patterns hard to modify. So I have to learn how to conform. Because I haven't practised emotional literacy, I will find it hard to control these powerful feelings. I may get a reputation for trouble-making or may suppress my angry feelings altogether and end up feeling depressed.

On the other hand, as is more likely in England, my family may have thought that anger was 'not a very nice emotion'. People were allowed to be depressed or sullenly hostile but they weren't allowed to be angry. To be angry was a shameful thing, showing both immaturity and inferiority. In some cases the loss of control associated with anger is confused with the loss of control experienced during passionate love-making. If control is an important issue in the family I may feel humiliated by my rage. I turn my anger in on myself and it becomes depression.

Yet another twist is added when different attitudes towards anger are permitted within the same family. Some family members are allowed to be angry and in fact are encouraged to be so. Others must not be angry because their role is to be reasonable. What happens is that the angry people end up doing all the angry work for everyone else and the reasonable people end up carrying all the depression for the others. It's not a satisfactory solution because people don't own their own feelings.

Sometimes these feelings are divided up between the men and the women. An example of this might be the irascible father who is continually angry and aggressive with his children. This man was frightened by his own father's anger but does not have the insight to break the pattern so he passes it on to the next generation. The mother will be the reasonable, peacemaking person who secretly drinks or who is less secretly depressed. Often the men will carry the anger and the women the depression. This stereotype is not always the case and one should be careful not to assume that all men are angry and all women are depressed. Women can be very angry and violent, too. Both sexes have the natural capacity for these emotions.

Look Back on Anger

Take a moment now and look at your own anger mythology. Ask yourself the following questions:

- **Do I believe that showing my anger is the right thing?**
- **Do I believe that showing my anger is the wrong thing?**

You will probably answer that it depends on the circumstances. Start to make a list of circumstances where you feel it's justifiable to be angry. When you've done that think back to your childhood. Have your beliefs about anger changed since you were a child?

THE CYCLE OF ANGER

Anger works, like other emotions, as a cycle. This means that as we go repeatedly round the circuit recognising familiar landmarks time and time again, we can choose to leave the cycle. Anger usually starts with an underlying feeling which may be anxiety, boredom, fatigue, fear or restlessness. This makes us vulnerable to the events which trigger anger. Often there will be more than one trigger, and so our anger escalates throughout the day as more and more fuels our rage. One thing seems to lead to another until there is an explosive outburst of uncontrollable rage. Losing control like this adds to our underlying feelings of vulnerability, stress and fear, and so the cycle is a self-perpetuating one.

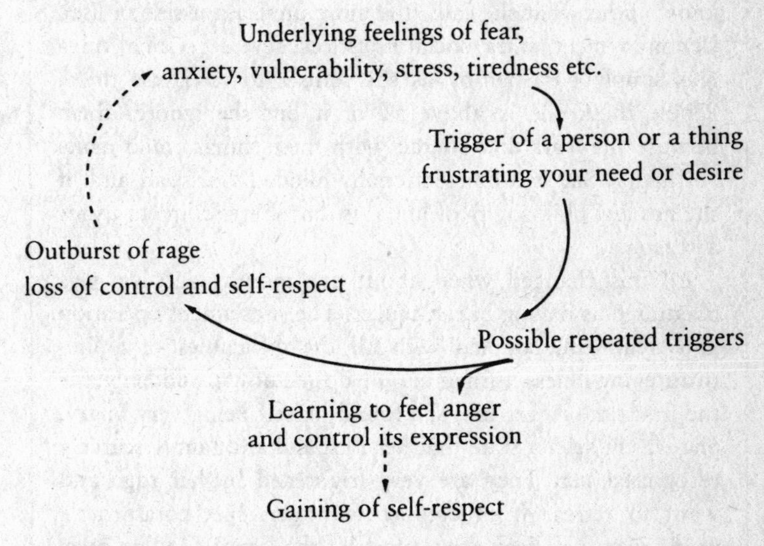

There are two important steps in breaking the cycle of anger. The first is to recognise what our underlying feelings are and to treat ourselves with extra care and love at these times. The second is to learn how to feel our anger and to focus it towards the right place. When we acknowledge that we're angry, we have some control over how we express it.

Learning to feel our anger takes time. It's usually best to start by looking at our family patterns (see the exercise 'Look Back on Anger') and see how much of the way we express anger is inherited. Then we can decide what we want to do about our anger. If you are frightened of your anger, as is very common, remember that by acknowledging it, you are taking responsibility for its expression.

Too nice to be angry – Cynthia's story

Cynthia is now in her sixties and lives a comfortable retirement life with her husband. She was married young and has three grown-up children and six grandchildren. She lives in a pin-neat village in the country. She prides herself on her personal appearance and her house is always spotless, well organised and well stocked with food. She does not want to know about what she calls 'the more unpleasant side of life'. Unemployment, wars, social injustices, severe personal traumas simply pass her by as she refuses to recognise them. People think she is above all of it but she ignores them because she fears that contact with these things could make her angry. She is a conventionally-minded Christian and, if she has any philosophy of life, it is that things come to us for a reason.

All this changed when about five months ago she was diagnosed as having breast cancer. The subsequent operation and treatment, coupled with all the difficulties of a life-threatening illness, turned her life upside down. Suddenly, for the first time in her life, she found herself being very angry. She was in such a state that her husband and family scarcely recognised her. They are very frightened by her rage and want to retreat from contact with her. Her comfortable world-view has been torn apart by the illness. As she says, 'The enemy invaded my own body – I could no longer carry on with the denial of my anger. I had to admit that life has unpleasant things in it which make me very angry. I can't see a reason for my cancer and I feel powerless.'

As a child Cynthia had been very frightened by her mother's rages. Her mother was angry and alcoholic and Cynthia spent much of her childhood attempting to pacify her and head off some of her more terrifying outbursts. As an adult, Cynthia married a man who was similarly frightened by anger and they constructed their life as an 'anger-free zone'. Because her life has been built around the fiction that 'everything's all right really' her whole life is threatened by this new state of being. As well as dealing with her illness, she also has to learn to deal with her newly thawed feelings.

A raging volcano – Mark's story

Mark is now seventeen. When he was a baby his mother abandoned him and he never knew his father. Mark has survived a childhood in a children's home and a succession of foster homes. He learnt various ways to cope with the pain of this. One was to use anger as a weapon against anyone in authority.

He rarely experienced anyone caring about him and he assumed he was unlovable. The bitterness fed his resentment against the parents who hadn't wanted him. Because he has never met his parents, he almost doesn't know he's angry with them and instead is angry with anyone who tries to act parentally towards him. His anger is displaced from its real focus. He treats his girlfriends casually and without any regard for them as people, tossing them aside when he has had sex with them or they start to make any emotional demands on him.

He has also learnt that anger can be used manipulatively to get what he wants. He smashes anything to hand while shouting abuse and using bad language. In such situations it's often easier to give into his demands. His foster parents have often been terrorised by his anger. 'He's like a raging volcano,' said one of them as they admitted defeat and asked Mark's social worker to find him another place to live. Mark finds it difficult, if not impossible, to talk about his feelings. 'What feelings,' he says dismissively if you ask him. 'That crap's for girls. I'm not going to get involved with that.' The dismissiveness is only a mask for his fear.

Part of Mark is also terrorised by his anger. He doesn't want to be so aggressively angry but he doesn't know how to stop. When he goes on a rampage, a little boy inside him is intensely frightened. Mark's condition needs the help of someone who is both kind and firm – kind to the wounded and hurt side of him and firm with the manipulative and destructive side. It needs an adult to be able to say consistently to him, 'The buck stops here and you will not manipulate me but I care about you and know some of the pain you've been through.'

WORKING THROUGH ANGER

Both Cynthia and Mark have the same task – to find out what is really making them angry and to learn how to express it cleanly and clearly so that it falls onto the right target. Learning some assertiveness techniques can be very useful here.

Cynthia has never been able to ask for what she really wants in life, she has always fallen in with what other people have wanted for her. First with her mother and later in her marriage, she conformed to outward and conventional notions of her duty and her role. Her illness is now offering her a chance to discover who she really is. When she sits down and starts to think about her life, she is angry with herself, her family and with God. God should have protected me from this illness, she thought, after all, I played the game by the rules and although I sinned, I never did anything really terrible. She realised that although she could be angry with God, it wasn't part of the deal that, if she were a good girl, she would have no suffering.

Then she was angry with her family for trying to 'push me around and run my life' as she saw it. Her family found it hard to bear her anger and irritation with them and blamed it on her illness. Finally Cynthia was angry with herself for living in a cocoon of denial all these years. There were many things she had wanted to do but had prevented herself because other people always came first. Now she felt it was too late and that she had wasted her life. After she had experienced her real anger she fell into a depression. This often happens and it is a way of dealing with the feelings of grief and loss of our unlived lives. The depression was short-lived and when she came out of it she decided to live every day as if it were a precious gift. She learnt to be assertive and to ask for what she wanted. As she says, 'What really made me angry and what I denied was the fact that I was never allowed – no I'll change that and take responsibility and say instead that I never allowed myself – to be angry.'

Mark's anger is calculated to drive everyone away and he would say this is what he wants. But he is really hungry for attention and love and if he gets it, he may be able to use the safe space to look at some of the issues that have been too painful to explore up until now. Although Mark might be able to work on these things by himself, it would be much easier and quicker if he has someone, such as a therapist, social worker, or otherwise experienced adult to help and guide him.

He realised that he was primarily angry with his mother for abandoning him. He was encouraged to imagine his mother was sitting in a chair opposite him. For a long while he hurled at the chair all the abuse that he could think of and shouted every kind of obscenity. When he had finished that he asked himself, I wonder why she did it? This opened up a new line of thinking and he happened to meet an older woman who had given her child for adoption and she spoke about the pain it had caused her. She had been told it was for the best and had always regretted it. Mark realised that his own mother might have left him because she genuinely thought he might have a better life without her. He also realised that he had repeated the pattern of his own abandonment by angrily dumping all his girlfriends as soon as there was a possibility of a real rapport and tenderness.

He started to see that he used his rage as a manipulative weapon so that he could get his own way. When he learnt how to ask for what he wanted, he was surprised to find it was so easy. He also learnt techniques for dealing with his rage safely. Apart from speaking to an empty chair (in which the person he was angry with was sitting in his imagination), he practised free expression drawings, shouting in open spaces, hurling cushions onto a bed and kicking stones against a wall (checking first that nobody would be hurt).

ASSERTIVENESS AND ANGER

There is really only one golden rule – do not express your anger in a way that might harm yourself or others.

There are many books and training courses on assertiveness and what follows is only a brief overview of the subject. The following guidelines may be helpful:

- speak from your own experience. Use words like 'I think', 'I feel', 'I am angry', 'I am experiencing such-and-such'.
- express anger as soon as you can – don't store it up as resentment.

- ask for exactly what you want. Other people aren't mind-readers. Say, 'I would like x – is that possible for you?'
- be prepared to negotiate – other people have needs and agendas, too.
- don't put the blame on other people and say accusatively, 'You didn't or did.'
- find the true target of your anger – but don't always accuse them of it. Don't allow your anger to come out sideways.
- find a safe way of expressing your anger. This might include speaking to an empty chair, beating a cushion, going for a long walk, playing a highly competitive game of squash.
- take responsibility for your own life and happiness.

If you can practise the above, you will find your anger is much cleaner and less contaminated by other emotions such as vindictiveness, violence, resentment and fear. You will also find that the anger of other people is much easier to deal with as these techniques work well both ways.

RULES FOR DEVELOPING AN ENVIRONMENTALLY FRIENDLY FORM OF ANGER

1. Clear the air
2. Express your rage safely
3. Respect yourself and others
4. Stand your ground and ask for what you want
5. Practise clean anger

Inner Work

Referring to the 'Look Back on Anger' exercise, what do you do with anger that isn't justified? Do you translate it into depression, resentment or some other emotion?

How do you feel about your anger?

What anger do you allow yourself to express and how do you express it?

What would you like to change about the way you express your anger?

What do you feel about other people's anger? Does is frighten you? Does it make you angry?

Are you prepared to take responsibility for your anger? If not, who should?

Creative Task

There are two tasks in this section.

The first is for you to do when you're in a rage. You might like to prepare this beforehand so that you've got it to hand. Take a very large sheet of paper and pin securely to a large drawing board. Now select two wax crayons (and the choice of colours is always interesting). Put one crayon in each hand and close your eyes firmly. Scribble with the crayons on the paper like this until your hands stop. Now open your eyes and see the map of your anger. You might like to keep it by your bed or your desk for a few days or weeks to remind yourself that your anger's out there and no longer trapped inside.

The second task is to do after you've been angry. Anger is like a giant and it lifts us up. We have to come back down the mountain to sea level. If possible go for a quiet walk amongst some trees or by a river. Imagine yourself descending a stone staircase leading down a mountain. With each step downwards, you are getting closer to your normal state.

THE TRANSFORMATION OF ANGER

'The tigers of wrath are wiser than the horses of instruction.'

William Blake

Anger is one of the greatest teachers that we can have in the pursuit of emotional intelligence. Wisely expressed, it shows us what we really want and opens up a path to freedom. Being able to express our anger safely, assertively and effectively means that we have more choice in a situation. As we become practised in anger, we usually find that we less frequently fall into a rage and are no longer frightened by the rages of others.

Anger transformed leads to wisdom. We realise that we are not one person but many living under one roof psychologically speaking. In a large family or communal living situation it is quite likely that one person will be angry. The others can then minister to that person. When our 'inner people' are emotionally intelligent, they won't all catch the anger from the one angry person and fall into a collective rage. Instead they will look for the thing that is behind the anger, which might be powerlessness, vulnerability, loss of self-esteem, and they will work gently with that.

There is a further pay-off in the work with anger. There are world situations which rightly make us very angry. These are starvation, massacres, ecological catastrophes. Most of the time we feel angry about them but feel powerless to act. As we deal with our own personal anger, we may find the strength to confront these wider issues.

9

Anxiety

'Anxiety is the price of a ticket on the journey of life; no ticket, no journey, no journey, no life.' James Hollis

WHAT IS ANXIETY?

Anxiety is a state which is aroused when something important to us is uncertain and perhaps not within our control. It's closely linked to success because it generally comes when we're moving into new areas of change and growth. In many ways the ability to feel anxious, but not be paralysed by it, is crucial to becoming successful in any field. Anxiety is a normal part of the human experience and exists in the space between fear and excitement. The trick is to steer it away from the former and towards the latter. If we go towards the excitement end of the spectrum, anxiety will give us energy to perform at our peak but, if we get stuck in fear, then we will find the experience of anxiety disabling.

We're never really anxious about the outcome of a situation we are totally indifferent to or completely in control of, and so the experience of anxiety is a litmus test of what is most important to us. For instance, if you have just fallen in love with someone wonderful, do you feel anxious if you don't know what his or her feelings are? If you don't, then you are probably not in love. Similarly, if you have just been given a new and exciting project at work which has many difficulties and problems to overcome, is it likely that you'll feel excited but also anxious? We get anxious when a situation or event stretches us, never in one where we are totally at ease.

Probably all of us have experienced anxiety at some time but only in some of us does this feeling become a state of being. These people are the chronic worriers and there is always something to worry about. As anxiety is a reaction to a stressful situation, it's natural to feel anxious, for instance, about the outcome of an exam, a pregnancy test, or the size of one's tax bill. Once the stimulus for the anxiety has passed and the uncertainty is resolved, usually the feeling goes. But for some of us anxiety exists as a constant and unwelcome background companion. It's connected with a personality type which is liable to depression and worry, and occasionally panic. It's also closely linked to the desire for perfection and the need for high achievement. Those who want to do well will reach high, and then risk falling flat on their faces. Perfectionists, in particular, find that very hard to do.

COPING AND CONTROL

Understanding the way we cope with anxiety is an essential step in transforming a distressing feeling into a powerful tool for change. One coping strategy is to attempt to desperately control everything but this is never a satisfactory solution. Our underlying belief structure and personal self-confidence will play a large part as well. If we don't believe we have the resources or don't deserve the positive outcome we desire, we will tend towards the fear end of the spectrum and our anxiety will become repetitive and ultimately disabling. An example of this would be a waiter who, desperately anxious to please the table of important guests, carefully takes their orders, but forgets them by the time he reaches the kitchen door. His anxiety takes up all his energy and ability to perform his job. He is then compelled to return to the table and ask for the order again – and again. Terrified of letting these guests down, his anxiety brings about the very outcome he most feared – the humiliation of failure. Only by breaking the cycle of fear, and paradoxically by allowing himself to fail, can he ever succeed.

Coping mechanisms can also become rituals. A ritual, in this sense, is an action which is performed because it once had the power to alleviate a painful situation. A smoker may say that they smoke because it makes them less anxious. But, in fact, it is *not* smoking which makes them anxious. They are dependent on smoking which makes them more anxious because anything you're dependent on can be withdrawn. The former crutch becomes the device that breaks your leg again and again. Addictions have more complex causes than anxiety. Nevertheless, understanding the mechanics of our own anxiety can help us in dealing with addictive patterns.

The ability to tolerate feelings of stressful anxiety has much to do with issues of control and trust. When we're anxious, we say in effect, 'I don't know the outcome of this particular situation and I can't control it either. That frightens me.' The next question is can I turn the anxiety into a concrete fear which I can deal with or am I going to remain in a state of undefined and nameless anxiety? Anxiety always concerns the future, it is about what *may* happen. If we can find the fear at the root of our anxiety, then we can either deal with the situation, or else come to terms with it. Trust replaces anxiety when we believe we can handle whatever comes our way. It can then mutate into excitement as we develop our self-confidence and our belief in our capacities. We may or may not have the help of our family, friends and colleagues, but we will certainly have the help of the inner family that has been unfolding through the developing work of emotional intelligence.

HOW DOES ANXIETY FEEL?

The German word for anxiety is *Angst* which carries the meaning of not only fear but also anguish and constriction. Anxiety often has this almost physically constricting feeling about it. Maybe our chest feels tight, or our throat dry. Our stomach may have butterflies and our legs feel shaky. There is usually a reduction in ability to concentrate. We may go into repetitive actions such as nail-chewing, hair-pulling, smoking or compulsive eating. Our voice may quaver or go faint. As one person put it, 'It feels very like fear but there is no focus – only a feeling of nameless dread'. These physical manifestations are the primitive remnants from the old fight-or-flight mechanism which served well in mankind's more physically dangerous past.

Anxiety is related to stress and we are all different in our ability to deal with stress. Some of us feel it more acutely than others. It can range from a feeling of apprehension to a worried state and can erupt into full-blown panic. What will stress one person will be easy for another. The important thing is not to compare ourselves with other people but to compare ourselves with ourselves – over time. So as time goes by you may find that you can handle situations which before would have fazed you. This emotional mastery brings the gift of increased self-esteem and a larger life.

WHAT ARE THE ROOTS OF ANXIETY?

The roots of anxiety lie in a fear of the unknown. In a way it's a bit like the early maps of the world which showed in detail the coastlines that sailors had come to know. Their knowledge wasn't complete and, in the parts they hadn't been to, they drew dragons and frightening beasts. We project our fears onto the unknown. Everything in the future is unknown for, in truth, we do not know that we will live to draw our next breath. Despite all our plans for the future and all our hopes and fears, the future is an unknown and uncharted territory. In order to deal with this rather uncomfortable state of affairs we often fantasise about the future, imagining that we know what will happen tomorrow. Quite often, based on past performance, we're right and this reinforces our belief that we do know. In this fallacy a lot of our pain and suffering are located because much of the freshness and spontaneity goes out of life.

We noted earlier that people who are by nature perfectionists tend to become anxious. That's because their perfectionism tends to make them fantasise the faultless outcome to the situation they're in. At the same time they know that it may not happen that way and that they haven't the power to make it happen. This makes them very anxious as they run through all the scenarios in their head which could influence the outcome and try to work out what do in each eventuality. In a way this is a very sensible and imaginative activity. The difficulty arises when the false belief arises that their actions will determine the outcome – whatever it is.

HOW IS ANXIETY TRIGGERED?

The trigger for anxiety is a situation whose outcome is uncertain but very important to us. Anxiety is intensified when we react to anxiety by trying to control the outcome instead of letting go. If we don't let go of our fantasy at this point, then we are doomed to repeat the cycle. If we don't get what we think we want, we are disappointed, but believe that, if we try harder next time, we will achieve what we want. This makes us more anxious for the future. But even if we do get the result we desire, it doesn't show us how to get off the cycle of anxiety. It merely reinforces our belief in our own power and sets us up for another round of anxiety – in which we could lose all that we've gained.

THE CYCLE OF ANXIETY

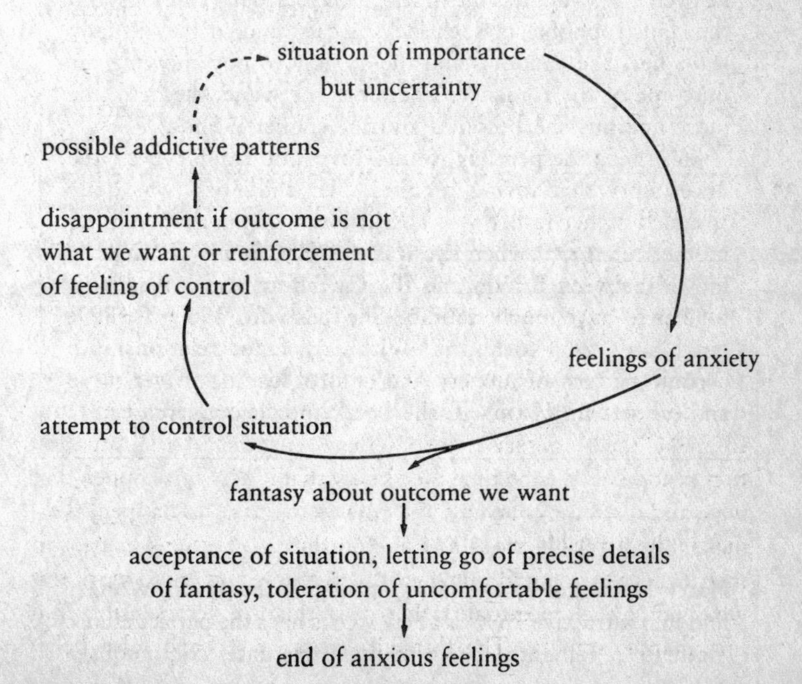

The control freak who wants to be loved – Bathsheba's story

Bathsheba is a pretty woman with what appears to be a good life. On the surface she doesn't appear anxious but in fact she is. She has a good job and a full social life. She is very well-presented with beautiful clothes and has a charming manner. She says, 'Most people think I'm a success. They don't look beneath the surface and see what's really going on. I'm anxious and lonely. I can't seem to connect with anybody.'

She has many men flocking around her and has passionate affairs with some of them. She longs to find 'the right one' and to settle down and get married. When any of them look as if they will get serious, the affair comes to a sudden and abrupt end. Bathsheba ends the relationship by trying to control the other person's actions and activities. She makes rules about what they can do and wants them to account for all their time. She worries when they are late that they have been in a car accident and have been killed. She demands that they have to ring up and tell her where they are and if they'll be even a few minutes late. Her partners usually cannot stand the claustrophobia of such lack of trust and so they usually leave her. She cannot stand the anxiety of not knowing the outcome of the romance. The more she wants the man, the more anxious she becomes and the sooner it ends.

Bathsheba desperately wants love but cannot bear the uncertainty that loving requires. Her childhood was quite troubled as her father was absent much of the time and her mother remarried when she was ten. The family continually moved between Britain and the Caribbean and it was hard for her to have much stability. She tells you, 'I long for love but I can't seem to find it.' With each failed relationship a chronic pattern of anxiety and control leading to yet more anxiety sets in. How will she break the vicious circle?

In flight from life – Harry's story

Harry is around forty and is an eligible bachelor. Women find him attractive and for a few weeks he is the perfect escort – attentive, romantic and passionate. He dates continuously and is a member of several singles' clubs and up-market dating agencies. As he is well-established financially in life, he can afford to go on a variety of holidays where he encounters many potential mates. He will tell you he is looking for 'the perfect women' and he hasn't found her yet. In fact women make him very anxious and sex makes him even more anxious. For him, it means surrendering a part of his body to a woman's control. If the woman is a casual acquaintance and he doesn't know her, it is just about bearable but if she is someone he knows and could fall in love with, then sex becomes a threat.

The roots of Harry's sexual anxiety lie in his childhood. His mother was very controlling (we may hazard a guess that she was anxious, too) and he was controlled through feeding, nappy changing and potty training. She could touch him intimately as a baby (as mothers have to with small babies) but she gave him no space or respect of his own. As he grew up he felt his body didn't properly belong to him but could be used by another person at any time.

Harry knows his own patterns by now and is starting to find them slightly sickening. First there is the meeting and wooing of a new woman. Then there's the sex. If there's a real connection between himself and the woman, he leaves immediately, making her feel perplexed and rejected. Then it's on to the next. He would like to change the pattern. He says, 'I want more from life. I want someone to be there for me. But she has to be perfect or I'll feel cheated.' With the myth of the perfect woman, Harry keeps himself perpetually in flight.

HOW DO YOU REACT TO ANXIETY?

In the examples of Bathsheba and Harry we have seen different reactions to the stress of anxiety. We have already noted that anxiety is one of the older, more 'primitive' emotions. Let's imagine ourselves back in time a few thousand years ago. We are part of a tribe living with stone-age weapons, hunting and trapping whatever we can. One day we see a large predatory animal in a grove of trees some way off. We are small, alone and unarmed. In those circumstances a number of reactions to this anxious situation might flash through our minds. We might wonder whether we should stay absolutely still and hope it wouldn't notice us, or run away, possibly provoking the animal to chase us. Or we might consider the best method of defence as attack and go up and try to frighten the animal. Or, if it is a large dominant male of our own species and we are weaker, we might go into a submissive pose and offer the other animal sexual gratification so as to defuse its hostility. All these responses are potentially valid in terms of the threatening situation in which our ancestors found themselves. The judgement would be in deciding which was the most effective in the unique set of circumstances.

The interesting thing is that these responses are still with us. The stimulus of the large frightening animal is no longer present of course (except in very exceptional circumstances) but the reactions to anxiety are the same. The sight of the powerful animal filled our ancestor with anxiety until he or she decided the best course of action. They then carried it out and were either eaten or survived. In making the action, they got rid of their anxiety and their choices. Once the incident was over, the anxiety was gone.

Because the threats to our survival are so much more subtle and usually involve a psychological dimension, we usually don't have the resolution of our anxiety that our ancestors enjoyed. We can't return to our cave and say to our mate: 'I was downwind of the most enormous sabre-toothed tiger. I was terrified and I stood stock still for twenty minutes. He never even saw me! My heart was in my mouth the whole time. But he went off in the other direction and here I am back safe and sound. Perhaps I'll paint a picture of it on the wall this evening if I have time.' We don't have the physical means of processing anxious reactions the way our ancestors could but we are still stuck with the reactions. They are:

- **The freeze response**
  People who habitually adopt this means of coping with their anxiety usually become paralysed by it. They are frightened to do something, but also frightened not to do it. Quite often people become trapped in a job they no longer enjoy and have in fact grown out of but are too frozen by their anxious feelings to move on. They are in a sense trapped on that

prehistoric savannah, waiting for the beast to pounce. They think if they don't move, then the feared thing won't happen. Perhaps it won't but it will be very hard for anything else to happen, so their lives are, so to speak, on hold.

- **The flight response**
  People who usually adopt this means of coping are forever on the run from one thing to the next. They will get into a relationship and be very excited about it and then when you see them a few days later, it is all over. Often those who flee will justify their actions and can sound deceptively rational. They may say, 'I don't think this is quite it.' Sometimes it is best to run away, but if your habitual coping mechanism is running away, you may end up with nothing at all.

- **The attack response**
  Some people attack when they feel anxious. Probably many wars have been started this way with a collective anxiety in one country being dealt with by attacking another country. In the sphere of intimate relationships, people who habitually attack are very trying to their partners. In the context of work, this is a very destructive response because it usually undermines colleagues and fellow team-workers. You can usually spot an attacker as they will say something like 'nobody puts one over me'. Another variant of this response is the turning of the attack onto the person themselves, rather than the outside world. This usually leads to depression and lack of self-esteem.

- **The submission response**
  Some people choose to submit when they feel anxious. They choose the outcome they most dislike and then accept it. They refuse to fight for what they really want because they are frightened of not getting it but also of being injured in the process. The key phrase of the submissive is 'anything for a quiet life'. As with all the above responses, it is sometimes valid but if it becomes a habitual coping mechanism, it can lead to a passive and rather masochistic attitude to life. Submissives believe they have no choice and this ends up being a self-fulfilling prophecy.

Most of us are not pure types as described above. We have bits and pieces of all these responses in the way we behave, depending on what threats we face. It is worth working out what anxieties provoke what response in you. Do relationship anxieties make you want to run away or anxieties in your workplace make you want to submit? Or perhaps conflict of any kind makes you freeze?

Inner work

What situations make you anxious? Describe them in as much detail as you can, imagining that you are telling a close and trusted friend about them.

Do you have rituals that are connected with feeling anxious? Describe them and how they help you to become calm.

What is your response to feeling anxious (freezing, fleeing, attacking, submitting)?

What effect do these responses have on the quality of your life? Do they stop you getting what you really want?

Can you name the fear your anxiety is masking? (It doesn't matter if you can't – that will probably come with time and practice.)

Keep an anxiety diary for a week and note down when you feel anxious. After a week review it. Does the act of noticing your anxiety change your experience of it? In what way?

Creative Task

Write a letter to your anxious self. It is, after all, part of you and it is frightened. You may like to tell this part of you that you will look after it and are not cross with it for being anxious. In the letter, explore the possibility that you are more than your anxiety and other parts of your personality can come to help and soothe it. You may like to answer the letter from the perspective of the anxious person within and so set up a dialogue. The fruits of such an exchange could be far-reaching and transformative.

THE TRANSFORMATION OF ANXIETY

Through their inner work both Bathsheba and Harry realised that the real problem with their anxious natures was not the anxiety as such but their response to it. Bathsheba attempted to control and lost. Harry fled and lost. Both wanted love and neither would find it while they allowed anxiety to rule their lives. They had to find a way of tolerating anxiety and surrendering control.

Existential philosophers have had a great deal to say on the subject of anxiety. According to them, there are four types of anxiety which all human beings experience. They are the anxieties which surround the following facts of existence:

- death – inevitable but fearful because it involves the unknown
- freedom – free choice is scary because it makes us responsible for our fate
- aloneness – human beings are basically alone, despite all our attempts to merge and fuse
- meaninglessness – the world is a random accident and it is up to us to make sense of it. We impose meaning on our situations

For many people existentialism presents an unnecessarily bleak view of the world. However, this way of looking at anxiety can be useful. If our personal anxiety touches on an existential anxiety, it reinforces the personal anxiety. For instance, Harry's fear of sex is derived from the fact that he cannot trust his body to another person who's close to him. When he was a baby his mother was large and powerful, he was small and defenceless. She appeared to be in total control (but of course was really feeling nervous and anxious). He feared that because she could totally control his body, she could cause him not to exist. Bathsheba realised that much of her anxiety was fundamentally centred on her aloneness. She feared separation from people more than anything else and so brought it about in order to end the uncertainty. When she realised that everybody else also feels alone but that there are possibilities of connection despite that, she feared it less.

For both of them, the transformation of their anxiety was long-term work. A turning point in Harry's journey came about when he realised that, although he had been frightened of annihilation and death at his mother's hands, his fear had not actually been realised. He was still here. Nothing could make up for his difficulties in early parenting but he could still become a good parent to himself. When faced with a situation in which he felt like bolting, he decided to adopt a different strategy. He would withdraw for a while from the woman he was with, explaining that he needed some personal space for himself but that he would be back. He then nurtured his inner child, reassuring it and being with it. He would carefully explain to it that this relationship was not going to lead to annihilation and death. That was only a very understandable but actually unfounded fear. He had now far greater resources than he had had as a baby and together all the parts of his personality would cope with the situation.

Bathsheba learnt to let go. When she realised that the mechanism she had been using to cope with anxiety was defeating her, she was amazed. But she was also relieved because it made sense. She realised that she had to give up control and trust whatever life brought. That didn't exclude making sensible and rational choices, but it did exclude imagining that she could be in control of the future. As she says now: 'I've learnt to expect the unexpected. Well – not always. I'll always have my control-freak side but I can laugh at it more now. The unexpected changes my life every day and brings me new things. I can't wait to see what's going to happen next.'

10

Boredom

> 'And my mother taught me as a boy,
> Ever to confess you're bored means you have no
> Inner Resources. I conclude now that I have no
> Inner Resources because I am heavy bored.'
>
> John Berryman

WHAT IS BOREDOM?

If you're reading this chapter because you're bored, then there must be a small part of you that doesn't want to be bored. This is very significant because when you're bored it feels as though all power to will has been drained away. The animation seems to have gone out of life and you can't make it come back. All you can do is work with that little bit of you that isn't bored and use it to charm and persuade the rest of you back into the stream of life. But the very act of opening a book, and starting to read it, is enormously encouraging and maybe the next few pages will help you to recover sparkle and interest in the present moment. Because, ultimately, a commitment to living in the excitement of the present, with all its uncertainties, possibilities and hope is the best antidote to boredom. There's no magic carpet to take you there – it's part of a step-by-step process.

There is a need to distinguish between a genuine reaction of something being boring and a blanket of being bored. The latter is what this chapter is about – not the momentary flashes we all have in response to a boring event. The opposite of boredom is a connection with the energy of life. The Greeks called this quality eros, a term that has become almost synonymous with sexual passion. It's easy to see how energy and sex have become linked because the overwhelming feelings of passionate sex are the polar opposite to boredom. A similiar word for boredom is apathy, which revealingly means to be without feelings. Feelings give colour to life and so to be bored means that somehow we've lost touch with what we really feel. As Tolstoy said, boredom is 'the desire for desires', and we may need to uncover the desires which have been hidden or repressed.

There is both pride and shame in boredom. We may feel pride that a situation or a relationship bores us because it shows the level of our sophistication and self-development. 'It's boring and dull' we may say when in fact we're really beyond it but haven't quite moved on yet. So to feel boredom in these circumstances may be really an indicator that you should find a bigger canvas to work on. A degree of self-awareness is necessary for boredom and, therefore, it is quite a sophisticated emotion. The important thing here is not to get stuck on how sophisticated and knowledgeable one is, but to move onto the next level where one may feel like a beginner all over again. It may mean changing a job or taking a different career path. It may mean leaving a relationship, or perhaps looking at an existing one in a new light. A patch of boredom can be seen as an encouragement to a greater challenge.

There is also a potential sense of shame in boredom. I shall never forget my English teacher saying very firmly to me when I was fifteen, 'You know, to feel bored is a condemnation of yourself.' I can see her argument even now but I find it a punitive statement which doesn't help me get out of my bored state. But it is true that, if you find yourself interesting, then there is always something of interest to occupy you. John Berryman's poem, quoted at the beginning of this chapter, is of the same ilk when it speaks of boredom being the lack of inner resources. I don't nowadays believe that it does mean a real lack of inner resources but that the access to those inner resources has been blocked. The blocks can be:

- limiting beliefs
- conflicted or confused values
- hidden desires
- physical causes e.g. exhaustion or overwork

Whatever the reason is, this chapter looks at ways you can unblock your emotional inner resources, connect with your life and banish boredom.

HOW DOES IT FEEL?

As we've already noted, boredom feels as if you have no feelings. Of course you do but they're hidden under a blanket, a rather wet blanket perhaps, of denial. A woman told me, 'It feels as if you are in wasteland. Everything is colourless, black and white at best. You don't want anything because as soon as you might think of something you want, you decide either you can't have it, or it's no good anyway.' There are probably fewer physical feelings associated with boredom than with other more passionate emotions. Your body might feel a bit heavy and sluggish and your thought-processes slow and lacking in creativity.

There is an interesting connection between being bored and being boring. Boring people are usually bored, as Dylan Thomas said, while giving a talk, 'Somebody's boring me – I think it's me.' We often say people are boring but what does it mean? Perhaps it's to do with the fact that as their life force has gone out of the situation, they have nothing to offer to others, just as they have little to offer to themselves? Sometimes boredom precedes depression and some people would describe a mild depression as a patch of boredom. It signals a detachment from life and a lack of engagement. It could be useful to learn how to stop boredom from going into full-blown depression if this is your pattern.

One cause of being blocked and therefore bored can be simply tiredness. Overwork and constant stress play a part here. If you're too tired to engage in some interesting activity, then it can seem as if you're bored. Quite often we work so hard that we almost switch off our tiredness and lose track of how tired we are. If you suspect this may be the case, make sure you give yourself a weekend off with plenty of time for sleeping.

UNBLOCKING INNER RESOURCES

It is always worth looking first at the physical causes of boredom such as tiredness and stress, but if this does not resonate with you, the following possibilities may be useful avenues of exploration.

Limiting beliefs

All of us hold beliefs but only in some of us have they become so hardened that they actually limit the area we can think and feel in. Usually these limiting beliefs hide sneakily under our mental stones whenever the subject comes up. If they have to be looked at, then we will suddenly find ourselves justifying them with a number of rational arguments. The point is that they are built into the way we have decided to live our lives and it is hard to change them. We may feel they don't want to be changed but, of course, the reverse is true. We don't want the effort of changing ourselves. When our beliefs limit us, they can cause us to be bored and dissatisfied with our lives. Dissatisfaction is a key precursor of boredom but it can also herald major life changes and new horizons. Limiting beliefs cut off our possibilities, making our imaginative view of the future short-circuit into a repetition of what has already happened.

Everyone has their own set of limiting beliefs based on the way they process events and the actual events themselves. Some examples of limiting beliefs (in italics) include:

- *You can never get the job you really want.*
  Rationalisation: There's always a fly in the ointment, a hidden catch. And even if it's any good, there's sure to be an internal candidate that the job's been earmarked for. So it's no good even applying for that post I saw advertised – someone else will get it anyway.
  Result: I won't even try and I'll stay where I am even though I'm utterly bored with my current job.

- *There are no available single men (or women) over the age of thirty-five years.*
  Rationalisation: They're all married, or gay, or if they're single, they're no good. If they do get divorced or widowed, then they're snapped up immediately. So there's no point in hoping for a partner at my age – it just won't happen.

Result: So I won't go to parties or have a positive, open attitude to romantic possibilities – I'll just be sulky, cynical and bitter.

- *You can't make new friends once you're fifty.*
  Rationalisation: It's a sort of cut-off point and then you're stuck with what you've already got. You become a boring person anyway – look at the people that I know who're in their fifties, sixties and seventies. I don't want to grow old.
  Result: I won't try to find new and stimulating people – and if one came my way, I'd reject them before they rejected me.
- *I can't go on holiday alone.*
  Rationalisation: For one thing it's dangerous. My money might get stolen or I might be attacked. And, anyway, I wouldn't enjoy it. Can you see me alone at Niagara Falls or the Taj Mahal? I'd hate it because I wouldn't have anyone to share it with.
  Result: So, no holiday because there's no-one to go with.

You can never defeat these beliefs by logical arguments. They are much too cunning for that. There is simply no end to the rationalisations that they can produce. The only way to get around them is to outgrow the fears they conceal. In the first example, there is a hidden fear of success. In the second, a disguised fear of both commitment and rejection and, in the third, a not-so-covert concern with death and ageing. The fourth example speaks in a veiled way of a dread of aloneness and a lack of self-esteem. The theme of disappointment runs through these examples and one has the impression that at one time, these people tried to live more adventurously. Their defeats led them to generalise that it wasn't worth trying any more. If you don't try, you won't get hurt, but life does become mega boring.

You might like to pause and make a list of some of the beliefs that limit you and the resulting narrowing of your life that comes in the wake. Start to look at some of the fears and disappointments that may have played a part in concretising these fears.

Conflicted or confused values

The second major root cause of boredom is a conflicted or

confused personal value system. Values determine goals and without goals life lacks excitement. Values can be spiritual or material but they will reflect our unique and individual paths. The choices we make on the journey of our life reveal our values. Our values become conflicted if they are not consciously articulated and placed in some sort of hierarchy. We must decide what we want most. Otherwise we will find that the goals we do reach are not truly our own and therefore are not fulfilling.

If, for example, I decide that an important value for me is an art form in which to express my creativity, then I must do it. If I refuse this task, then I will become disappointed and bored. Our values can also be conflicting. I may decide that I need a good house and plenty of money to enjoy it. My value will then be to provide a good standard of living for myself. But hang on, I've just said it's very important for me to find a creative outlet and I haven't the energy for both. Unless I decide which is the more important and consciously aim for that, I will feel unsatisfied by whatever I achieve in either arena. If I make wonderful art but have no money, I will feel frustrated. If I make plenty of money and have a good standard of living, but do not exercise my creativity, I will feel similarly frustrated, though in rather more comfort. If I don't act on this feeling of frustration and resolve it, the energy will go out of my life and I will become bored.

Resolving such a conflict of values may or may not require major life change. I could give up my well-paid day job and embrace the life of an artist with all its consequent financial downsides. A less dramatic resolution might mean that I make space for a creative hobby while pursuing my less creative, but well-paid career. I might have to give up the option of winning (one day) the Nobel Prize for Literature in favour of, perhaps, writing some short stories for my local literary magazine. This could be equally fulfilling but only if the loss (whether it be financial or creative) is actually acknowledged by me. If I deny the element of loss which is present in every choice, I'm bound to have conflicting values which could very well lead to my becoming bored with my life.

Hidden desires

Sometimes we hide our desires very successfully from ourselves.

This can be for a variety of reasons. It may not suit our image of ourselves to admit them. We may consider them unworthy or shameful and thus we don't acknowledge them. It's a bit like meeting a very disreputable acquaintance in the street when you're with some very smart friends whom you want to impress. In such circumstances, it's hard to say hello and introduce them. They belong to different worlds and you don't want to mix them. The only trouble is that the disreputable acquaintance is part of you and by denying this, you cut yourself off from this energy. Emotional intelligence is ultimately about being able to bring the two sides of our lives together.

Why do we hide our desires from ourselves and repress them? There are a number of reasons which include:

- shame – the desire doesn't fit my self-image. For example, I might find myself wanting to have a relationship with someone who's married to someone else. Because I believe this is morally wrong, I will not allow myself to admit that I'm very drawn to this person.
- pride – the desire shows that I am needy. For example, I might have a desire for companionship but feel that I can't contact my friends when I'm lonely. I am too proud to admit that I need them.
- despair – the desire can't be fulfilled. For example, I might want my father to show some sign of affection towards me but he never has and it's unlikely he ever will. I despair about it and it's easier to deny that I want this than to acknowledge the pain of not having it.
- fear – if I show my desire I'll get punished for it. For example, if I've been brought up in a family which ridiculed people's desires instead of respecting them, I'll be very careful about admitting them. By the time I reach adulthood, I have internalised this mocking family so successfully that I don't dare admit what I want – even to myself.

For each person the mechanism of repression is different but the end result is the same. Desires make life fun and without them, life is flat and dull. It can be useful to look at your most honest wish list and decide what might hold you back from trying to get it. The very act of being truthful with yourself can have a profoundly liberating effect. It may not bring what you want into life immediately but you may feel freer to be excited about the possibility and to aim for it.

If what we want is unattainable, we may have to find a reasonably satisfactory alternative. In this case, the exercise 'Finding our true hopes' (Chapter 17: Hope, page 191) could be useful. At the bottom of all our desires is a wish for an emotional feeling which might be love, security, self-esteem or just simply happiness. Sometimes we have to refine our hopes down to their emotional roots and find other ways of achieving what we really want.

THE CYCLE OF BOREDOM

Boredom usually needs an event to trigger it. This might be a set-back or a challenge of some kind. The trigger is not very important and can't be avoided. It might just be stress and tiredness or they may actually work with the trigger to produce boredom. The important thing here is to recognise that it's not the trigger that's made you feel bored, but the underlying pattern of root causes: limiting beliefs, conflicting values and hidden desires. Without the root causes, if you have a boring trigger event, like going to a dull play, you will simply say, 'That *was* a dreary evening', but you won't get trapped in the emotion.

Trigger event
+
Root causes: limiting beliefs/conflicting values/
hidden desires/stress and fatigue

boredom reinforces
beliefs, confused values,
hidden desires

withdrawal of life energy

boredom

getting behind root causes and
constructing a personal value system

end of boredom and beginning of excitement

Boredom prevents him from finishing anything – Mark's story

Mark will go on holiday to an expensive resort and leave after a couple of days because he's so bored. He will drink himself to excess because he's so bored. He will end a potentially good relationship on a whim because he's so bored. In fact his whole life is governed by responding to his boredom and almost all his decisions are taken in response to this emotion.

He's still in his twenties and, despite talent and promise, has not yet made anything of his life. Instead he flits from one project to the next. He has been a jockey, a landscape gardener, an estate agent, a would-be scriptwriter. In all these careers he had some possibilities but when the going got tough, he simply left it and went on to the next thing. Because he never finished anything, or saw it through to its natural conclusion which might be to admit defeat, he has no feeling of any satisfaction which leads to yet more boredom.

Mark's childhood was not obviously difficult but he was indulged without being supported. His parents vaguely let him do anything he liked without mentoring him as to the wisdom of it. He has no underlying value system to fall back on except the idea that if doesn't feel good 'it means that I shouldn't be doing it'. The truth is that, without application, he will never reap the fruits of his talents and make some sort of worthwhile success, he has to cross his boredom threshold and learn to tolerate the feeling.

He is on the verge of wanting to break this cycle of boredom and defeat leading to new things which seem exciting but just repeat the cycle. He represses the desire for real change because he is partly afraid that it will mean real effort and partly because he is afraid of failure. As the cycles seem to be getting shorter and shorter, he feels some pressure for change.

The party's happening the other side of the hill – Daphne's story

Daphne is a successful woman in her early fifties. Successful, that is to say, in everybody else's eyes but her own. She is an attractive woman and owns a chain of craft shops. Over the years, her capacity for hard work, her excellent nose for young talent and her commercial flair have developed this enterprise into a highly original and successful business. On the surface this achievement is enviable but it doesn't satisfy Daphne. She admits to being restless and bored and the two things are linked in her mind.

Her personal life looks pretty well-ordered. Her children have grown up, her marriage has ended very amicably, and she has a charming companion and lover. She says: 'Having all these things, whether they are material or to do with people and relationships, does not make me happy or content. I always feel the party's happening on the other side of the hill and that I'm not invited for some reason. The party I actually go to is pretty good by everyone else's standards but I know somewhere there's a better one.'

This belief limits Daphne's enjoyment of her life and frequently makes her bored. At the base of it is a fear of death. If this is all there is to life, and she has it, then there's nothing left to strive for. If there's no more striving, then death has to be faced. If you reach the top of the tree, there's nowhere else to go except down. Daphne fears the loss of her powers and the gradual physical decline of old age. To deal with this she has created a restless and bored mood, which is actually less painful than facing up to her existential anxiety around ageing and death.

There is another strand to her belief that she's not been invited to the best party and that is a lack of self-esteem. She judges herself by other people's standards and not her own. Therefore she will always feel excluded. She says, 'I want a genuine experience of life and not this vague feeling that I've been given second-class goods.'

BREAKING THE CYCLE OF BOREDOM

There are several stages in breaking the cycle of boredom. They can happen in any order and include:

- Finding yourself interesting again. This is crucial because bored people are fundamentally bored with themselves. Doing things to boost your self-esteem could be useful here.
- Understanding the root causes. This comes from doing your inner work. Being conscious of the root causes and admitting them to yourself is more than halfway to alleviating boredom.
- Constructing a personal value system. If our values are confused, conflicted or even non-existent, we may need to do some work with clarifying our personal values.

Daphne found that one of her limiting beliefs was based on her lack of self-esteem. She simply didn't believe that she could be invited to the best party because she wasn't worth it. This made her think that whatever she had was second-best. She had to allow a little reality into the situation and acknowledge some of the wonderful things that she did have in her life. Mark discovered that he did not have a personal value system. He lived in a chaotic world and the only yardstick he had was his feelings. Although these could be useful feedback, they weren't, by themselves, enough to live on. He also uncovered some repressed desires, particularly the need for excitement, and achievement. Underneath he was very ambitious but also quite depressed because he believed deep down that he had wasted his life. Part of his work was self-forgiveness and moving on.

Inner Work

Make a list of any limiting beliefs that you may have and the rationalisations that go with them.

Think back to your values – are you in conflict with any of them?

Are you repressing any desires – and why?

Do you relate to either Daphne or Mark? Does either irritate you?

When during the reading of this chapter have you felt especially bored or even angry? Can you relate this to something you might not want to acknowledge?

When you construct your personal value system – what are your most important values?

THE TRANSFORMATION OF BOREDOM

Although we've said that the trigger event is not the cause of boredom, it can still be a useful marker of the thing we're trying to deny. For example, a man who was very anxious about money became so bored that he fell asleep during a lecture on financial affairs. Sometimes we switch ourselves off very dramatically to avoid facing the thing we most fear. The switch can be much more subtle and has a corresponding result of a loss of conscious life. The transformation of boredom is a reconnection with the inner resources and passions from which we have detached ourselves.

Daphne's life was transformed when she realised that her sense of boredom was linked to her limiting belief structure. Because she had worked hard at the rest of her life, her progress in developing her self-esteem was remarkably rapid. Her fear of death and ageing was subtly linked to this. If she thought she was only just coping, then any diminution of her powers would mean a dramatic decline. Realising that she was coping well, and that she was loved by others and herself (perhaps the more important realisation), gave her the strength to face the future. As she said, 'Death is unthinkable and unknowable and therefore very frightening. But I'm not going to waste a second of this precious life waiting for it.'

Mark created his own personal value system. Interestingly he put himself at the centre of it. But instead of putting his indulged self at the centre, he put his potential self. He realised that much of his boredom had been a mask for his fear of adult life. He started to see that he had been no more than a child psychologically playing with the toys of his career. When they disappointed or frustrated him, he threw them away. That behaviour may have been all right at three but is not appropriate at thirty. He started to appreciate consistency and sticking to things. A major theme was his infantile desire to have everything his own way and to reject whatever didn't go his way. A few years down the track of self-development, he is no longer a bored person but an alive and committed one. As he says now, 'Commitment to anything – yourself, a child, a creative work, or even a tree – is the true antidote to boredom. You cannot defeat boredom, you can only change yourself. I would like to get to a state where I want nothing but am prepared for everything.'

11

Depression

'Yet through depression we enter depths and in depths we find soul. Depression . . . brings refuge, limitation, focus, gravity, weight and humble powerlessness. The true revolution begins in the individual who can be true to his or her depression.'

James Hillman

WHAT IS DEPRESSION?

Depression is many things and is not strictly speaking an emotion, but as it has a strong emotional content it has been included here. It is rather a state of being in which the normal energy of life seems curiously drained. It can range from a feeling of being a bit down or having the blues to a full-blown suicidal despair. It's not just something that people get – economic situations and weather systems have depressions, too. Perhaps there is a clue here to depression being in some sense a natural process and part of the cycle of life. And this is important because what we think and feel about our depression colours our experience of it.

People have very varied reactions to depression. It can be seen as a potentially creative rite of passage, as a nuisance to be got rid of, as a sin, as an illness, as something to be overcome or as an unbearably destructive and sad burden. And one person may go through all those reactions and find that their views on depression vary from hour to hour. The crucial element in finding depression bearable seems to be the unique meaning which the individual is able or not to find in it. This chapter is not about curing depression – it would require a whole book and many useful books have been written on the subject. Rather it's about looking at ways in which we can find depression's meaning for us and could be helpful not only for those suffering depression but also their relatives and friends.

In order to see the various perspectives on depression I would ask you to imagine a dinner party where four people are sitting round a table talking. They are: a psychiatrist, a personnel manager, a priest and a mythologist. They have eaten well and the wine has flowed. At that expansive time of the evening, let's look at the sort of things each person might be saying about depression.

The Psychiatrist

Depression's very largely a medical problem. People lack certain chemicals in their brains – it's been scientifically proven. With the right drug regime you can replace the missing chemicals and then the patient feels better. They regain a more hopeful outlook and begin to restart their lives. The drugs we use to treat depression are getting better and better, and more and more people are able to take them without side-effects. Even quite normal people are taking Prozac to feel better than just OK. I don't decry the role of psychotherapy as a talking cure but depression's obviously a chemical problem which has got to be attacked and beaten.

The Personnel Manager

When I see a depressed person come into my office I know that there's much more to it than just what's happening within them – their whole environment plays a part, too. They may be depressed because they aren't able to be productive in their job or because they've got problems at home. I had one girl in my office recently who was very depressed. She was just about able to come into work but her performance had dropped off and her colleagues had noticed it. When I asked her how things were at home, she burst into tears and told me a horrendous story about her mother being bedridden with multiple sclerosis and how she had to both care for her and do a full-time job. She was exhausted and at the end of her tether. No wonder! I helped her to get some support and her depression lifted.

The Priest

I see depression from the perspective of faith. Many people in the Bible were depressed and deeply troubled. They were tortured by guilt, self-blame and doubt. They fought it alone but were only helped when they put their problems before God and surrendered to His will. The act of submission seems to be what enables healing to take place. Of course not all depression has a spiritual content – I also see many people who are seriously depressed because they've lost a loved one or can't find a meaningful path in life. We've moved a long way from the view of the Church in the middle ages which saw depression as a sin. It's obviously not that because people can't help it. But God can and He's the person to go to, as it were.

The Mythologist

Myths are a distilled form of the struggles that human beings have gone through. One of the most potent myths about depression is the Greek story of the Goddess of Fertility, Demeter, and her daughter, Persephone. As you may remember, the young maiden Persephone is picking flowers when she is abducted by the God of the Underworld, Hades. Her mother is distraught and stops everything growing, so no crops ripen, no new animals are born, a frozen state of never-ending winter. After a lot of suffering, a compromise is worked out that Persephone will spend six months of the year in the Underworld with Hades and six months with Demeter. Persephone returns to our upper world with a little boy in her arms. The myth may be saying something about the experience of depression. It feels like a dark, underworld state, where we mourn for our losses and growth of any kind seems impossible. But if we can work out some sort of a deal with our depression, we will return to our everyday life with a gift and hope for the future, which is symbolised by a child.

The interesting thing is that all these points of view may be valid although they appear mutually exclusive at first sight. Depression is not just a surface problem but a complex system in which physical, environmental, spiritual and mythological factors all play their part. If we understand this, we can start to educate our *emotional* reaction to depression, whether we experience it in ourselves or in others.

HOW DOES IT FEEL?

Julie is depressed and when you ask her how it feels, she replies angrily, 'That's just it – in some ways you can't feel at all. And then at other times, you fall into uncontrollable weeping.' Other people have described it as 'the only feeling you have is one of pain and that's not enough to live on'. Some call it a 'black dog', who is persistently at their heels, negatively colouring their experience of life. A chronic feeling of low self-esteem is often present as well as a heightened sensitivity to criticism, which is often seen as a personal attack. A key characteristic of depression is a sense of hopelessness which can verge on despair. From an objective standpoint the depressed person's situation is usually not as hopeless as they think. Quite often people with far worse circumstances can survive and not become depressed.

The key factor here is the person's attitude to their circumstances. One of the most frustrating experiences when you're with a depressed person can be that they present you with a problem to be solved. As Julie's husband said, 'I used to spend a long time suggesting practical solutions to Julie's problems but she found one reason after another to rubbish them. I felt her negativity getting to me and I gave up after a while. What I found helped more was to listen to how she felt and ask her to talk about that – and if that happened she would usually find the right solution for herself.'

The specific symptoms of depression vary but can include:

- apathy – lack of interest in life
- difficulties with sleeping
- problems with concentration and performing tasks
- loss of appetite (or occasionally overeating)
- lethargy and feelings of hopelessness
- anxiety

- suicidal thoughts

If a person has a number of these symptoms to a moderate or severe level, they are said to be clinically depressed. This is not a hard and fast condition but it could be an indication that some help is needed (in the form of medication, counselling or other support) to enable the person to get better.

HOW IS DEPRESSION CAUSED?

The fundamental experience of depression is loss of power but there are many ways in which it can come about. Many people experience a period of depression after a major life change, such as having a baby or starting a new project. Often the change is seen as for the better and may well take the person by surprise as they thought they would thoroughly enjoy the new state. Depression is sometimes a way of coping with the transition and, as long as it is not excessively prolonged or particularly heavy, can be quite a healthy way of adjusting to a new reality. Events which commonly trigger depression can include:

- loneliness and social isolation
- financial problems
- separation and divorce
- a major change e.g. house move, marriage, retirement
- redundancy
- childbirth
- bereavement or loss
- shock and trauma

If you experience some form of depression following a life event such as one of these and it is bearable, it may be time to give yourself extra nurturing and allow the depression to pass. If you feel yourself getting stuck then it may be worth investigating depression further.

Depression can also arise from emotional causes. The denial and suppression of certain emotions, particularly anger, grief, resentment and fear, often leads to depression. If we believe certain emotions are unacceptable, then we tend to pretend to ourselves and others that we are not feeling them. Many people who recover from a long-term depression have to be able to feel the anger they have suppressed and to acknowledge that even though they are angry, they are still good people. Most people who have a depressive temperament believe it's important to be thought a good and lovable person. Perfectionism often goes with this temperament because the person feels that they could not bear to be found wanting and to be criticised.

Depression seems commonest in those who have already become vulnerable to it through losses in early life. If an infant has been loved unconditionally, she believes that she is lovable and so builds a store of self-acceptance which can be later drawn upon. Psychologically speaking, this is one of the major bulwarks against depression in later life. For those not fortunate enough to have had this kind of nurturing, substitute ways of building self-esteem have to be found. This can include creating a loving adult relationship or a job in which your contribution is highly valued, or the love and companionship of friends.

Depression is quite an advanced state. Some people, because of the deprivations of their infancy, never reach the stage of depression. However, the key thing with depression is not to become stuck in it but to see it as a stage which we pass through, discovering its meaning and message.

DEPRESSION AND THE POWER DYNAMIC

As in aggression, a crucial factor in depression is to do with power. When our life circumstances change, there is a time of transition. If we are used to being very capable, then it is difficult for us to be struggling to learn a whole new way of doing things. When circumstances force an attitudinal change and we have to let go of a view of ourselves that we have long cherished, the result can be that we feel we have lost our power.

We need to draw a distinction between power as might and domination and power as energy and enabling ability. If we see power as might then we will hang onto the old way of doing things because it's established. If we are able to see power as energy, then we may be able to let go some of our conservatism and allow life to bring us to the next thing.

DEPRESSION AND ELATION

Interestingly, the opposite of depression is not health but mania. Many people who cannot tolerate their depression flip into an excited state of mania. At the pathological end of the spectrum, this is manic-depressive illness. An example of the less extreme form might be the person who despairs of ever finding a relationship. In the morning they might ring you up in the depths of despondency and then, later that day, call you excitedly to tell you they've met someone. They then pass into a state of elation where they fantasise about this new person being the one for them. This person becomes the solution to all their problems. You are taken aback because you don't know what to say and if you present a reasoned view of the situation, your friend gets upset. A few weeks or months later, the relationship is over because the real issues which caused the depression have not been addressed, and your friend is back to square one. Of course, life can change in an instant and it's a wonderful blessing when it does. But if an elated fantasy is a repeated pattern of avoiding the real lesson of depression, then it is not a healthy response.

THE CYCLE OF DEPRESSION

As we have seen, there are many cycles taking place in depression and most of the problems occur when the depressed person attempts to short-circuit the experience of life. Anyone can get depressed given the right circumstances but a person who is vulnerable to depression will need less of a trigger than one who is not. Whatever the event is, the situation makes us feel powerless and we may react in a number of ways. If we are able to feel the rage and fear which feeling powerless can evoke, then we may not get depressed or, if we do, it will only be for a short moment of transition. We will then progress to a stage where we can incorporate the knowledge and things we've learned and carry on with our lives. If we don't, we have a choice between chronic depression and mania. When the bubble bursts on elation, it leads us back to being vulnerable to the next depressive trigger that comes along.

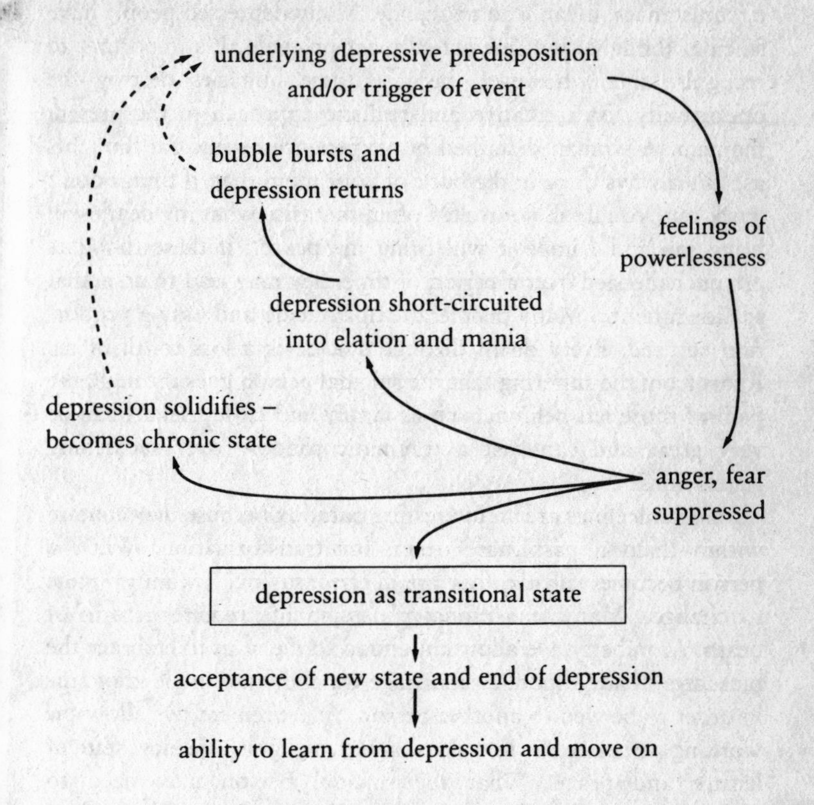

How do you feel about depression?

Take a moment now and look at the way you feel about depression. Is it something you have ever experienced? How do you feel about it? How long does it last? Have you gone through any major life events recently? How did you cope with them? Do you stay with your depression or do you flip off into mania?

Have you seen depression in other people? How do you react to it?

How do you react to criticism? Is it important what other people think of you?

SUICIDE AND DESPAIR

One of the grave risks with depression is that, in extreme circumstances, it can lead to suicide. Many depressed people have suicidal thoughts but few actually act on them. It's important to recognise them, however, because these fantasies destroy the opportunity for a creative and realistic approach to the present moment. A woman described her experience of suicidal thoughts as, 'It's always there in the back of your mind that, if things don't work out, you'll kill yourself. I often fantasise what my death will bring me and I hope it will bring me peace.' If these thoughts are unchallenged over a period of time they may lead to an actual suicide attempt. Many people attempt suicide and only a proportion succeed. Every death through suicide is a loss to all of us. Apart from the suffering that the suicidal person goes through, the pain of those left behind, such as family and close friends, can be very great and can cast a traumatic shadow over succeeding generations.

Suicidal feelings are an interesting paradox because they contain within them a passionate desire for transformation. When a person becomes suicidal they are in effect saying, 'I want my state to change.' Many transitional phases in life require a form of death. At puberty, we allow childhood to die in us to embrace the pleasures of adulthood. At marriage we allow the single life to die in order to be wed to another person. At retirement, we allow the working person to die in order that we may grasp the new state of leisure and peace. What the suicidal person may need to understand is that they may not need to be literal about their death. We can change state by allowing a part of us to die rather than the whole person. We may find the strength and support to move into the new state, shedding our old skin in the same way a snake does. If this wish for transformation can be grasped positively, then the suicidal person may not literally have to end their life.

A woman tried to commit suicide by jumping out of a high window. She landed on a ledge and her life was saved. Afterwards she said, 'As soon as I was out of the window, I didn't want to die any more. I realised I could do my transition from the perspective of life, rather than death.' She was fortunate to be able to live to tell the tale. There is much help on offer for people who have thoughts of committing suicide. One particularly good example of this is the Samaritans, a voluntary organisation that operates a listening telephone counselling service in many countries across the world. By providing support and befriending at a critical moment, many lives have been altered and probably many lives have been saved.

A necessary evil – Gordon's story

Gordon is now fifty. He is a clever man who says of himself, 'I find it easier to deal with machines than human beings.' In his late thirties he suffered from a particularly bad bout of depression following the break-up of his first marriage. When their child was six, his marriage broke down and he returned home to live with his mother. He went through a period of bleak depression. He was unemployed and in a bad state financially and found it difficult to eat and sleep properly. He had very little to keep his life in any kind of pattern or connection.

Gordon is vulnerable to depression as he has had the experience of feeling abandoned by his parents. His mother was hospitalised for six months when he was a baby and he was cared for by a relative. This was a critical time for his development as he bonded first with his own mother and then had to suffer the loss of her, and then bonded with his aunt and then had to suffer the loss of her when he returned to his mother. He was abandoned for the second time when he was eleven years old. His parents left him with the same relative when they went to live abroad for five years.

Despite this rather shaky start, Gordon was able to marry and establish a family. He married a much older woman by whom he had a child. She was his tutor at university and presented herself to him as a sort of parent substitute. Gordon was looking for someone to take care of him on a permanent basis because he had not had reliable care earlier on. But, as he said, 'I found that the price for this kind of care-taking was that I had to play the role of the totally submissive and obedient child.' It was not ultimately satisfactory and the marriage ended amidst much bitterness. Gordon's return home to his original mother was an attempt to get her to understand that he needed to have some secure base in his life.

After recovering from his initial experience of depression, Gordon found that he was much more vulnerable to feeling depressed in the future. He used overwork as a coping mechanism and dreaded any holidays or leisure time. He neglected his own creativity because it brought up too many painful feelings. After a while be began to search for some sort of meaning to his depression.

Born to a depressed mother – Emma's story

Despite her lively and extrovert temperament, Emma has been depressed much of her life. Her depression is founded on the despair of ever being an independent and yet related human being. She is now in her forties and has developed a flourishing and original career in the academic world. She is liked and respected by her friends and colleagues. She is also a talented painter. Despite her outward successes, she has suffered from chronic low self-esteem and inner loneliness.

Her mother was clinically depressed before she was born and Emma's birth was seen by her parents as a way of healing her mother's illness. Her mother loved her but almost too much, without recognising that Emma had her own life. She used to smother her, saying, 'You and I are almost like one person.' The result was that Emma identified with her mother's problems to an overwhelming degree and she took on the suffering of her mother's depressions. She described it as 'Feeling I had the life sucked out of me. Anything good that came my way was destroyed by my mother's negativity.'

Emma felt she was no good for anything but looking after her mother and let her own career and life pass her by in her twenties. She was chronically depressed herself and achieved very little. When Emma was in her early thirties her mother committed suicide which was a terrible blow to her. She felt she had failed to take adequate care of her mother. This led to a feeling of deep guilt and also a profound fear that history would repeat itself and that her depression would eventually lead to her own suicide.

She began to go to a psychotherapist and discovered that family patterns, if they are not examined, tend to repeat themselves. She had to come to terms with her anger against her mother who, without meaning to, had stolen a lot of her life energy. Anger in any form was hard for her to express as she had been born into the role of being the healing, helping person to whom the whole family would turn for advice. She had been expected to be the perfect miniature therapist and to intuit and sort out other people's uncomfortable feelings. Part of her inner work was to learn how to express her anger at the role she felt she had been forced into before she was able to choose who she wanted to be.

FINDING A PERSONAL MEANING IN DEPRESSION

Emma and Gordon are now in their middle years and after much struggle both would say that, despite the pain, their lives have been deepened by the experience of depression. Gordon started to do inner work and to look at some of the issues around his first marriage and his problematic childhood. He realised that his choice of mate had been an attempt to provide himself with a substitute mother. When the relationship ended he felt that he had been abandoned again and through the experience of depression he found that he had to examine the pattern of repetition in his life. As he put it, 'If I hadn't have become depressed, I would have carried on with the same old life and never grown up.'

He managed, with help, to recover from his initial depression and to restart his life. He went to see a psychiatrist who prescribed a mild drug to help him cope with the worst of his symptoms. He retrained and eventually started his own successful small business. He married again, this time to a much younger woman, with whom he could have a more equal relationship. He was able to work more effectively because he managed to create a good and supportive environment for himself. Although he still bears the scars of his experience of depression, Gordon now thinks that it had a meaning. Ultimately it forced him to heal himself and move from wanting to be a dependent child all his life. As he says now,

'Depression is a black dog but it can become a friendly black dog and that is the great difference.'

Emma's work had to do with finding a voice for her long-suppressed anger. She had to learn how to break the mould of her perfectionism and allow herself to be seen as less than perfect. She had always been the care-taker of her mother, but now she had to learn to take care of herself. Anger is a difficult emotion for many people who are prone to depression to express. By saying that they are angry, they are acknowledging that the world isn't perfect and that they cannot control the outcome of the situation. This makes them feel very powerless and Emma had to learn to trust that if she let go of trying to control things, life would not fall apart. This was difficult for her as she had also experienced the major trauma of her mother's suicide. Feelings of powerlessness are hard to cope with.

Much of her work was carried out through recording and analysing her dreams. She noticed that, over a period of years, she dreamt of her mother. At first her dream mother looked like and behaved like her real mother. But gradually she began to change and to behave in a more mature way towards Emma. She became the loving, but separate, parent that Emma had never had. In the dream world, the mother figure developed her own capabilities and had her own connection to her life energy. She respected Emma's uniqueness and independence but gave her support and nurturing as well.

The myth of Persephone and Demeter referred to earlier was especially meaningful for Emma. She progressed from either seeing herself as the abducted victim daughter or the sorrowing, depressed mother and realised that she had both voices within, so to speak. As she said, 'At times I can feel like my energy's been drained and I have been taken to the underworld. At other times, I can feel that I've lost a part of myself, which has gone away and I don't believe that I can function without it. But neither view is the complete truth – they are just the way I feel at a particular moment.' Emma still has depression but she is able to see it as separate from herself. She is able to ask it what it wants from her and she often finds the answer leads her on to the next thing in her life.

Inner Work

Think back to the people we encountered at the beginning of the chapter: the psychiatrist, the personnel manager, the priest and the mythologist. Which approach to depression do you have most sympathy with and why?

Did you have a depressed parent and has it affected you?

How do you cope with your own depression? Do you try to short-circuit it or learn from it?

What things make you depressed?

Have you identified any particular life circumstances which could be triggering your depression?

How do you see power? Are you a powerful person and in what sense?

Which person did you feel more sympathy with – Emma or Gordon? Why?

Creative Task

This is an exercise for you to do when you are depressed. Sit down and pull up a chair beside you. Locate the part of your body where your depression is situated. Very gently, as if it were a real thing, lift the depression out of your own body and out on the chair beside you. Keep sitting together for a while. Your depression is now separate from you. If you like, ask your depression what it would like you to do for it. You might like to ask what changes in your life it wants to bring about. Don't necessarily act literally on what it says but respect and consider it.

This exercise is called personifying the emotion and can be done with any emotion.

THE ALCHEMY OF DEPRESSION

Both Gordon and Emma would see the views of the psychiatrist, the personnel manager, the priest and the mythologist, expressed at the beginning of this chapter, as having had a relevance to their situation. There are times when depression needs to be seen as an illness and times when it needs to be seen in the context of our environmental stresses and strains. Although the priest was a Christian priest, many of the world's major religions advocate a similar form of ultimate surrender to the divine. Myths, too, have their role in connecting us with the different, often conflicting, energies and needs within us.

Depression and despair are closely linked but despair is allied to hope. It is possible to be depressed but not to suffer from despair. The ability to tolerate depression and to learn from it requires giving up a certain kind of hope and cultivating attitudinal hope instead. Despair comes when we have had a specific hope dashed, depression is about learning to endure and be transformed. The ancient art of alchemy is relevant here. The alchemists believed that you could transmute base metal into pure gold through a process of refining. Although they conducted their experiments on a physical level, there is a psychological truth here. In order to change, you have to allow yourself to go through the blackness of total despair. Only when the old self dies will the blackness gradually turn to white and then gradually, ultimately, to gold – the colour of joy and one of the the most precious substances in the world. Acceptance of depression and its lessons leads finally to the ability to be joyful. Depression has the ability to refine us into the greatness of the people we are destined to be.

A final comment ends this chapter. Gordon experienced his mother as abandoning him but he still had an idea that, underneath that behaviour, she was a good and altruistic person. Emma experienced her mother as a smothering and controlling person who never let her be herself but she ultimately came to feel sorry for her. They are two very different views but the irony is they are both views of the same person for Gordon and Emma are brother and sister. Perhaps it underlines the fact that each person has a unique perspective and, to be emotionally literate, we must individually explore and trust our own interpretations of our lives.

12

Envy

'It is certain that envy is the worst sin that is; for all other sins are sins against one virtue; whereas envy is against all virtue.'

Chaucer

WHAT IS ENVY?

Envy has traditionally had an exceedingly bad press. The Christian Church described envy as the deadliest of the seven deadly sins because of its corrosive quality. The Latin word for envy, *invidia*, contains overtones of malice and evil. Psychoanalysts, in particular the followers of Melanie Klein, also regarded it as a highly destructive and particularly nasty emotion. But envy also has potential value. Although its manifestations can be very harmful, it also contains the seeds of creative possibility. If we look at it in the right way, envy can be a stimulus to personal development. The thing we envy is the thing we might actually create or achieve but for some reason haven't. For example, if I envy you because you have an MBA and I don't, this might be seen as a prompt for me to explore the possibility of getting one for myself. Envy is a dreadful emotion when denied but, if acknowledged and worked with, may lead us to what we truly desire. As Susie Orbach said, 'Envy is a signpost to wanting.' Envy is profoundly potential unrealised.

Envy makes us believe that, if we had the thing that we see someone else having, we would be all right. We may wish to take it from them and have it ourselves, or we may deny that we are envious and say that the thing is worthless. In many ways, we are profoundly ambivalent about envy. It is a shameful emotion but one which, in some ways, forms the basis of modern capitalist society. Some of what drives us to acquire money, status and possessions is envy of those who have them, a fact which is ruthlessly exploited by the media. There is, for example, even a glamorous perfume named Envy. Many advertisements play on envy in their portrayal of an almost impossibly luxurious and stylish lifestyle. We can start to feel that our lives are a bit shabby without these glittering accoutrements. In order to feel good, we may have to go out and buy them. So we act on our feelings of envy without making ourselves fully aware of them and discovering what our envy is really about. Envy is disguised, even from ourselves, because we feel ashamed of being envious. The shame comes from the realisation that we lack something, that we are not as whole or as successful as we thought we were. Shame tends to make us hide things, even from ourselves and so makes us more vulnerable to the seductions of advertising.

We can be envious of all sorts of things, not just material possessions. Gender envy is a very strong theme in current culture, for instance. Both sexes can go through a period of envying the opposite sex. A man may be envious of a woman's ability to bear a child and her comparative social freedom to express her emotions. A woman may feel envious of the fact that men, on the whole, have freer lives and usually a greater capacity to earn money. Of course, this is changing now as some men are attempting to develop the more feminine side of themselves and women are becoming very successful in the working world. But the stereotypes persist, even in the imagination, and fuel envious feelings. In this state we only see the opportunities the other has, and none of the responsibilities, downsides and drawbacks of their situation.

The warnings about envy should be heeded. It is a destructive emotion and corrodes not only the person who experiences it but, occasionally, the person who is the object of envy. If you have ever been seriously envied, you may react with a measure of pride that you have managed to capture something that someone else wants. This feeling of satisfaction can swiftly give way to a feeling of strain and discomfort when you realise the potentially unremitting nature of your friend's or colleague's envy. In vain, you may try to tell them that what you have isn't really that valuable or good, or you may try to devise ways for them to achieve it, too. But envy isn't rational in this way and envy may destroy the relationship between you.

HOW DOES IT FEEL?

Envy is an extremely painful emotion and often involves elements of anger, greed, hate, resentment, loneliness and depression. A person who is in the grip of envy often feels that they are hard done by and that life is profoundly unfair. The person who has the thing that we envy is railed against and may indeed become hated. Sometimes we imagine the person losing the thing that we desire so much. For example, we might say to ourselves, 'I wonder how she'd feel if she didn't have her big house.' There may be greedy fantasies of having the coveted big house for ourselves. There may be a spiteful wish to take it away from them or, alternatively, to disparage it and declare it worthless. We may (secretly) rejoice to hear that the envied person has had some misfortune, such as a serious illness or a car crash.

Envy is often accompanied by feelings of depression and shame. Ovid gives a vivid portrait of the horrible way envy feels when he describes in his poem 'Metamorphoses', 'the filthy slimy shack where Envy dwelt . . . a gruesome sunless hovel, filled with heart-numbing frost, forever lacking warmth of cheerful fire, forever wrapped in gloom'. And envy without the enlightenment of understanding does feel utterly dreary and depressing.

Envy and jealousy are all linked but there are differences between each emotion. Jealousy is similar to envy but always involves three people. The person who is jealous fears that someone else will take away the person they love. For example, a man may be jealous of his wife's piano teacher. He thinks, they have ample opportunity for intimacy under the guise of the music lessons to make love. A suspicion grows that he is being cheated on by his wife and he tries to trap her verbally into admitting this. Or he may come home early and try to 'catch them at it'. Quite possibly what they are doing is innocent and the husband's jealousy is stimulated by fear rather than by a rational view of the facts. As one person put it: 'The tragedy of jealousy is that it either comes too early (when our fears are groundless) or too late (when the thing we fear has already happened).'

Another twist to jealousy is when a third party is jealous of a couple and wants to take one partner away from the other. A woman, for instance, may be jealous of her best friend who has just formed a new relationship with a man. She may think that she wants her friend's boyfriend for herself and this could well be the case. But it might also be that she doesn't want to lose the close friendship of her best friend. She may act seductively towards the boyfriend. If he responds she may try, unconsciously, to break the couple up so that she doesn't have to face the loss of this close friendship.

THE ROOTS OF ENVY

The roots of envy are complex and it can be seen as having both an inherited and an environmental component. People seem to vary as to the amount of envy they're born with but adverse circumstances, especially in early life, probably increase our chances of becoming an envious person. There are several theories about this and put simply they are as follows:

Envy as a result of not having our needs met as infants

Imagine the complete helplessness of a tiny baby, dependent on his care-giver for food, warmth and love. If this is not given, the baby experiences extreme distress. The breast (or bottle) becomes a symbol of the longed-for food and the baby becomes intensely envious of the power of it. This pattern is then repeated with other situations where the person has to wait for something and is not sure that they will receive it. Another person's power to give or withhold love, status or other important things will be very threatening to him.

Envy as a result of the birth of a sibling

The blissful world of the only child is shattered by the arrival of a baby brother or sister. No longer is she the centre of her parents' love and attention. She has to fight for her rights and becomes bitterly envious of her small sibling. She may want to return to the baby state of having everything done for her and is resentful that she has to grow up. In later life she may have problems accepting adulthood and maturity as she wishes unconsciously to be taken care of. She may be envious of people who have lifestyles where they are looked after e.g. dependent partner in a marriage.

Envy as a result of dissatisfaction with the position of our parents

If we feel we have been born into a family which isn't good enough for us, socially, financially, intellectually or in some other way, we may respond by feeling envious of other families who seem to have what we lack. This is compounded when there are very real problems in a family. It may seem quite reasonable to fantasise about a mother who is not alcoholic or manic-depressive, for instance. But the fantasies of having different parents are potentially dangerous because they take us away from reality. As we grow up we may try to create a false history for ourselves, or leave out the bits we hate.

Envy as an archetypal force which can act as a spur to our development

In this model, envy arises when we realise that we are not fulfilling ourselves sufficiently or have got stuck in a rut. We feel that we have failed in some way. We look around and see other people doing rather better than ourselves in terms of achievement, and we feel envious. This feeling can make us go one of two ways: either we will become depressed and bitter, or we may decide to compete for what we want. If we can have the courage to look at the thing that we actually want which lies below the surface of the thing we envy, we may be able to achieve it.

Whatever the roots of envy in our personal circumstances, the emotion is always accompanied by a feeling that we lack something.

CYCLE OF ENVY

The event which triggers envy is probably not of any great significance. It is a knife touching on the envious, still-open wound. A woman who longs to be rich, for instance, may walk down a street perfectly happily until she sees a Rolls-Royce pull up and an elegant couple get in laden with Harrods shopping bags. This event will activate her dormant envy. She will shiver slightly and look down at her own coat which now seems hopelessly out of fashion. Her sharp eyes will have taken in the other woman's slim ankles which she will mentally compare with her own. She notices the attentive way the man held the door open. Suddenly she feels very alone in a cold and bleak world. All the joy and life in her world seems to have driven away in the car. She imagines being in that car herself and dispossessing the occupants, or perhaps just the other woman. What our hypothetical woman doesn't know is that this couple is as likely to envy other people as she is to envy them. As they drive away their thoughts may be very different from her imaginings. Instead of feeling perfectly peaceful and happy with themselves, they may also be caught in the cycle of envious wanting.

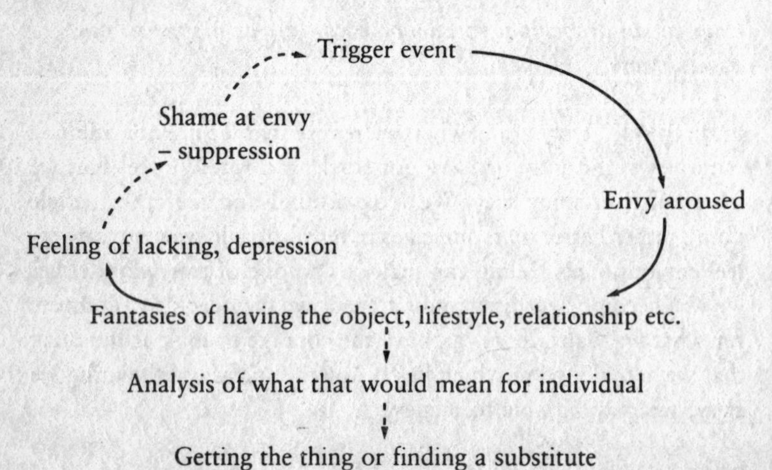

Our hypothetical woman has a way through this very painful experience. The moment her envious fantasies arise, she can ask herself what having this lifestyle would mean for her. Is it freedom, security or beauty she craves? Are there practical ways she could develop what she has already in order to experience these feelings more often. In other words, is she making enough of herself? It may not be feasible for her to acquire a Rolls-Royce but maybe she could aim for a better job with more money. That might enable her to buy a pretty little car which she would feel good driving around in. Is she taking enough pride in her real achievements? Perhaps she is denigrating herself and needs to list what she has achieved.

HOW WE PRETEND ENVY DOESN'T EXIST

Because envy is such an uncomfortable emotion, we often go to great lengths not to feel its bitter pangs. There are a number of ways in which we can deny or suppress our envy. Here are some of the major types:

The Belittler

Belittlers tend to react to feelings of envy by saying that what they envy is no good. Mike, who secretly envies Sally's flat, may find himself criticising it in quite harsh tones. 'The kitchen's too small, and the bathroom needs doing up and, anyway, who would want to buy a property in that neighbourhood?' All these negative statements are attempts by Mike to convince himself that he didn't want the flat anyway, so there's no point in being envious of it. But we are not really easily persuaded by such arguments ourselves and so the envy goes on, in an underground way. An acute listener can usually fairly quickly detect the envy in such belittling criticism, which can be extremely hurtful to the person receiving it.

The Self-Denigrator

The self-denigrator also uses criticism as a defensive weapon against envy but in this case they turn it inwards on themselves. Sue is deeply afraid of her envy because she recognises what a powerful and destructive force it can be. She would rather say, 'I'm no good', than risk destroying her relationships with other people. She never puts herself forward for promotion, saying quietly that she 'doesn't think she'd be up to it'. She never believes a man is genuinely interested in her, she says to herself, 'He's really keen on my best friend and is using me as a way to get to know her.' Another thing she does is to spoil anything that she does that is creative or good. She might, for example, tear up a painting which she has just done, saying that it isn't good enough. Self-denigrators tend to place a great store on relationships but they usually end up without the things they really want.

The Provoker

Provokers have recognised that envy is very powerful and also painful. They have developed a strategy to deal with it that involves getting other people to feel it. Provokers attempt to show off their attributes, wealth, attractiveness or talent. They choose carefully and only display them to those people who they perceive have less than they do. Ted is a provoker. He cultivates the friendship of Alice and Mary and often asks them round to his house. He casually lets it drop that he is going to Paris for the weekend. Then on to New York '. . . for a business conference . . . what a hard life!' he exclaims. 'By the way, Alice, where are you off to for your holiday this year?' Alice, who hasn't much money or status, feels humiliated and envious of Ted's good fortune. Whatever she says in reply Ted will indicate that he's already been there but doesn't think much of it. He can then enjoy Alice's feeling of envy towards him. Provokers appear to be dealing with their own envy by foisting it onto others but they pay for it in the loss of meaningful relationships with other people.

Sometimes we encounter a pure type, either in ourselves or in other people. Usually, though, people will mix their types according to their circumstances and personal history.

Having everything but the thing she really wants – Bettina's story

Bettina is a very envious person but she skilfully hides it, even from herself. She is in her forties and outwardly successful with a good job and a reasonably happy marriage. She has two children, who are at boarding school, and she lives in a well-appointed house in an exclusive suburb.

Her early family life was troubled and her mother died when Bettina was very small. She says, 'I prefer to draw a line under that. I don't want to speak of it. I have everything I want now.' As a child she experienced great pain following the loss of her mother, but she had no words to express it and no kind adult with whom she could talk about it. Her father said little about his own emotions and remarried fairly quickly. Bettina was left alone with her grief and, as a result, she became very envious of those other little girls who had mothers.

In order to deal with her envy, Bettina uses a mixture of provoking and belittling techniques. She decided fairly young that being well-off financially was of paramount importance to her. She married a man who was also interested in money and who had the same goals. Although they haven't much in common, their marriage works because they both want the same things. One of her tricks is to display her wealth to her less fortunate friends, asking them round for bridge or tea, but making sure that they know that there's an exclusive party she'd been invited to later in the evening.

Her other technique is belittling. Because she didn't have the mother she longed for, she downgrades the importance of mothering. The victims of this are her own children. Deprived of maternal affection (because she couldn't bear them to have something she didn't have) they were packed off to boarding school at a very early age. If Bettina is to break the cycle of envy – and it will be passed down through the generations if she doesn't – she must first acknowledge the pain of her own loss and then the depths of her subsequent envy.

The underachiever who wants to be top dog – Tom's story

Tom is still in his youth but has been dogged all his life by the spectre of underachievement. At school, he consistently did less well than his teachers expected and now he is struggling to hold down a job. He is the middle child of three brothers. His elder brother, Joe, is very brilliant and the younger, David, has learning difficulties.

Tom deeply envies his older brother his success. He said how glad he was when Joe won a scholarship to Oxford but inwardly he couldn't help feeling bitter. Most people would relate to Tom's envy of his older brother but what is not so obvious is that he deeply envies his younger brother, too. Tom was two when David was born, and it was immediately apparent that he was going to need a lot of extra care. Tom saw that both brilliance and disability got attention whereas he did not. He is caught in the trap of not being able to succeed because it might challenge Joe and not being able to give up completely because David is the one that gets looked after.

He developed a strategy for himself that he must always be kind, helpful and liked, and he must never show his envy. His mother says, 'He's the one that's never given any trouble', but he's never had his needs met either. He is a classic self-denigrator and chooses to be a failure rather than risk challenging the status quo. Recently though he has begun to think that this half-life is not good enough for him and needs to be able to face the envy he really feels.

Inner Work

What are you feeling at this moment? Take some time to describe your feelings. Remember that your journal is private and that it's your companion.

What has triggered this feeling now?

What other emotions are you feeling/have you felt? Remember that naming them takes the sting out of them.

If you are feeling envious right now, who is your envy directed towards?

Reading Bettina's and Tom's stories, did you notice where you felt angry, impatient or pitying, or any other feeling? Is there some message here for you?

Which person did you feel more sympathy with – Bettina or Tom? Why?

What techniques do you use to cover up your envy? Are you a belittler, self-denigrator, or a provoker? In what situations do you employ these techniques?

ENVY AND SELF-REALISATION: THE STORY OF PSYCHE AND EROS (I)

There is a very important classical myth about love, self-development and envy. It is the story of Psyche (meaning soul) and Eros (meaning life force or sexual energy, which is a manifestation of it). Psyche is the youngest of a king's three daughters. She was so beautiful that her fame grew far and wide. Strangely, no-one wanted to marry her and her father asked the oracle at Delphi what was to be done with her. The answer comes back uncompromisingly: Psyche is to be left on a mountainside for death to claim her as his bride. With great sadness this is done and her family bids the beautiful Psyche farewell, leaving her on the rock as night falls. In the darkness, something sweeps down and carries her off to his palace. Here she enjoys all the delights of being a princess and all the joys of love. One condition is attached to this bliss, however. She must never see her husband (he visits her only in total darkness) and she mustn't know who he is. The darkness is a metaphor for being unconscious. This state of affairs goes on for a while and then Psyche's sisters hear that she is still alive and decide to come and visit her.

Psyche's two elder sisters have meanwhile married local kings but their marriages haven't brought them any happiness. They arrive at Psyche's palace and are terribly impressed by the splendour of it. But when they hear about Psyche's sex life, their envy knows no bounds. They pick on the one thing Psyche is unsure about – the identity of her husband. They plant poisonous suspicions in her mind, saying they are sure that he must be a loathsome and ugly snake and that's why Psyche is forbidden to see him. They persuade her to light a candle in the darkness and cut his head off if he is, indeed, a snake.

Psyche follows their suggestion and sees that her husband, far from being a snake is, in fact, the magnificent god, Eros. She falls passionately in love with him. But he is furious with her for breaking his rules and leaves her. After a long time and much suffering, Psyche and Eros are reunited and can then have a conscious relationship where they can see each other as unique individuals. The rest of the story is told in the chapter on Love (page 214). Psyche's sisters are in fact, part of herself, the little voice inside that wants to destroy our happiness. The wisdom is to realise when envy will lead us on to a greater sense of self-realisation and to recognise when it merely wants to demolish the good things in our life.

THE TRANSFORMATION OF ENVY

Envy can be the spur for a greater self-development and this usually involves the loss of the status quo. As a result of envy, Psyche becomes a more developed person because she realises the truth of what is going on. In their own ways, both Bettina and Tom have to realise the truth of their situation before they can move on. Part of this is to recognise that their envy has come about through pain and loss, which wasn't their fault. Envy has been a totally understandable response, given the circumstances they were in at the time. In many ways, the original emotion is not so troublesome as the coping mechanisms they have developed to deal with it. When Bettina can say, with great sorrow and shame but also honesty, that she is envious of the fact that her children have a mother, which she didn't have, much of the pain of envy drops away. With support for these deeply uncomfortable feelings, she can begin to find her own source of generosity. She may find that she no longer needs to arouse her friends' envy but can actually use some of her material good fortune to help and encourage them in their own self-development.

Tom's envy had stifled his creativity. He was not the academic type that his elder brother was but he had considerable skills in a different direction. When he realised that he spent most of his energy being a nice person, he decided to stop that for a while and to act more in his own self-interest. His family didn't like this much and were angry with him for, as they put it, 'becoming rather self-centred and selfish'. Tom lived through this time, realising that he couldn't make major changes without upsetting the family's status quo. He went on offering support to his younger brother, but increasingly out of love rather than duty. The sting of the comparison between the way David had been nurtured and the way he had been neglected became less when he realised that his response to become envious was completely understandable. The coping mechanism of self-denigration no longer served him, however. He could let it go and pursue his own creative life. Now he has what he really wants, he is no longer envious.

13

Fear

'I believe that anyone can conquer fear by doing the things he fears to do, provided he keeps doing them until he gets a record of successful experiences behind him.' Eleanor Roosevelt

WHAT IS FEAR?

A would-be suicide sat on a bridge, waiting to jump. He said, 'I'm afraid of life and so I want to die, but I'm afraid of death, so perhaps I want to live.' These are the two paralysing extremes of fear: fear of life and fear of death. In its most basic form fear is about existence. The very fact that we exist makes demands on us which can be fearful. On the other extreme, contemplating death, which means the ceasing of our actual life, is similarly frightening.

Fear of life may come out in all sorts of ways. One form of it shows in the person who is never committed but always moves on seeking constant new beginnings. Another form of it involves undertaking ever more dangerous activities, such as fast driving, drugs, risky sex or excessive alcohol. It's a form of 'dicing with death'. The physical feelings of fear are translated into thrills and highs.

On the other hand a person who is afraid of death may find themselves taking no risks and living a constricted, narrow life. 'Safety first' is their maxim. They are afraid to marry, or leave a dead marriage, or have children or not to. They live lives that involve as little change as possible or else follow a conventional, well mapped-out path. They choose not to feel fear but don't have much excitement either. Somehow we have to find a middle path, learn how to take 'safe risks', and use fear as a feedback mechanism rather than allowing it to run our lives.

Fear is one of the most unpleasant emotions to feel and yet to choose a life where we feel little or no possibility of being afraid is to choose a diminished life. Fear is a friend as well as a foe because it contains within its miserable and debilitating wrapper its transformational opposites: excitement and courage. You may be reading this now because you live in chronic fear, which washes over you frequently, or you may sense that you are so afraid of feeling fearful that you have limited your choices to those things which are utterly safe. Although fear can be very uncomfortable to feel, it is better to feel it than to suppress it. Apart from limitation of life choice, suppressed fear can lead to depression, anger and oppression of others.

Everybody has been afraid at some stage in their lives. Those people who can say honestly 'I'm afraid of such-and-such' are often less fearful than those who cannot. For some of us, fear is such an unpleasant and powerless feeling that we short-circuit it and cut out of our lives anything that could make us fearful. But fear is not always what it seems. Sometimes we carry as adults fears that crippled us as children. Our current fears may only be symbols of earlier terrors. In fact we have probably outgrown them. If we unmask them, we allow ourselves more freedom to live and enjoy ourselves.

DIFFERENT SORTS OF FEAR

There are various degrees of fear from the mild 'I'm rather afraid of that possibility' to a full-blown, almost paralysing, terror. In between are panicky feelings which we can have several times in a day when we remember the consequences of things we have or haven't done. Sometimes a word or a place or even a smell can trigger fearful feelings. There are many guises of fear and they can include:

- a shiver of anticipation
- a sense of consternation or dismay
- a feeling of annihilating terror
- phobias of various sorts e.g. hydrophobia (fear of water)
- anxiety and worry
- shame
- hope
- hate

Many of our fears are masked by other fears which are easier to deal with. A woman told me that she had only to hear the word 'pension' mentioned on the radio or television for her to feel so anxious that she would switch the set off. At some level she felt ashamed of not having a pension and she wanted to deny any possibility of hearing about one. She said that, because she hadn't got one, she was afraid of being old as she wouldn't have any money. She then added reflectively, 'Perhaps it's because I am afraid of growing old and want to deny that, that I haven't got a pension.'

When I asked her what being old meant she replied after much hesitation, 'Loss of power, beauty, strength, health and the feeling that I'm inevitably going to die.' When she had accepted that she was going to die (as much as any of us can accept this difficult and unpalatable fact), she was no longer afraid of the mention of the word 'pension'. Fear of death reduced her competence to deal with life but making that fear conscious gave her the ability to make the choices she needed to make.

Similarly, many phobias (the Greek word for fear) are masked fears. Common ones include agoraphobia (fear of going out and being in open spaces), claustrophobia (fear of being enclosed and suffocated), as well fear of flying, spiders, snakes and darkness. At some stage in our lives we have come to associate the particular thing we're phobic about with a fear of the worst thing that we can think of. As we've said, for each individual this is different but usually involves a fear of life or a fear of death. The actual phobia is only a symbolic representation of the ultimate fear. Some therapists use desensitisation techniques to help a person come to terms with a fear of spiders. This could involve actually touching a spider and allowing it to run around on your hand. It is a successful treatment in so far as it encourages a person to break the link between their specific fear and the greater fear it masks. Confronting a fear breaks its power. The next step (which is often left out of this sort of treatment) is to address the existential fear.

WHAT DOES FEAR FEEL LIKE?

Fear is a very physical emotion to feel. Feelings can include: a pounding heartbeat, a dread feeling in the pit of the stomach, a severe headache, as well as sensations of shakiness, sweatiness, tingliness. The evocative phrase 'shit scared' sums up another very common physical manifestation of fear: the need to visit the lavatory repeated times.

Fear is very useful when we have to encounter a physical threat like running away from a charging bull in a field. Fear gets us into action – to run fast or to leap the gate. In the past when daily life was more dangerous, our ancestors had either to run away from a dangerous situation or to fight for their lives. Facing a physically dangerous situation meant that extra hormones were needed to enable the person to run faster or to fight harder. These hormones slow down many of the normal processes of the body such as digestion to enable us to use the maximum energy to cope with the threat. This response to danger is called the flight-or-fight syndrome.

The trouble is that, although this response is magnificent and life saving in physical danger, it is crippling when the danger is psychological. When the threat is not physical, a flight-or-fight response is not appropriate and we are left with strong hormones flooding the body. These hormones themselves make us feel panicky and afraid and the fear becomes a repetitive cycle.

THE CYCLE OF FEAR

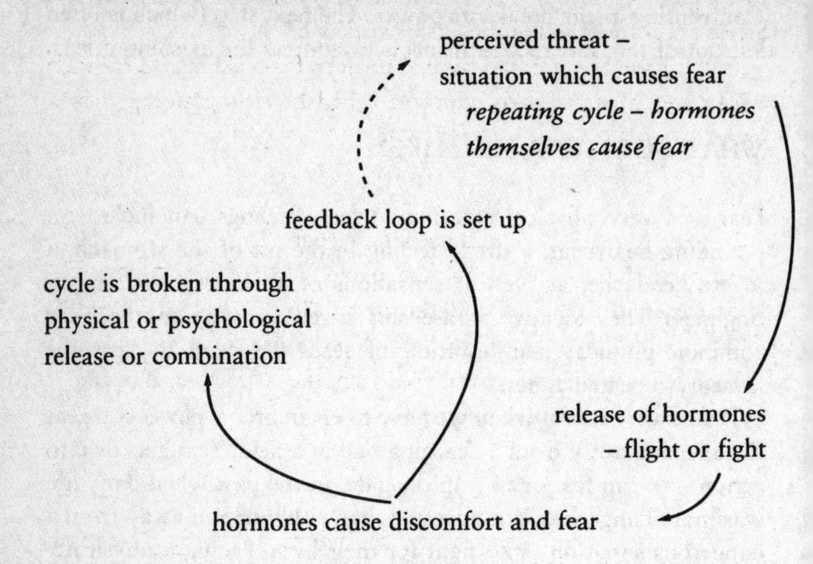

There are three ways to break this cycle:

- through physical means – by strenuous exercise which 'works' off the unpleasant physical effects of the hormones
- through psychological means – by understanding the nature of the threat (and what the fear really represents)
- holistically – by a combination of physical and psychological means

WAYS TO PHYSICALLY RELEASE THE FEAR CYCLE

The body and mind are part of one system and what occurs in one will affect the other. Most of the rest of this chapter is devoted to understanding fear from a psychological perspective but it is important to work holistically and to balance both body and mind.

People vary in the ways they cope with the fear cycle. I find that fairly slow repetitive exercise such as a long walk or swim is very effective in reducing my symptoms of fear. It needs to be done long enough to feel the body to get into its own rhythm. Others find the cut and thrust of competitive sport helpful and some prefer to do yoga and breathing exercises which are calming and ensure that every part of the body has sufficient oxygen to work effectively. Stress relaxation techniques also work well.

If you have not tried a physical form of fear release, do try it. It works much better than lying on a bed or sitting slumped in a chair.

Quintessence of Fear

Stop reading the text now and name a fear. Write it down and make five boxes underneath as the things that would flow from that fear are realised. Keep asking yourself what each fear would mean until you reach the quintessence of the fear (literally refining five times).

For example

Fear: *being made redundant*

↘

What would that mean?
Answer: *I'd lose my money*

↘

What would that mean?
Answer: *My wife would leave me*

↘

What would that mean?
Answer: *I'd have to live alone*

↘

What would that mean?
Answer: *I'd be very lonely*

What would that mean?
Answer: *I might give up on life*

If you go on long enough the quintessential fear will probably be around life or death (sometimes it needs more than five 'refinings' to get to this point). Our everyday fear derives its hidden power to terrify us by attaching itself to fears of life and death. You see how one thing leads from another in the fear chain of your mind. Now ask yourself if these steps are entirely logical. You may need to ask your wife, for instance, whether she would leave you if you had no money and if she says no, that breaks the chain. Most of the steps are based on fantasies. Use logic and facts to break the fear chain.

Control at all costs – David's story

David is an ultra-neat man in his late twenties. He is intelligent, professionally qualified and has a secure job which he neither likes nor dislikes. He simply does it because he feels it's expected of him. He owns a flat which he has put little of his own personality into. He dutifully visits his parents once a month. He has a girlfriend of five years' standing. They occasionally go out and spend time together without much interest or excitement on the part of either of them. It's more about convenience than love.

David's tastes and attitudes are conventional and as much like everyone else's as he can manage. He rarely allows himself to hope for anything. He says, 'I prefer to deal with life as it is, not as it might be. It's easier.' Because he defends himself against fear, he also denies the possibility of feeling hope or desire for change. Likewise, he has never really fallen in love as this would bring up the fear of losing someone he cared about deeply. Instead a succession of girlfriends (who mostly have similarly muted emotional needs) are his companions.

When you're with David you feel an impenetrable skin around him. If you asked David what he was frightened of he would probably say he never felt afraid. However the price he has paid for this is that his life is very bland. In fact, he pushes his fear so far down that he never consciously has to feel it. It comes out in other ways: in an impoverished life with no excitement and a lack of love or any similar strong emotion. He never thinks of the meaning of his life or of the fact that it will end one day. If someone he knows dies then he pushes the thought out of his mind as fast as possible.

Because he cannot acknowledge his fear let alone feel it, he is oppressive to those around him, especially to those he works with. He criticises and humiliates the people at work because he is unconsciously frightened that they will become better at their jobs than he is at his. David's life can be summed up in one word: control. He controls his feelings and other people's as much as he can. David's fear of feeling fear and his fear of death have become one and the same thing.

Pursued by fears – Catherine's story

Catherine is in her thirties. She is afraid of many things. Although a vibrant and attractive woman, she has not committed herself to a relationship, a career or a creative purpose. Instead, she flits from one thing to another, driven on not so much by love of exploration as by repetitive patterns of fear.

'I'm bored of this job,' she says, as she hands in her notice. 'It's so ultra d-u-l-l, you can't imagine!' she says entertainingly, throwing up her hands with a withering look on her face. She might do an imitation of the boss at this point. All her friends will laugh but they will miss the real point. She is not bored so much as frightened. An inner voice says to her, 'You are a failure here. It's a dismal place. You will spend the rest of your life here slowly decaying and never do the creative things you want. Probably you're not capable of them anyway.' This brings up her fear of failure. Because she can't cope with the uncomfortable and distressing feelings that arouses in her she represses the emotion and translates her fear into boredom.

It's a similar picture with relationships. She tends to date men who enjoy on-off relationships much as she does. Occasionally she will humiliate a man who gets too close. She may even be falling in love with him which makes her more afraid because it brings up the possibility of pain and loss. Part of her wants and likes the man and would like to be with him. But her unacknowledged fear gets in the way. So she humiliates him so that she doesn't have to respect him any more. Then she can end the relationship.

The interesting thing about Catherine is that her fears seem to follow her wherever she goes. Because she doesn't turn and address them, they reappear in a different form. It may look as if her fear is pursuing her, but in reality it is always there, merely taking on the local colouring of her particular life circumstances. Her method of coping, which involves a continuous moving on, worked quite well for her in her twenties because everyone else in her age group was similarly experimenting. As she grows older, she is finding her mode of life unsatisfying.

THE ROOTS OF FEAR

Like most emotions, fear has its roots in the sort of family we were brought up in. If the messages we received as child were 'be careful – the world is a dangerous place' then we may find ourselves with a whole raft of limiting fears. For example, if your mother always picked you up from school when it was raining, you may find that you have a fear of getting wet. This can limit your life as an adult as you find yourself avoiding situations where you *may* get wet and not be able to control it. The reason why your mother was frightened of getting wet was because she had pneumonia as a child. She was told that it was dangerous to get wet and it may well have been dangerous for her. But it is not dangerous for you, as you haven't had pneumonia. But by protecting you against the thing that she has had to protect herself against, your mother has given you a fear of it.

Social and economic factors play a part in the transmission of fear through generations. In the 1930s there was a major economic depression. People who were young then picked up the message that poverty was to be feared and guarded against at all costs. Similarly with people who have gone through an experience of war, terrorism or famine. These fears are often passed wordlessly from parent to child. When you did the 'Quintessence of Fear' exercise described earlier, you may have noticed that some of the fears that you refined were based on what happened in your family's past rather than what is likely in the present.

Another root of fear lies in the very fact of being a small child in an adult world. Being small, helpless and in the power of adults can be very frightening. If they loved and nurtured us, it was good. If they were ambivalent towards us, sometimes being loving and sometimes being angry or indifferent, we became fearful as we didn't know what to expect. If we had an experience of one of our parents abandoning us (for whatever reason), then our greatest fear may be that we will be abandoned again. If we were overprotected and never allowed space to experiment and make mistakes, then our greatest fear may be being 'smothered'. As adults, we have the opportunity to review our fears and to discard those we have outgrown.

And yet another root of fear lies in the existential conditions of life. Life and death are the two fundamental unalterable givens. We are born and we will die. Fear of life (leading to inability to make commitments and in some cases to extravagant risk taking) and fear of death (leading to stagnation and excessive control) are present in us all to some degree. It is normal to feel afraid of the mystery of life and the profundity of death but they are separate issues from our everyday concerns. Part of the work of emotional literacy is to learn how to separate the two. In the 'Quintessence of Fear' exercise, the refining of fear usually comes down to a fear of life or a fear of death. These powerful archetypal fears then give false energy to our lesser fears which is why it's important to break the chain of fear. It puts our everyday fear into its true perspective.

THE DENIAL OF FEAR

The denial of fear is very widespread but very damaging to those who deny it but also to those around them. Both David and Catherine deny their fear and their lives are less exciting, creative and fulfilling than they might be. At the same time, other people are hurt and humiliated by them. When they start their inner work, they have to realise that not only are they responsible to themselves but, to some degree, to other people.

David and Catherine represent opposites, but all of us have elements of fear of life and fear of death. David's work is to realise that every change he makes doesn't necessarily lead to his death. Catherine's work is to realise she doesn't have to kill every creative possibility because she is frightened of failing at it. Fear of failure is related to fear of life because it relates to a failing at the demands of life. (This may manifest itself as wanting to die because you don't feel good enough but shouldn't be confused with fear of death.)

Fear is a very infectious emotion. It can only take one person in a room to spread fear very fast amongst the others. If fear is passed on in this way, it lessens the pain in the person who spreads it. Rumour, gossip and half-truths are very powerful modes of transmission. Truth and logic can defeat the onslaught of transmitted fear. Sharing fear openly and honestly can bring relief to others. When you say, 'I am really afraid of such-and-such' without trying to make the other person fearful too, the results can be remarkable. It releases in others the ability to be with you in your fear, and to acknowledge their own fear and not to catch yours.

Inner Work

What are you feeling at this moment? Take some time to describe your feelings. What has triggered this feeling now?

What were the messages you received as a child? What were your parents most afraid of? You may also like to think of what your grandparents were most afraid of?

What would you most like to change about your current life circumstances? What are the fears that hold you back? How realistic are they?

What messages does your inner voice give you?

When you did the 'Quintessence of Fear' exercise, were you more afraid of life or death? Do the exercise again with another fear and see if you get a different result.

What defences do you use against fear? Is some of your boredom a form of fear?

Have you humiliated or belittled someone lately because you were afraid but are denying it? Has someone done this to you?

Has your world shrunk because of your fears? In what ways? Could you start to move into those areas?

Creative Task

Take a large sheet of paper, the bigger the better. Put yourself in the middle of it. You might like to draw or paint yourself. It doesn't have to be realistic – only you or someone you chose will ever see this. Then draw a circle around the representation of yourself. The circle should take up about a third of the available space. This is your safe zone. Starting with the activities you feel most comfortable with, put them inside the circle. Again you may want to draw or paint them.

Once you have done that, start to think of things that you are a bit afraid of doing and put them outside the circle. Then add those things you are more afraid of and finally end up with the things you are terrified of which you will put in the 'outer darkness' of the corners of the sheet of paper. Starting with the things that are nearest your safe zone, imagine yourself doing them. If that seems just about bearable and, if they are not dangerous to yourself or anybody else, practise doing them until it feels comfortable. Then extend the safe zone to include them. Review your map regularly. You will be surprised at how the safe zone's boundaries change. Remember that each change of outline represents the transformation of your fear into courageous action.

THE TRANSFORMATION OF FEAR: COURAGE AND EXCITEMENT

Catherine's realisation that her boredom was only a mask for her fear was an exciting revelation. She did the 'Quintessence of Fear' exercise and realised that her failure to be creative or make a satisfying relationship was related to her fear of failure. She could then detach that fear from her fear of life. This gave her the strength to start to face her fears and begin to notice when her inner voice whispered something frightening. Instead of listening to it uncritically, she befriended it. She spoke to it as a friend and mentally said, 'Hello, how are you?' (If she had been angry with it, it might have tried to make her more frightened.) Facing the inner voice took courage but once done, the thing she was frightened about seemed less fearful. The voice started to become a friend and to say less threatening things. The problem was to do it on a daily basis before a dull pall of boredom crept over her. Keeping a journal was a very useful activity for Catherine as it reminded her that the inner voice could become a friend. She now could be more courageous about living life and expressing her creativity.

David realised that he had not felt any excitement in his life since he was a little boy. He could just remember a dim distant past when the world had seemed full of golden possibilities. Just remembering this brought up feelings of huge loss for him as he realised he had wasted much of his life in being cut off by fear. It took some while to mourn this 'unlived life' but as he did he noticed that he needed to control people and situations less. He could take risks and allow some of his human warmth out of its long suppressed hiding place. We do not know what the incident in David's childhood was that caused him to choose control and safety rather than fear, possibility and excitement. Some people need to find out what the actual incident was and some people need only to know that it has happened but that they can change. One of the problems he experienced in changing was that the people around him expected him to be a certain way. When he became kinder and more empathetic, they had to adjust, too.

14

Grief

'No one told me that grief felt so like fear. I am not afraid, but the sensation is like being afraid. The same fluttering in the stomach, the same restlessness, the yawning. I keep on swallowing.'

C. S. Lewis

WHAT IS GRIEF?

Grief is the natural reaction to loss and is an emotion which requires the application of profound imagination to resolve. As we go through life, we lose things: looks, youth, parents, friends, jobs, possibility, mobility, love and, in the end, life itself. In order to come to terms with these losses we mourn them until we're ready to let them go. Grief is a doorway from one state to another and is essential for change and development. Grief doesn't feel very comfortable but it's exactly this discomfort that's needed to force us to move on. If it was too easy, we would stay stuck. The goal of grief is to achieve an integration at a higher level than we were before we lost the thing we mourn. The fear in grief is that, having lost the thing, we are forever diminished. This is where our imagination training comes in. We may indeed be physically, or perhaps financially, diminished but we can be emotionally, and maybe spiritually, enriched. Imagining the new state gives us the power to move into it.

For example, if I am made redundant from my job, I will have to go through the process of feeling that I've really lost something very valuable. I may have lost status, a company car, economic security, a place to go to during the day, a sense that I am needed. These are all important things and it would be very surprising if I didn't feel something. If I can go through this honestly and feel the pain, I will be able to let it go. A year later, when I have created the business which I always wanted the courage to start, I may perhaps say that being made redundant was the best thing that ever happened to me. It made me change and find something better. If, on the other hand, I haven't learnt to grieve and let go, I will cling to the wish for the past, perhaps desperately and miss all the good things in the present. People in this state put on their business clothes and catch the train every morning although they have no job to go to. Sometimes they don't even tell their partners that they have been made redundant. They can't let go of the life they once had. They are caught in denial and can't start the grief process.

Grief is like a dark tunnel which we must go down into in order to see the sunlight again. At the entrance to the tunnel, we have three choices:

- to deny that the loss has occurred
- to acknowledge that the loss has occurred but deny its importance to us
- to accept the loss and work through the grief

If we opt for the third choice we enter the tunnel. Once into the tunnel, however black it feels, there is usually a glimmer of light somewhere. As a woman who had lost her husband said, 'It feels bleaker before you accept it and once you do, there is some form of relief.'

WHY DO WE RESIST GRIEF?

We resist the work of change that grief requires for a variety of reasons. It can be through sheer laziness or a form of pride but it is more likely to be because we haven't resolved the losses of the past. If a person builds up a portfolio of losses that they've successfully negotiated, then they can face the next loss with some degree of equanimity and, perhaps, courage. If, on the other hand, the experience of loss is catastrophic, then a person will find it very difficult to grieve and move on. Trust has a great deal to do with this and those people who, on the whole, have a trusting attitude to life will find grief easier to work through. But even if we haven't had the best of past experiences, we can still build up a reservoir of trust by looking at the good things that have come to us as a result of change. These can be the small, often unlooked-for benefits. For example, I might get promoted at work to a job I really enjoy. In all the excitement, I may forget to be sad about the job I am leaving. There will be some loss in the change, but it will feel minimal if it's a change for the better. It's worth making a list of the positive changes that have occurred in your life. Remember that change can be very good and that all loss potentially leads to change.

Different cultures have different rituals surrounding bereavement. In ancient China people were expected to mourn the death of their parents for thirty-nine months. During this period, they would have to retire from public life and go and live quietly in the country. It could be extremely inconvenient for their careers. Gradually the strictness of mourning was relaxed and by the end of the three years, they returned, ready to take up their life again. This period of contemplation and retreat gave them a chance to come to terms with their loss in peace. In Mediterranean cultures, wailing in public is an important part of grief. This enables people to express their grief in a very physical way and, most importantly, to express it together with other people. By contrast Northern Europeans are more reserved and private about their mourning but it's nevertheless important that it takes place.

WHAT DOES GRIEF FEEL LIKE?

As C. S. Lewis noted, grief can feel like fear. Other feelings closely associated with grief include: shock, numbness, loneliness, anger, disbelief and guilt. Immediately after the loss, there is usually a sense of unreality. People say things like, 'It feels like a bad dream and I want to wake up now' or 'I just don't believe she's dead – it must be a mistake.' Often a person who's recently been bereaved feels very confused. One moment they may feel relieved and elated and the next they are crying their eyes out. Emotions can swing around like a weathervane in a gale. The smallest things seem ludicrous, such as the fact that one still needs to carry on one's bodily functions at such a terrible time. People can, for example, feel ravenously hungry and then deeply ashamed that they're eating when their loved one has just died. There may be attempts at black humour and laughter as well as crying.

As time goes by and the loss is assimilated, there are specific markers of the mourning process which include: denial, anger, depression, resignation and, finally, acceptance. The nature of the loss will determine how long each process takes. The loss of a close family member will probably take longer than the loss of a friend because the relative is more closely entwined within the bereaved person's life. The loss of a parent is a terrible thing but somehow within the natural order. By contrast the loss of a child, who should take life forward beyond their parents' death, is very hard to bear. The grief process for this type of bereavement can take considerably longer. If the loss is, for instance, of a body part, such as an eye or a limb, the loss may never be fully assimilated, but a state of being can be reached in which the pain is no longer active and there is the possibility of deep joy in life.

THE JOURNEY OF GRIEF

Working through grief is like going on a journey. The landscape changes and it can be helpful to recognise the landmarks. There are many ways of looking at the stages but this is a model that I've found useful. Although the stages are presented as separate events, they are not like that in reality. We go back and forth and don't be surprised or upset if you find yourself 'regressing' to an earlier state. It's a healthy part of the process. The stages are:

Finding yourself at the entrance to the tunnel

This is the period immediately following the bad news when the doctor says your loved one has just died, or that you must lose your breast, or you get a letter saying that you've failed the exam or been refused a job. It is the moment when the judge sentences you, either literally or metaphorically. It is the ending of a hope for the future for now the future is irrevocably changed. It feels as if you're walking around in a daze, you're numb and the news can't really sink in. This is nature's way of protecting us against the full force of the pain we feel at the loss which dramatically alters our future.

At this stage, there is a temptation to say, 'This is not happening' or to take refuge in drugs or drink. Another form of denial is to acknowledge what's happened but to minimise it, and say, 'I'm fine really . . . I'm not too affected by what's happened. It will be all right.' This often confuses people who are trying to support the bereaved person as they feel their help is being rejected. Denial is a form of being stuck and we can be stuck at the entrance to the tunnel for a long time.

Going into the tunnel

It takes real courage to enter the next phase because it looks so dark but it is a necessary next step. It is dark, dank and bleak. This is the time of real depression. As one person put it, 'Emotionally it feels like my own personal nuclear winter.' No sunlight penetrates this state but if it did, through some deep shaft in the tunnel ceiling, the source of light would seem so far away that it would only mock us. Anger and depression possibly alternate at this time. Questions like, 'Why me?' and 'It isn't fair' come here. Although company often is sought, the negativity of the grieving person can prevent people getting close. If we have been bereaved we are often angry with the dead person for leaving us and rejection and abandonment can be important themes in this phase.

At this time everything seems black and hateful. Any comforting words that are offered are usually rejected and turned away. In this state a person can be hopeless (which is quite good) or despairing (which is less so). Hopeless really means that we have given up on our specific plans for the future which opens the way to finding later the attitude of trusting hope within. Despairing means that we have fallen into a pit of agony because things are not the way we would like them to be. Whatever the loss, some part of us has died and we start to shed and let go of our past life. We come to realise that things will never be the same again.

The valley beyond the tunnel

Acceptance of the reality of the situation ultimately leads us out of the tunnel. We have arrived in a new land. This might be the time of the first Christmas after a bereavement or the sunny morning when we can look down at a mastectomy scar and face the fact that this is the way it is from now on. At first we don't like this new land very much and want to return to our old country.

Little by little, we notice that there are pleasant features to this landscape. Some of our old pleasures are still with us, others have changed and some new ones start to creep in. At first we may feel guilty if we notice that we quite like having Sundays to ourselves and no longer having the duty of visiting our elderly mother. Moments of peace alternate here with pendulum swings back into the black emotions of the tunnel. The valley is a turning point when we begin to look forward to the future and to hope for good things in it.

Crossing the river

If we negotiate the valley sufficiently well, we will find ourselves at the point of crossing a river. The river is symbolically a passage between two states and crossing it represents an acceptance of the situation. At first we are merely resigned. We may say things like, 'You have to accept it' or 'It's fate.' But our hearts are heavy. We know the truth and can face reality but there is no joy in it. This is another time we can get seriously stuck for it is an act of faith to take the next step. We have to imagine ourselves beyond the wounding into a state of integration. At this moment, we can get very angry with the person who we perceive wounded us. It is also often the time when a therapeutic relationship will be left or a supportive friendship cooled.

If we can summon the courage and energy to wade across the river, we enter into acceptance. Resentment often thwarts us at this moment as we can feel that we have to agree that whatever wounded us was *for our own good.* This isn't true, of course, some things just happen. The personality which is restlessly seeking reasons for things will often make a story out of an event which attempts to supply this sort of logic. It is worth recognising that there are things we do not know the reason for. Trying to make things fit often hampers us from moving on. The river is a kind of washing of the soul and many of the grievances we've been holding onto can flow away in the water. At the other shore of the river there is the possibility of integrating the loss. At this moment we have truly entered into the new state beyond grief.

SHORT-CIRCUITING THE CYCLE OF GRIEF

At any stage in this process we can get stuck but there is one stage which is the most likely. This is the stage of denial. There is a temptation in denial to short-circuit into a state of resignation. Because the descent into the tunnel of grief has not taken place and all the unpleasant feelings have not been experienced, the resignation will be shallow and phoney. Moira is an example. A few years ago, she fell in love with Ted and he left her, just before their wedding. It was a shock that she has never recovered from. She coped with it by denying that he was ever important to her and that she ever loved him. This enabled her to achieve a fake state of resignation. She said things like, 'If he hadn't left, I would have and it's for the best really. It would never have worked out.' But because she was in denial about Ted's importance, no other man could be important to her. She was not free to love anyone else.

Not so long ago, Moira had a dream in which his dead body blocked her path. When she discussed the dream, she realised that she couldn't go on without acknowledging what was truly dead and needed burying. Burying the relationship required facing the pain of the loss of it and going through the grief process. She also had to face the social shame of being an abandoned woman. As she wrestled with these deep and uncomfortable feelings, she discovered the power of paint and she regularly painted whatever came into her head, without censorship. After many 'adventures in colour' as she called them, the image of a phoenix came to her. The phoenix is reborn from the ashes of its dead parent. Only when something is fully acknowledged as dead can new life spring forth from its ashes. Moira recognised that this image meant that she could carry on to a new future.

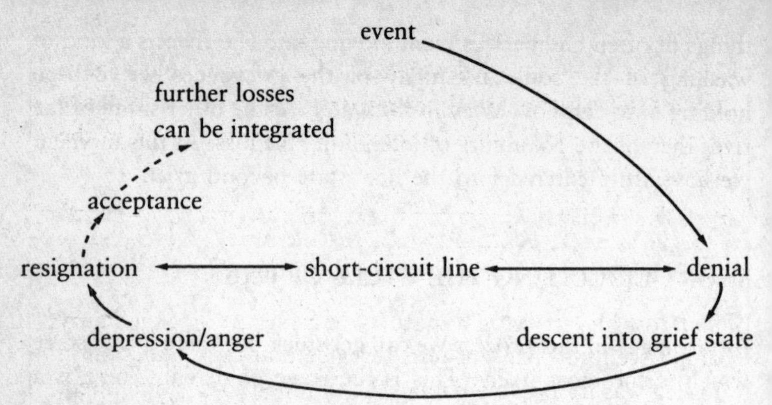

Looking for her lost twin – Maureen's story

Maureen lost her twin sister when they were born but has only recently realised that she has never been able to integrate that loss into her life. She is in her late twenties and has a promising career and lives with her partner of five years' standing. She is a jolly young woman but is prone to fits of black depression during which time she will weep uncontrollably.

Her mother never spoke much about the death of the baby, beyond saying casually when Maureen was a teenager that she had been a twin. Maureen has always had a sense of incompleteness and loss which she has never been able to account for. Outwardly, her life is flourishing but inwardly she feels bereft. When she planned to start her own family, she asked her mother about her gynaecological history and then the truth came out that the twin had died at birth. Maureen felt a sense of tremendous guilt that she had been the one to survive. She says, 'Mum really played it down, saying it was sort of nothing but my sister was a person and it is so sad that she hasn't even got a name.'

Maureen prepared herself to enter the tunnel of grieving. She had to mourn not only the loss of the sister with whom she had spent nine months in the womb but also her sister's unlived life. Her partner opposed this grief work, saying that all this dwelling on the past was no good and instead she should get on with her life. Maureen was very tempted to short-circuit her grief into resignation. Matters came to a head when her partner threatened to leave her unless she gave up 'all this psychological navel-gazing' as he put it. Will she preserve her relationship or complete her mourning? Can she do both?

Man of metal with a wounded heart – Stan's story

Stan lost his left leg in a motorcycle crash. At first the injury didn't seem too bad but tests revealed that the circulation in his leg was irreparably damaged and it had to be amputated. Stan was furiously angry and blamed the doctors' incompetence as he put it. As he is an active young man of twenty-six, the loss of a limb came as a deeply felt blow. Stan went into a form of denial. He decided to become, as he put it, 'A tin man. Now that part of me's going to be made of metal, I might as well all be made of metal.'

His friends said that he was very cut off to which he replied bitterly, 'Well, I have been cut off.' He refused to love anyone or anything but adopted a mask of cynicism. Anyone, particularly if they were female, who came too close, was treated with scorn and sarcasm. In fact, Stan longed for the comfort of a woman and for the joys of a passionate sexual relationship. Because he now found himself so ugly, he believed that no woman could ever love him. He became hostile to any attempt to befriend him because he felt that anyone could be interested in him purely out of pity and not out of any genuine interest.

Stan also had to face a future in which his plans had been irrevocably changed. He had to give up the idea of many things a two-legged person can do and recognise that life would be different from now on. This was very difficult for him and he became increasingly isolated as his friends gave up on his negativity and bleakness. They realised that he was facing a very difficult situation but they could no longer put up with his wounding comments. As time went by Stan developed a strategy of laughing at his stump. He would wave it at people to shock them and then make a horrible joke out of it. One day he did this to a little girl and she cried. Stan, to his great surprise, found that he was crying, too. He had entered the tunnel at last.

Inner Work

What are you feeling at this moment? Take some time to describe your feelings. Remember that your journal is private and that it's your companion.

What loss(es) are you grieving for now?

What fear is holding you back from beginning the grief journey?

What losses have you had in the past that have gone on to better things? What good things have come your way as a result of change?

What other emotions are you feeling/have you felt? e.g. envy, fear, depression, anger. Remember that naming them takes the sting out of them.

Reading Stan's and Maureen's stories, did you notice where you felt sympathetic, angry, impatient or pitying, or any other feeling? Is there some message here for you?

What do you hope for in the future? How is that future changed as a result of your loss?

Creative Task

Take the largest sheet of paper you can find, a set of coloured felt-tip pens, a tube of glue and a pile of magazines. Spend some time leafing through the magazines and cut out any images that you are drawn to. Do this without thinking too much about it but just trust the process and don't try to control it. When you have done this, take a break and have a cup of coffee. Then return to the pictures and sort them into some sort of a journey. Although I have described the journey of grief in terms of a tunnel, a valley and a river, these images may not work for you. You may see the journey in terms of a sea voyage, a journey across a mountain range or a desert, or whatever. Make the map on your large sheet of paper and sketch or describe the bits in between the pictures. When you

have finished you may start noticing all sorts of things about your grief journey.

THE TRANSFORMATION OF GRIEF

Although Stan's and Maureen's stories are very different, they had the same task. They both had to risk the pain of the grief journey. Maureen risked a further loss as her partner was antagonistic to her going through this process. At first Maureen reacted to this by agreeing with him that everything was fine and that there was no need to start digging around in the past. 'It's best to let it go,' she said brightly. But it would not let her go. Her depression continued, now accompanied by bad dreams. She had to face it. There were a number of issues. She had to acknowledge her guilt in being the twin that had survived. Then the anger that her mother had never told her about it properly. Then the fact that she would never see her sister and that she had no name and no grave.

This work was hard for Maureen and her partner was opposed to it. She asked him why and he said, 'Look what it's doing to you. You're in a complete state all the time and I want to be with a happy person.' After a while she began to realise that he and her mother both did the same thing with unpleasant facts. They both tried to sweep them under the carpet and bandage over any unhappiness with a smiling face. Maureen decided that she wanted a life that was much more out in the open and where painful things could be accepted and worked through. She and her partner, after much discussion, decided to split up, and Maureen mourned his loss. A year on, she felt she had crossed the river and had integrated both the losses. A new country opened up before her.

Stan had a great struggle with accepting the reality of his amputation. When he realised that he could begin to cry about it, he started to mourn his loss. Many things would now not be possible. But after a while, he realised that some things still would. Strangely the little girl's tears, when he frightened her with his stump, made him realise that he could still feel, too. He told his counsellor that he felt his amputation would be bearable if he felt he could still attract a woman, and still give and receive love. His counsellor challenged him to explore the possibility that someone might find him attractive and together they found many examples of people who had found love despite greater disabilities than Stan's. Stan summed it up one day saying, 'I think what's unattractive about me is my attitude and not my missing leg. By refusing to feel, other people are shut out and they react to that, quite understandably, by moving away from me.'

C. S. Lewis writes movingly about the parallels between physical loss and emotional bereavement in his magnificent book, *A Grief Observed*. He contrasts the pain of the amputee with the pain he felt after his wife's death. C. S. Lewis had suffered the loss of his mother while still a child and had not been able to trust in life sufficiently to fall in love until he was in his sixties. Joy, the woman he finally married, had cancer, but she had a long remission during which they had several years of happy married life together. Her death devastated him and he struggled with God to find some meaning in the experience. Although *A Grief Observed* is written from a Christian point of view, it is a book about grief which is of great value to the non-religious reader as well. The struggle with God can equally validly be seen as the struggle with what is, with reality. Stan found the following paragraph particularly helpful and he realised that many people have suffered a devastating loss of one kind or another. He resolved to make contact with other people and to share the pain and fruits of his own journey.

> 'To say that the patient is getting over it after an operation for appendicitis is one thing; after he's had his leg off is quite another . . . There will be hardly any moment when he forgets it. Bathing, dressing, sitting down and getting up again, all will be different. His whole way of life will be changed . . . At the moment I am learning to get about on crutches. Perhaps I shall presently be given a wooden leg. But I shall never be a biped again.' C. S. Lewis

15

Guilt

'When a white man in Africa by accident looks into the eyes of a native and sees the human being (which is his chief preoccupation to avoid), his sense of guilt, which he denies, fumes up in resentment and he brings down the whip.' Doris Lessing

WHAT IS GUILT?

Guilt is a great inner adversary with which we have to do battle in order to reach our fullest potential as human beings. The ability to feel guilt is a sign of psychological development and is very much allied to conscience. Conscience enables us to choose between right and wrong and to correct our course when we go off track. The uncomfortable pricking of guilt is the way that we tell ourselves that our actions do not tally with our moral code. Tragically, some people appear never to develop the capacity for guilt and they are called psychopaths or sociopaths. The absence of it enables them to act without feeling or remorse. Many mass murderers and torturers, though not all, are psychopaths and it is a great mystery why this should be. For the great majority of us, however, guilt presents a series of problems throughout our lives which we must resolve to reach the next stage. Guilt has the potential to encourage us to revise our actions or our belief structures, or both. At the further end of guilt is the possibility of forgiveness, reappraisal of our values and a fresh start.

Guilt and shame intertwine but are subtly different. Shame relates to the person we are, to our very identity. Guilt relates to our actions, behaviour and thoughts. Shame tells us we are bad, perhaps irredeemably so, guilt tells us that what we do is bad. In developmental terms, shame is an earlier emotion than guilt. If an infant feels that he or she is bad, they will feel shame. If a slightly older child feels that they have done a bad thing, they will feel guilt. Shame is about the very core of our existence, guilt is about the way we relate to the world about us. Guilt can be used to cover up shame because, paradoxically, guilt can make us feel better. If we feel guilt, however uncomfortable it is, we can say to ourselves: 'What a good person I am to feel this troubled, I must have a finely developed conscience.' Often guilt and shame present themselves together in our emotional lives.

When we have unwrapped shame from guilt, a nest of Chinese boxes presents itself as guilt itself is a complex emotion which calls for great discernment to unpack. One aspect of it has a very positive potential, the other, rather less so. It can be a call to conscience, action and integrity, but, on the other hand, it can also be a trap which justifies inaction and stuckness. To become a conscious human being, a certain amount of guilt is necessary but we also need a mechanism for processing our guilt otherwise we risk drowning in it.

Mary is an example of this. She is a guilt-ridden person. She flits from one guilty thought to the next. Her inner dialogue goes something like this: 'Oh God, I didn't ring Mum although I promised. I can't now, the moment has passed and, if I explain why I delayed, I'll feel embarrassed. I'll just have to leave it. Perhaps she will ring me and I can pretend that I forgot. I hate Jack (her boss) and I wish he would suffer for all the pain he puts me through. Oh that's not a very nice thought. I mustn't think that – it's not worthy of me. I really must take those library books back. I can't now, the librarian will notice that the books are at least two months overdue. I can't. I feel so ashamed and guilty. I'll have to leave it.' If we listen carefully we notice that Mary's guilty feelings flow from one source of guilt to the next. She feels shame and can't resolve her guilt by an action because she's paralysed by the feeling. Possibly many of us have a Mary-like figure within us.

This chapter looks at the things that guilt and shame are hiding, to distinguish between the various forms of guilt, and to suggest ways to move forward, taking notice of the valuable feedback that these emotions provide.

HOW DOES GUILT FEEL?

Guilt has been often called bitter and it can feel extremely piercing. Other words often used to describe it are guilt-pricks and pangs of guilt. A woman described it 'like having a hungry animal inside you, always wanting to gnaw at your vitals'. Repetitive physical actions like wringing of hands, hanging of the head and avoidance of eye-contact may also be present. Guilt can also feel like a queasy pain in the stomach, a bit like mild anxiety. A characteristic of guilt, however, are the fantasies that accompany it. We may run scenarios through our head of our transgressions, trying to change this or that. This is an attempt to make ourselves feel better because we feel so bad it must mean that we are very good. Remorse may be present, and much of what a guilty person is really saying to themselves or to others is 'if only'. *If only* I hadn't done that or *if only* that hadn't happened.

In general, the worse we feel with guilt, the more we are trying to avoid the message. Instead of changing our actions or our moral code, we pile the agony onto ourselves. Guilt is designed as a course corrector, not as a punishment. A man was tormented by guilt because his girlfriend had an abortion and he had to face a choice in order to resolve his pain. Although he hadn't wanted the abortion, he had recognised that it was his girlfriend's right to make the choice. He had been a party to it and he had to acknowledge that, in part, he was guilty of ending that life. As his moral code felt that abortion was a form of murder, he had no option but to think of himself as an accessory to murder. He could choose to change his moral code and permit, as the law does, abortion in certain cases, or he could recognise himself as a murderer in a sense and carry the burden. When he adopted the latter course, he sought to make amends by charitable activity and by rededicating his life to the principles he found important. This led to the transformation of his guilt from a raging pain to a bearable burden which deepened his sense of the sacredness of life and no longer paralysed his actions.

THE FORMS OF GUILT

There are various forms of guilt and they need to be distinguished from each other because they need to be treated differently. They are:

- real guilt arising from a situation of wrong-doing or inappropriate action
- neurotic guilt which is a defence against anxiety or fear
- existential guilt which is part and parcel of being human

Each has its own cycle and roots but all three are interlinked.

Real guilt

Real guilt is something everybody knows (unless they are a psychopath). I have stolen something from you and I feel badly about it until I own up and put the matter right. The difficulties with this form of guilt start to come in when the code which governs my moral life is not clear-cut. There are always grey areas. For example, if there is a murder going on in the next room and I do nothing to stop it, I would certainly feel a sense of guilt about my non-intervention. But if, on the other hand, I hear a scream in the night which sounds as if someone may be being hurt, and I do not stir from my warm and comfortable bed to investigate it, I may feel a sense of guilt. This may depend upon my sense of my own ability to defend myself (which will vary according to age, strength and sex). If I have the sense of myself as a person who always helps and I do not on this occasion, then I may feel far more guilty than if I have decided that it is not my task in life to risk myself physically. Real guilt relates to our personal value system and offers us a stark choice: either to change our behaviour or to change our values.

With real guilt we also have the possibility of making a reparative or expiatory act which will absolve us from our guilt. This will vary according to our circumstances and the action which has made us guilty. If I can confess to someone, this may be a great help. In the Catholic tradition, penitents confess to a priest, make an act of repentance and are forgiven. In more secular societies, psychotherapists and counsellors have often taken on that role. In a sense, it doesn't matter who the person is, all that matters is that our guilt is acknowledged. We need to say it out loud so that we hear it. This involves taking responsibility for it and that is where the possibility of forgiveness comes in. Forgiveness (whether it is self-created or comes from a priest) is the key to the healing of guilt.

The questions to ask yourself with this form of guilt are:

Am I responsible for this situation? Why am I responsible?
What moral code or belief system have I transgressed in order to feel this guilty?
Can I change any of these beliefs?
Can I change my actions in future?
How can I repair my fault (in some way which does not bring further harm)?

If your guilt feels manageable as a result of understanding or activity on your part then it is real guilt and not neurotic guilt.

The cycle of real guilt

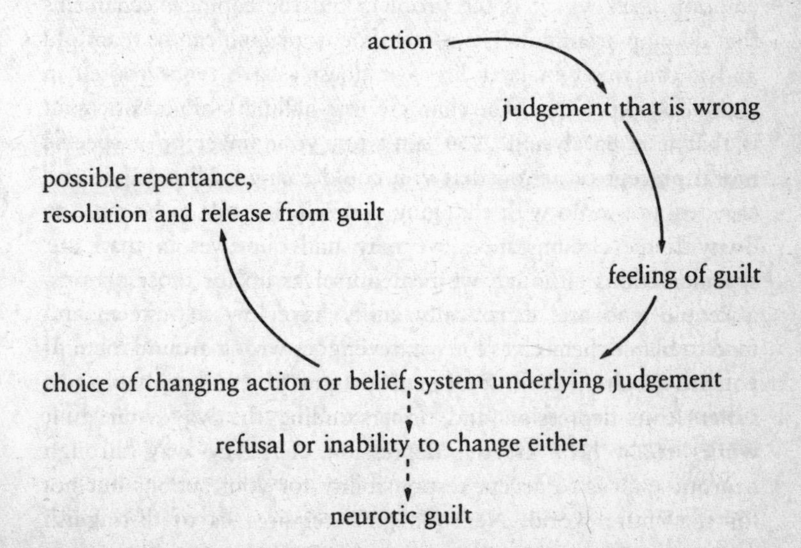

Neurotic guilt

Neurotic guilt looks deceptively like real guilt but has no true focus. It can lead on from true guilt and may in fact be a chronic form of it. The same physical feelings and the same fantasies may be present but there will be no clear action that will resolve them. Even if an action is undertaken, the feelings of guilt will remain. This is because guilt has become imbedded in our psyche as a means of dealing with anxiety, anger or fear. What happens is that, as small children, we become anxious if our environment is disturbing or ambivalent. For example, our parents may row destructively with each other. A child may very naturally feel anxious or afraid at the sight of adult anger and aggression. The child may develop a mechanism for coping with this that says, in effect, 'My parents are angry with each other which makes me feel very afraid. In order to deal with this fear, I must find a way of controlling the situation. The only thing I can control in this uncontrollable situation is myself. It must be because of me that they are rowing. I must be a very bad little girl. I feel guilty because I am so bad.'

This pattern repeats itself endlessly whenever we come across a situation which terrifies us or makes us enraged, and it is beyond our power to deal with. As with most emotions, it is not the emotion itself which is the problem but the coping mechanisms that develop around it. The roots of neurotic guilt can be manifold and it can onset in later life – it doesn't have to be rooted in childhood experience. The characteristic hallmark of neurotic guilt is that it is paralysing. You can't put your finger on a specific moral precept or action that you could change. All is vague and clouded and to do with changing yourself. It tends to be more to do with the circumstances we may find ourselves in than our specific actions although we beat ourselves up for those actions.

People who are neurotically guilty have low self-esteem and tend to blame themselves for whatever goes wrong around them. If you are caught in the trap of neurotic guilt you will probably also suffer from depression and understanding the way your guilt works could help lift the depression. The key way through neurotic guilt is to accept responsibility for your actions but not for the entire world. Neurotic guilt requires us to distinguish between what we legitimately may control but to allow a trusting acceptance towards those things we have no power over.

The questions to ask are:

Does my guilt stem from the sort of person I am (rather than my actions)?
What may have triggered my fear, hatred or anxiety?
What anxiety or fear may my guilty feeling be masking?
Can I accept responsibility for my guilt?

The cycle of neurotic guilt

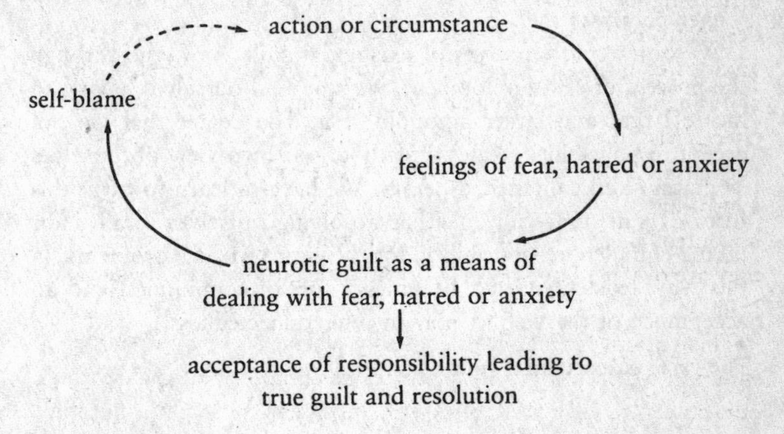

Existential guilt

All of us have an existential level of guilt which is latent in our psyches and which is activated by certain circumstances. Existential guilt, like neurotic guilt, is to do with responsibility. Existential guilt comes when we have to accept the consequences of our choices, *even though those choices were not made in the knowledge of the full facts*. This is one of the hardest things to bear and makes us feel the tragedy of life. In a deeper sense, yet, existential guilt is about accepting the very faults and flaws which make us human. This enables us to live in the present and not the past. Often the person we have most failed is ourselves. If we have missed the mark, we have pretended we were a smaller, pettier person than we in fact are. If we have cramped ourselves into a sad marriage or a dead-end job, we have lacked self-respect.

As human beings, we are responsible, to some degree, for the actions of our fellow human beings. In a sense, whatever is wrong with the world, is also wrong with ourselves. If we see an action which we judge to be evil, and we do nothing, where does this lead us? Many of us become bystanders in the tragedies of others. Immediate intervention may not be physically possible but some sort of moral outrage or ability to make a human statement may be necessary. This is what drives many voluntary organisations' activities. I may not be able to stop torture in a distant country, but I can support the condemnation of it and may be able to provide funds for helping the victims of that torture. In this way, I accept my guilt about being a member of the human race but it no longer paralyses me.

We cannot rid ourselves of existential guilt. As we go through the process of self-development, we may find ourselves having to tackle larger and larger amounts of it. The degree that we can accept responsibility relates directly to our own view of ourselves as mature and enlightened beings. We have to learn to carry this form of guilt gracefully, neither absolving ourselves totally, nor taking complete responsibility, for the entire world's problems. In this way, existential guilt becomes a sort of communion and an acceptance of the web of human interconnectedness.

The cycle of existential guilt

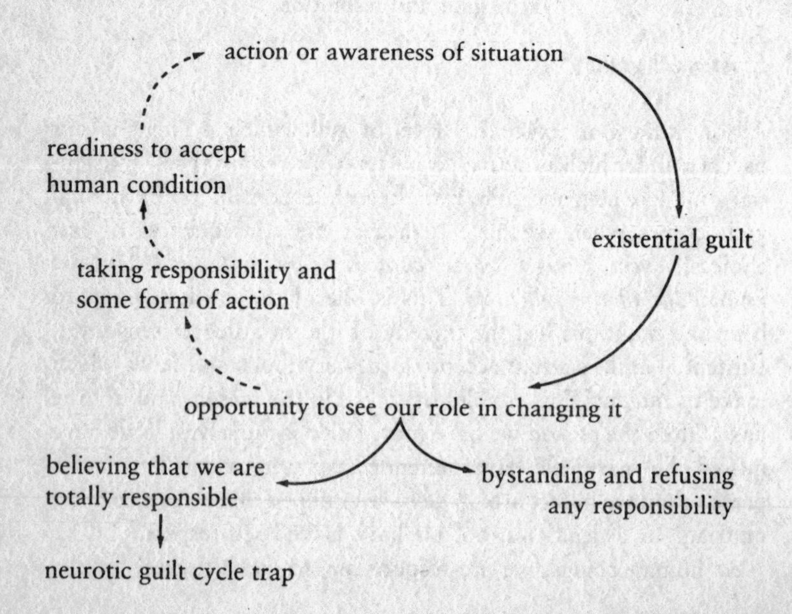

The way through existential guilt is to distinguish our true level of responsibility in the activity or event we feel guilty about. We may decide that we can't stop whatever is happening single-handedly but we can join an organisation which is involved with this particular issue. Or we may decide that some entirely private activity such as praying is more appropriate. Here are some ideas:

- Joining an organisation that addresses the problem we are concerned with
- Refusing to become bystanders and keeping alive our sense of moral outrage even if we cannot make an actual intervention in the situation
- Praying
- Helping another person or animal
- Taking part in a group activity
- Writing a letter to a relevant authority
- Peacefully protesting
- Committing ourselves to some form of reparative activity

Many great human achievements are outcomes of the existential guilt of men and women who have worked creatively to try to improve the condition of the human race.

Saying no makes her feel guilty – Jean's story

Jean is a pleasant woman in her early sixties. All her life she has been a people pleaser. She almost never says no to anyone's request, no matter how inconvenient it is to her personal life. She is retired now and runs several community activities in her local village. She literally cannot say no because she feels terribly bad about it.

As a result people put more and more onto her. Recently, she has come to see that there's more to life than running errands for others, putting up her nephews and nieces and baking endless cakes for charity sales. She avoids the feelings that these requests bring up by agreeing to them. The feelings are often of anger and resentment. At the bottom of her anger is a fear that she won't be able to control her anger, and so she creates a form of neurotic guilt to deal with these frightening feelings.

Jean says that she always agrees with people to avoid feeling guilty but in fact she experiences a low-grade form of guilt all the time. She is constantly looking over her shoulder to see what she should or shouldn't be doing. As a result she follows the most conventional line that she can take, the one that will offend the least number of people.

Jean's problems probably stem from a harsh and overbearing father. All through her childhood, he criticised her relentlessly. She became anxious and fearful, and as a result, decided that her best strategy in life was to attempt to please. Guilt became the driving force – but it was neurotic guilt. She felt that because she was a bad person, she must make up for it by becoming a doormat.

Avoidance of responsibility leads to an empty life – Steve's story

Steve is young and married. He works as a salesman which involves a lot of travelling away from home. Even though he loves his wife, Sonia, he frequently cheats on her. He doesn't do this out of any real desire for another woman but because, as he puts it, 'The opportunity came my way and it seemed a pity to pass it by.' After a bout of unfaithfulness, he returns to Sonia, highly contrite. He hangs his head and does the washing-up without grumbling for at least a month.

He says, if you ask him why he does it, 'I don't know why . . . perhaps you can tell me.' If you happen to come up with a hypothesis he would instantly reject it, shaking his head. 'No, that's not it. I don't know why.' Steve uses ignorance as a way of avoiding any responsibility for his actions. He will tell you, with tears in his eyes, that he is a good person, 'Otherwise I wouldn't be feeling all this guilt, would I?'

Steve's life is very empty and shallow. His guilt cuts him off from the possibility of a real relationship with Sonia. He never actually confesses his extramarital activities to Sonia, thinking that she would be hurt about it. But he avoids any confrontation with her about it. She wordlessly accepts his contrite behaviour, enjoying the power of it. But even more significantly, it cuts him off from a real relationship with himself. He could change his value system and decide that marriage is not meant to be monogamous, but that would not really solve his problem, because he knows that his guilt does not really stem from that.

Less and less motivates him. Even his work is suffering and when he has a serious car crash which confines him to a hospital bed for several months, he is forced to take stock of his life.

Inner Work

What are your personal *if onlys*?

Do they relate to true, neurotic or existential guilt?

What values does your guilt challenge?

Reading the stories of Jean and Steve, which did you feel more sympathetic towards and which were you more impatient with? Bearing in mind that we often find it harder to accept in others what we haven't accepted in ourselves, is there some message here for you?

Do you find yourself avoiding certain things? Can you link this with a denial of your guilt?

Can you identify the negative voice inside you that tells you that you're not a good person, or that you're very bad? It may be a mother, father, teacher or some other person you knew as a child?

If you are suffering the pangs of true guilt, what action could you do to put matters right? (Remember that making reparation must not hurt anybody.)

If you are suffering from the pangs of neurotic guilt, what emotion is underlying your guilt? How can you deal with that?

If you are suffering from existential guilt, how can you structure your life, so that you can be of benefit in some way, and not be a bystander?

THE TRANSFORMATION OF GUILT INTO POTENTIAL

Jean's inner work revolved around her realisation of what underlay her feelings of guilt. When she can unpack the fear and anger which her early life had conditioned her to experience most of the time, she can start to feel true guilt when it is appropriate. A lot of her work revolved around building up her self-esteem and her conviction of her right to exist. Then she started to look at her father's voice within her. Her actual father had, of course, long since died but she discovered that his negative attitude to her still lived in her head. His harsh criticisms of her appearance, behaviour and character were woven into the way she saw herself. Gradually, she started to be able to discern when this voice was speaking and when it was not. After a lifetime this took some practice.

She said, 'At one point I nearly gave up. It seemed so hopeless and such a mess, like a plate of spaghetti which I couldn't get round a fork. Then when I started to get a handle on it, I nearly gave up again. I realised that I had literally wasted my life hearing this negativity and it had stopped me from experiencing so much of the joy that life has to offer. I fell into a pit of grief as I mourned the life that I hadn't lived. But now things are much better.' Jean's problem wasn't bystanding as she took a very active role in her community. It was realising that she did the right things for the wrong reasons. She saw that if she acted less from guilt and more from love that the things she did for others would really bless and benefit them, as well as herself. Jean has come to say that, while we all are unique individuals with a personal destiny, nevertheless we are all connected up with each other. 'Forgiveness, even forgiveness of my father is possible. Some days I feel more forgiving than others and some days my old guilt comes back. But I know how to deal with it now.'

Steve had much work to do with understanding his pattern of unfaithfulness. As he lay in the hospital bed, encased in plaster after his accident, he had plenty of time to mull things over. A hospital counsellor started to come and see him and he found this very useful. He looked at the way he had used neurotic guilt as a cover-up for both his actual guilt and his existential guilt. Feeling guilty about cheating on his wife took care of his guilt as it could be hidden under the one umbrella. He noticed that a pattern had emerged. When he felt that he wasn't fulfilling his real potential either in his job or in his self-development, he was much more vulnerable to an affair. Then he could feel guilty about that and not about the fact that he wasn't the person that he knew he had the potential to become. He described himself as 'a small rat-faced person' but when he started to work on himself, his features filled out and he began to look more generous.

He said, 'In a way, feeling guilty gave me a sense of pride. I thought it meant I was a good person, and also, very much in control of the situation. Giving up guilt has meant a sacrifice.' As with Jean, Steve had much work to do around his self-esteem. He also had to confront the problems in his marriage to Sonia. He decided that, however painful it might be, he must discuss the truth of his life with her, risking that she might reject him.

This isn't necessarily the case with every act of infidelity as sometimes the guilty partner can work this through on his or her own. Sometimes a confession would give the other partner a great deal of unnecessary pain. These things have to be finely balanced. But in Steve's case, his infidelity and Sonia's tacit complicity were so bound up with the dynamics of their relationship that this area had to be brought out into the open. At first Sonia resisted this openness as she was used to the power that Steve's guilt had brought to her. When she realised that she could change, too, and live a broader life, she started to see that this could be a good thing. Negotiating this change in their marriage took many months and both decided that, as long as they could seek their true potential, they could stay together. They would not be bound by the power dynamics of guilt but by a spirit of honesty and respect.

16

Hate

'If you hate a person, you hate something in him that is part of yourself. What isn't part of ourselves doesn't disturb us.'

Hermann Hesse

WHAT IS HATE?

It is difficult to think about hate because it is a deeply distressing subject. Both to hate and to realise that you are hated are profoundly painful. In its purest form hate is murderous and annihilating. It can be focused on a particular person or it can encompass whole groups or indeed races. Human history bears the scars of these mass hatreds which have given rise to torture, war, persecution and genocide. Hate provides the motivating force for much of racism and sexism. It is beyond the scope of this chapter to discuss the broader sweeps of hate. However, if we start to understand this emotion in ourselves, we will be able to unhook ourselves from the collective feelings of hatred. First we have to feel our own hate and to begin to understand it – confronting it in ourselves which is anything but easy. If you are reading this because you are feeling hateful or, perhaps are feeling hated, then have the courage to read to the end. You are more than halfway to dealing with hate if you can recognise it and acknowledge it. This chapter will outline some ways in which we can understand hate better and learn to express it safely and constructively.

We have various ways of dealing with hate. One is to minimise the power of it by calling many things hate. For example, we may use the word hate when we're in a rage of not getting what we want. A toddler will say, 'I hate you, Mummy' when what he really feels is frustrated by her. A wife may say to her husband, 'I hate the way you leave the dishes unwashed in the sink' when she feels disappointed that he is not more tidy. Neither the toddler nor the wife really means that they hate the person, they just hate the way that person's behaviour is affecting them at the moment.

Another way of dealing with hate is to allow ourselves to feel it for a short period of time such as in the aftermath of the break-up of a relationship. 'I hate the bastard for leaving me and I wish he were dead at the bottom of a lake,' one woman told me. But she added in the next breath, 'I know by next week I will be getting over it and I won't feel this way.' She had loved this man very much and he had left her. She used her hate intelligently. By allowing herself to feel hatred for the jilting lover to sever the connection between them, while realising that the emotion was time-limited. After a week or two she would see things more clearly and have some forgiveness in her heart. She didn't permit her hate to take her over completely but allowed it to spring her into the next state which involved separation from her lover. She was also honest with herself as to the degree to which he had hurt her. She saw through her hate and yet used its emotional energy.

This is a positive example of hate felt truly and yet employed creatively. By contrast the real tragedy of unexamined hate is that while it may or may not destroy the hated person or thing, it certainly will destroy, in the end, the person who hates. Much of our hate is unconscious because we cannot bear to recognise it. It runs like a monstrous underground river beneath the city we have consciously constructed to live in. But if this river is not channelled then it will undermine the foundations of the buildings of our lives. People can literally be eaten away by a hatred that they have denied for years, possibly a lifetime. Sometimes it can erupt in full force in old age, giving rise to the terrifying spectacle of an old person's murderous monologues, literally filled with hate. Cursing people for leaving them alone, they drive all but the most persistent away. It is not old age that is making them like this. It is rather that their defensive masks have worn out over the years and their long-suppressed hate has come to the surface. By contrast an old person who has acknowledged their hate throughout their life and worked with it intelligently, will be at peace.

HOW DOES HATE FEEL?

Hate exists along a spectrum and so the feelings of hate similarly vary from feelings of frustration and disappointment to an intolerable and restless loathing and disgust. The more manageable it is, the more likely we are to be able to admit it. When our feelings of hatred reach a destructive level, we are likely to simply push them underground. Hate feels simultaneously both bad and good. It feels bad because there is so much anger and pain in it. It feels good on the other hand because it gives us power over those who have hurt us. As a woman described it, 'When I loathe my mother's behaviour towards me, I want to bite and grind my teeth. Perhaps I want to bite her – but it feels better to hate her than to feel depressed and powerless.'

If you hate someone you may be spiteful or nasty about them. Quite often this is behind their back because you are frightened of them. But if you are the object of another person's hatred, it may not be obvious to you. They may go through the motions of being very nice and polite to your face but there will be something wrong that you can't quite put your finger on. The only way to describe it is that you feel worthless, or frozen, or somehow useless in their presence although they are saying perfectly reasonable and pleasant things. It takes a lot of practice to detect this disguised form of hate but trust your intuition. If it feels as if there is a serious discrepancy between what is being said to you and what you are feeling, then look further. It may be to do with your own process, of course, so consider the situation carefully.

Often we tend to deny feelings of hate in ourselves and others because hate itself is frightening. So hate hides in other emotions which it is associated with. Sometimes these emotions lead to hate and sometimes they cover up hate. All the following emotions are possible indicators of the presence of hatred:

- Guilt is often aroused when we realise we hate someone. If we believe we are a good person, and good people do not hate, then we may feel guilty as a cover-up for our hatred.

- Envy and hatred are quite closely linked. If we are envious it means that we have noticed that another person has something which we don't have and which we passionately want. It is a short step tc hating them for it.
- Aggression can be founded in either love or hate. If it is hate, then the aggression is strengthened in a negative way. If we want or need to be aggressive towards someone, then we often allow ourselves to hate them first so that we can justify our aggressive actions.
- Fear can be an indicator of hatred. If we are afraid of someone and they have power over us, it is hard not to hate them. This is particularly true of children who often have little power over their immediate circumstances, and consequently often profoundly hate a bullying parent or teacher.
- Love and hate are remarkably close to each other. If we love someone, they have the power to hurt us by leaving us or humiliating us in some way. Then we may come to hate them.

SELF-HATE

Not all hate is directly outwards. Many of us experience forms of self-hate which cause us to devalue ourselves. It can often be confused with depression but it is not the same thing. Depression is a withdrawal of energy but self-hatred requires passion. Self-hatred often centres on a particular attribute, such as 'I hate the fact I'm slow' or perhaps a part of the body, such as 'I hate my fat legs'. The distinguishing feature of self-hatred is that it will supply plenty of reasons as to why the attribute or body part is hated but *they will not be the right reasons.* Underlying the hatred is a disappointment that the person is not perfect and a belief that, if only this fault could be corrected, then he or she could have a wonderful life.

If you find yourself persistently despising a part of your self, then it is worth looking at the accompanying fantasy. If, for example, you believe that your slowness prevents you from getting a good job, then check this against reality. Many good jobs require people to be steady and thorough rather than brilliant and, perhaps, careless. Perhaps you are aiming in the wrong area of achievement? And if, for example, you believe that your fat legs preclude you from finding the right man, then examine that fantasy. There are some men for whom fat legs are a turn-off. But many men, in fact, have fat legs themselves or are not bothered by them. Perhaps you need to look for men who are less hung up on physical perfection. Self-hatred, if properly understood, gives us the chance to refocus our goals so as to maximise our chance of getting what we want.

THE ROOTS OF HATE

The origins of both hate and love are very close. They are not opposites but are entwined within each other. Perhaps the true opposite of both of them is indifference. Hate is a perverted form of love, bent out of shape by woundedness. In some ways, all hate contains a portion of love, just as all love has a small grain of hate in it. Love and hate begin early in life. As babies we are very dependent on our parents (or parent substitutes). We feel warm loving feelings if our needs are met and hateful feelings if they are not. In earliest infancy we cannot really distinguish between ourselves and others so we just feel the pure emotion.

As time goes by, if our parents persistently do not meet our needs or disappoint us deeply, we start to hate them because they make us feel so vulnerable. But we can't allow ourselves to acknowledge our hatred because we are dependent on them. So we push our hatred underground. This cycle is then repeated throughout our lives. The trigger is something which makes us feel small and powerless but there has to be an environment of dependence. We can only hate those we are dependent on in some way. Some people, because of their innate nature or because of the lack of nurture they received as small children are more prone to hating as an emotional response to a difficult situation. But all of us are capable of hating, given circumstances which make us feel fearful, angry or vulnerable.

There are two further twists to the roots of hate: the presence of both sameness and difference. We often hate in other people the things we don't like about ourselves. For example, a child may say he hates a boy in his class 'because he tells lies'. When you examine this further you may discover that the first child in question is not always truthful but wants to believe that he is. So he projects his disliked quality onto another person. The other little boy may be a liar but we will probably only hate him if we haven't recognised the liar in ourselves. When we withdraw the projection, it doesn't mean we stop noticing that the other person isn't truthful. This would be stupid. But we notice it without animosity and take suitable action accordingly. Always examine accusations that you make for the presence of hidden projections. Not all hatred is projected outwards from ourselves but it's always worth looking at that as a root cause.

The other major cause of hatred is the perception of difference. People can vary in all sorts of ways, e.g. gender, race, colour, religion, morality, sexuality, diet, culture, customs, dress. If we believe that our own way of doing things is the only way and the right way, then we will find it threatening if other people do things differently. We may start to hate them because they undermine our sense that we are right and that our way is the true path. This is linked with the black and white thinking of our early life. As infants things were either good or bad. There were no grey areas. Good was what nurtured and loved us, bad was what rejected and disappointed us. The scars of this form of thinking are widespread and there are many examples of the bigot, the religious fundamentalist, and the racial fanatic. It is easy to see the damage their hatred causes. What is not so easy to see is that these people are, to some degree, dependent on the people they hate or they could not hate them.

Some of us who are perhaps a little more sophisticated practise this form of hatred much more subtly. We may be threatened by the difference of others but we may cover it up more successfully. It may come out as a piece of intellectual justification or maybe just a patronising remark. It is probably a lifetime's task to rid ourselves of the feelings that difference arouses. The important thing is to keep trying to recognise when a perceived difference is making us hate a person or group and to allow ourselves to have a healthy disagreement with them. By openly acknowledging our differences with others, we can avoid hating them. Emotional maturity involves not hating what disappoints or threatens us.

THE TRIGGERS OF HATE

To hate we have to have both a trigger and an environment where we are in some way, perhaps emotionally or financially, dependent. The triggers of hate are generally those things which make us feel vulnerable and helpless. Thus for some people, falling in love can be a trigger of hatred as love is a situation where we give up some of our power to another. Abuse of any kind is also likely to trigger hate. This is a particularly cruel twist as the person who is abused has to deal not only with the after-effects of the abuse but also the pattern of hatred and self-hatred it sets up.

Many work situations deprive people of their autonomy and independence. Whenever a person's freedom and sense of self-worth is threatened he or she is liable to hate the person or organisation who seems to have deprived them of it. They can't leave because they believe they are dependent financially on their job. Another trigger of hatred is marriage because, unless it is a relationship where both partners are respected, people can become trapped and dependent.

The only way out of the cycle of hate is through conscious recognition of our hatred and the end of the attempt to deny it. When we can see our hate and don't project it onto other people, we can start to understand the message it has for us.

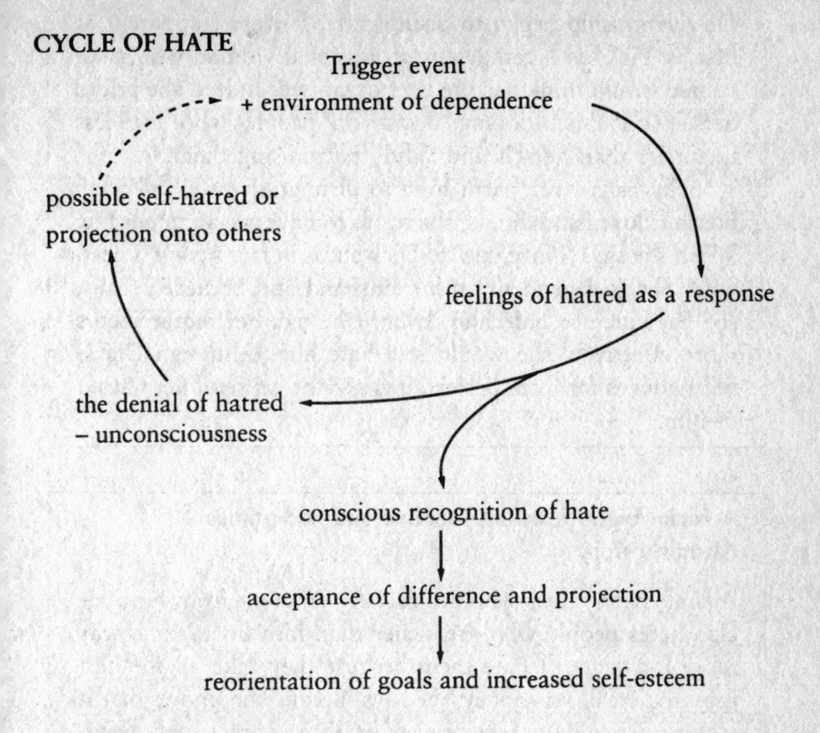

Hate and love inextricably bound together – Vicky's story

Vicky has been married eleven years and is now in her late thirties. She says she loves her husband, Dick, but she spends most of her time attacking him. When they are alone she screams abuse at him. She says: 'He despises me and prefers working to spending time with me. His family are very intellectual and exclude me. He doesn't help with the house at all and isn't a companion in any real way. I like spending time at home doing family things but Dick scorns this. I have given him my youth and my love and I feel very used by him.'

Vicky has in fact been married twice, the first time when she was eighteen and the second time when she was twenty-seven. In between her husbands there was a six-month gap which she describes as the worst period of her life. 'I hated being alone,' she said. When she met Dick, and he moved in with her three weeks later, she felt very relieved. But slowly the relationship began to disintegrate. It wasn't apparent at first as Vicky is a competent professional woman who most people would think has life very organised. Indeed she prides herself on this, looking down on people who are less fortunate than herself and subtly patronising them.

Vicky hasn't yet learnt how to distinguish love and hate. For her, love is neediness, she needs to have a man in her life. When she says 'I love you' to Dick she is in fact saying 'I need you'. She is dependent on her husband and because of this, she has come to hate him. Even if he met her requirements more effectively she would still hate him. Although Dick's behaviour is far from perfect, it is not the cause of her hatred of him.

A racial bigot yearning for love and acceptance – Alistair's story

Alistair hates those who are racially different from him. He also hates people who are richer than him or in some way more fortunate. 'I hate them because they take all the best jobs and steal our money,' he says. Because he knows that it is not politically correct or even legal to express such views, he tends to keep them to himself, and only express them openly when he is drunk. He is physically small, scruffily dressed and unemployed.

Alistair didn't have an easy start to life. He was born to a single mother, who had him adopted as a baby believing it would be the best thing for him. He grew up with Christian fundamentalist adoptive parents who controlled him ruthlessly. There was little love in the household but a lot of justified hatred.

Alistair has low self-esteem, thinking that he was so worthless that not even his mother wanted him. The atmosphere of repression and hatred that he grew up in reinforced his feelings of rejection and self-hatred. He copes with these terrible emotions only by projecting his hatred outwards onto those who are different from him. Alistair's views and his self-presentation are so unattractive that he has few friends and many people shun him. His isolation merely strengthens his hatred.

Although he repulses most people, one older woman, Jean, has been able to talk to him. She is so secure in herself that she can cope with his nastiness and not take it personally. She doesn't attempt to argue with him but neither does she agree with him. Instead she encourages the small part of him that actually wants to change and doesn't listen to his negativity too much. Under her guidance, Alistair has started to take more pride in his personal appearance and to think of getting a job.

Inner Work

Examine your self-hatred and apply reality checking to it. Are the grounds for your self-hatred realistic? Can you change your expectations in the light of this new knowledge?

Think of a person you hate. Are you projecting something about yourself that you haven't recognised yet onto them? Can you acknowledge this quality to yourself?

Look at the way you approach differences of opinion. Do you hate people who are different from yourself?

Can you define what triggers your hate?

Are you aware of your dependence?

Creative Task

1. Acknowledge that you hate someone or that they hate you, or both. Make a decision that you will deal with this *without causing any physical or emotional harm, either to them or yourself.*
2. Take yourself to a safe place. This should be somewhere you can't be disturbed and where, ideally, you can lock the door. Put the answerphone on or leave the telephone off the hook. Commit yourself to spending an hour there alone.
3. Light a candle. The point of this ritual act is that you want to shed light on the situation, and not live any longer in the darkness of hatred.

4. Allow the emotion to possess you but do not act on it. For example, if you feel you want to kill the person, notice that, but do not do it. Allow your fantasies of revenge to have full rein and to pass. Some people find they can express their feelings by pounding a cushion while others find a large sheet of paper and some poster paints a useful outlet. Use colour to describe the powerful feelings that are sweeping through you.
5. Take time to examine your hate. Why do you hate this person? What have they done? Are you projecting something you don't like about yourself onto them? You may find writing things down helpful at this point. Or you may just prefer to 'dialogue' internally.
6. Start to distinguish between the person you hate and their behaviour. Can you see that it is what they do rather than who they are that is causing the trouble? Do you see the need for you to separate from the other person in some way? If you feel you are hated, then look at some of your behaviour towards the person who hates you. Could you modify it in some way?
7. When you feel ready, imagine a large pair of shears. Isolate your hate in a bundle in your mind and cut it away from you with the shears. Acknowledge the truth of the situation – the person has caused you harm, disappointment and all the rest, but detach yourself from the feeling of hate. You no longer need it. It has protected you up to now and pointed you towards the truth you needed to recognise.
8. Thank the emotion of hate for bringing you awareness and ask it to leave now. Blow out the candle, open the windows, have a shower and change your clothes.
9. It's a good idea to keep this act private. Do not feel you need to tell the formerly hated person that you have done this – it may be seen as burdensome by them.
10. You will probably feel very relieved and at peace. You may find you have more energy. Do not be surprised if your hate comes back in a few days or weeks. Just quietly remind yourself of this exercise and repeat it if you feel it necessary.
11. In future, try to distinguish between the person and their

actions. Instead of saying 'I hate you', try to say 'I hate what you're doing but I don't hate you personally'.

THE TRANSFORMATION OF HATE

George Orwell's futuristic novel *Nineteen Eighty-four* describes a totalitarian culture which sets out to repress people's humanity. One feature of this nightmare regime is the compulsory time – the two-minute hate – during which everyone is expected to express open hatred towards the state's enemies. The rationale behind this is that hatred can be canalised to serve a political end. This is the extreme danger with hatred and only being intelligent about it can prevent the most hideous excesses which have been so apparent in the twentieth century. Simply expressing hate does nothing to resolve the painful issues underlying it. In all hate there is a component which shows us our own personal shadow. We should all be warned against collective manifestations of hate. It is an individual work. As people develop themselves they usually find that they are much bigger people than they have ever imagined. Their hate may stay the same size (and we will all hate from time to time) but it will be much smaller in relation to their overall personality.

When Alistair started to work on himself he had many things to face. His envy of those he regarded as more fortunate than himself, plus the hate-filled background he had been raised in, contributed towards the development of his hatred. Racism was merely an expression of his psychological pain not the cause of it. At the root of all of this was Alistair's belief that his mother had abandoned him because he was worthless. Encouraged by Jean, the middle-aged woman who had befriended him, he set out to find his mother. Instead of the hateful and indifferent person he had imagined she was, he found in fact a woman who had suffered much over giving him up. She had been told that it was in his best interest and so she had made the sacrifice. Although she was a simple woman she could express her love for him and her regret that his life had been blighted by her action, however well-meant. These two women, his mother and Jean, his friend, started to give Alistair a firm basis in life. The basis of his hate was challenged by the healing power of love. As time went by Alistair started to understand that what he hated in other people was his own self-hate projected outwards. When he realised he was lovable and that the two women cherished him in their different ways, his life started to change.

Vicky's journey was different. It was not love she needed to find but a sense of separation and selfhood. First she had to acknowledge the fact that part of her hated her husband. She had to realise that her hate was based on her dependence. This took a lot of doing because it was very threatening. But when she had done it she felt stronger. She learnt to stop blaming him for all his shortcomings and to recognise that if he did change, it would be because he wanted to not because she nagged him. She had to let go some of her crisp and coping exterior and acknowledge her own weakness. She started to confront the belief that she couldn't cope on her own and to look for examples of people who were managing to cope by themselves with reasonable success. Vicky also had to learn to separate from her parents, a psychological task she had never undertaken. She had looked for the outward form of separation but had looked for both her husbands to become parent substitutes. She needed to find a separate and adult way of expressing love which was less needy and dependent.

Hate and love are very close. The resolution of hate is in the acceptance of the constraints of adult love. Love when we are small is totally symbiotic, as we grow older this early paradise will come to an end. Mature love accepts the failures and shortcomings in the other person. Alistair began to heal when he could see that his assumptions about his mother were incorrect and that she did love him. Her actions were undertaken in the light of the best information she had had at the time. Vicky started to get better when she realised that, come hell or high water, she could love herself. She began to see that her hate offered her a way of separating herself from a situation of dependence. She says now, 'I think Confucius was right when he said that only a truly kind person knows how to love and hate. My hate has led to my leaving the infantile cocoon I called love and hate gave me the motive force to grow up.'

17

Hope

'In the factory we make cosmetics, in the store we sell hope.'
Charles Revson

WHAT IS HOPE?

Hope is a golden emotion to feel but one which calls for great wisdom. It can bring excitement and wonder to life and can be a tremendous motivator. It's central to emotional literacy because it shows us what we really want. At its best it is a life-enhancing energy which contains possibility, change, excitement and fulfilment. But at its worst it can swiftly metamorphose into disappointment and despair when what we hope for either doesn't come about or, if it does, doesn't fulfil us the way we expect it to. Being able to be disappointed and to be able to live with that feeling is part of being able to hope again. When we have repeated disappointments it can become easy to slip into despair, which is the refusal to hope for anything, or to turn to cynicism as a form of protection against the pain of hope.

You may be reading this now because you feel disappointed and fed up with the rollercoaster of emotions which go with hope. Or you may be feeling despairing or hopeless and want to learn how to hope for what you really want and need. Or you may be passionately hoping for something, hoping against hope, and want to know how to deal with the anxiety which you may be experiencing. What this chapter will tell you is how to understand the tension between hope and despair, how to develop an attitude of hope and, crucially, how to refine your hopes into the things you truly want.

WHY DO WE HOPE?

Hope in some form is essential to life. It is almost impossible not to hope for something. Even a person who is planning to commit suicide hopes for something because they hope that death will be better than life. And even if we're really enjoying something and want nothing more then we may catch ourselves hoping that this state of affairs will continue. So hope removes us from a true and total experience of the present.

Hope projects our lives into the future. It means we want something to happen and may put some energy into making it happen. Hope implies a *change* from the present situation but also a hidden criticism of it. We can hope for something to happen e.g. that we'll have the longed-for child, or that the sun will shine the day we've organised a barbecue, or that we will be short-listed for the fantastic job we've applied for. We can also hope for something not to happen e.g. that a friend's test for cancer won't be positive or that a lover won't leave or that the plane we're on won't crash. Whether our hopes are positive or negative, they nevertheless contain wishes and expectations for future change.

When we hope we are really saying to ourselves the following things:

- Something in my present life is either not satisfying me or the threat of something happening in the future is causing me anxiety
- I think that if a particular thing were to happen (or not happen), it would make me happy
- If that something doesn't happen (or does), I will be let down, disappointed, despairing, unhappy or fearful

It takes courage to feel hope because we are saying what we want to happen and we are opening ourselves to two quite difficult possibilities. It may not happen and we have to live with that situation or it may happen and we find that it is not the thing we really want.

HOPE AND DESPAIR

In the 1890s a Victorian artist, G. F. Watts, painted a picture called *Hope* that was for some years one of the most famous paintings in the world. Even Picasso had a reproduction of it in his studio. It is in subtle shades of blue and mist grey and shows a young girl blindfolded, with her head bowed. She is sitting on a half-visible globe, a representation of the earth, around the equator of which are clouds which also hint visually at the foam of a rising sea. Her eyes are bandaged perhaps to show that although her plight is hopeless, she refuses to see this and relies instead on her inner vision. She has in her hand a lyre which has only one unbroken string left on it. When Watts was asked why the painting was not called despair he explained that, 'Despair gives up but Hope, however great the odds against her, never gives up. She is trying to get all the music possible even with only one string left.'

We have looked at positive and negative forms of hope. There is a third form of hope, which is not tied to a specific outcome but is an attitude. This hope is an orientation of the heart towards the future even when our reason might be telling us it's literally hopeless. Watts's picture shows a situation where the chips are really down, things are as difficult as they can be, the way ahead is invisible and yet, even with slender resources, there is the courage to go on.

Despair is a rational emotion which comes when we have had our specific hopes dashed and our analysis of the situation indicates that we are highly unlikely to be able to achieve the particular goal we want. Attitudinal hope, on the other hand, is irrational, because it persists in believing that there is the possibility of something better in the face of all the evidence. What attitudinal hope does is let go the particular hoped-for outcome and embrace an enduring perspective of patience. T. S. Eliot wrote of this ability to wait without a specific hope 'for hope would be hope of the wrong thing' and yet, he said, 'faith and love and hope are all in the waiting.'

EMOTIONS ASSOCIATED WITH HOPE

Although despair and disappointment are the emotions most often associated with hope, other feelings connected with it include:

- wishing – our hopes are those things we wish for
- expecting – when hope becomes concrete and counted upon
- longing – more nebulous and less focused than a wish
- dreading – a version of blurred fear without the focus of a specific outcome
- fearing – if the hoped-for thing doesn't materialise, we can be fearful of the alternative
- anxiety – if we are hoping for something very much we may feel anxious, especially if we fear what will happen to us if the hope is not realised

Please take a moment and list the five things you hope for the most. Give each a 1 out of 10 rating and put a timescale on when you would like each hope to be fulfilled. In a separate column make a list of what you fear will happen if these hopes are not realised. Put a 1 out of 10 rating on your fear as well. Do this before you read on.

Hope against hope – Anna's story

Anna is an attractive single woman in her early thirties who has been involved with Ian for a couple of years. He represents everything Anna wants in a potential mate: he's fun, tender, amusing, interesting, successful, attractive. He already has a family but he has told Anna he loves her and wants to be with her. He doesn't say when he will be able to be free but hints at vague future possibilities. In between their times together she lives on hope.

Unlike some single people who are involved in a relationship with an otherwise committed partner, Anna actually wants to be married herself. She looks forward to the day-to-day life that she and Ian will lead. 'Once we're properly together then we can be really happy,' she says. She hopes for that future and she hopes (and expects) that Ian will decide to leave his family and make a new life with her. She fantasises about that new life and has in effect constructed a private cinema in her head where she runs imaginary films about the future.

Her energy is focused on the achievement of only one outcome. Gradually during the time that she and Ian have been seeing each other, the other parts of her life have withered away. She is no longer really interested in her career, her own creativity, her friends – everything has become sacrificed to this one hope. Her close friends are becoming bored with the tête-à-tête dinners in which she pours out some significant detail of the relationship. He said this, he said that – is it more hopeful? Does it mean this or that?

If a friend starts to speak about the reality of this present – that Ian is still living with his wife and has made no definite plans to change this – then Anna reacts by being angry with the friend. The friend then has two choices: to withdraw from the friendship, or to go along with Anna's fantasies in an increasingly half-hearted way. Most friends choose a sort of combination of the two which leads to a weakening of the friendship bond because it is no longer based on honesty.

Whenever Anna starts to move away from hope, she falls into a pit of despair. In order to 'rescue' herself from this painful feeling, she creates more hopeful scenarios in her head. When the films are running, she feels hopeful. She starts to notice that it takes more and more fantasy to keep the despair at bay. She may get her hope fulfilled ultimately – but how long can she wait as the years slip by? She admits she does feel fed up sometimes but is frightened of living without hope.

An attitude of hope – Karen's story

Karen is fifty-four and divorced. Seventeen years ago she was involved in a car crash in which she was paralysed from the waist down. Her husband, who'd received only minor injuries, left her soon after it was discovered that Karen's paralysis was permanent. He quickly remarried and moved to another city. Karen was left alone on the verge of middle age with a condition that required day-to-day physical support and massive courage to face.

Karen spent the next few years after the accident alternating between hope and despair. Her despair, loss and grief were very profound but at times she still hoped for a cure for her condition. But after trying various treatments and therapies, it was realised that her paralysis was permanent. Short of a miracle she would never walk or do any of the things that able-bodied people take for granted. Like Anna, Karen also fantasised about the future – a future in which this miracle cure was invented.

After a while she decided that she couldn't wait for this hoped-for thing to happen. Either it would – and she would take advantage of it when it did – or it wouldn't – in which case it wasn't really worth thinking about. Despite the difficulties and losses of her present life, she decided that life was too precious to simply wish away. She realised that she had survived the accident for a reason and that her life could still be valuable to herself and other people.

With this insight, Karen learned to live in the present moment and not to put too much energy into wishing things in the future. She still hopes for a cure (which may yet come as medical science advances) but she no longer expects it. She practises hoping for small things such as a sunny day, a visit from a friend, a good and absorbing book. These are achievable and realistic things which will bring her emotional satisfaction. She says, 'Expectation and despair are like two sides of a coin, they're both futile attempts to control life. And it won't be controlled . . . you have to let it live through you.'

REACTION TO DISAPPOINTMENT

Both Anna and Karen have had to cope with disappointed hopes: Anna's to be married to Ian and Karen's to walk again. They have dealt with them in very different ways. Anna has constructed a hopeful fantasy which protects her against real despair. Karen has been able to face her despair and the reality of her situation, given up her expectations and moved forward into the attitude of hope.

There are several reasons for this. Everybody is different and lives their life uniquely as part of their own development. If you have a friend who sounds a bit similar to Anna (and it might not be a love relationship that they are involved in, it might be a work situation or some other ongoing story) don't be impatient with them. They can't help it – yet. One day they will. In the second place Karen's situation is much more clear-cut – there is physical and tangible evidence of her situation whereas Anna's is much more nebulous. And in the third place, Anna's hope is being constantly reinforced by contact with Ian. If he were honest and said, 'I have no intention of leaving my family but I really value the times we spend together and I want the relationship to continue as long as possible on these terms', then Anna would be devastated. When she got over this then she would no longer hope that Ian would be with her.

Another reaction to disappointment is not allowing ourselves to hope for the thing we truly want. Often what holds us back is fear. 'If I hope for a thing I really want and I don't get it then it'll be terrible,' we say to ourselves. So to protect ourselves against this catastrophic disappointment we hope for something that is half right but not the thing we really want.

Yet another reaction is cynicism. This is when a person denies that there is such a thing as hope or else dismisses it as completely naive. 'It's all random, anyway, so there's no point in hoping,' they might say. What is really being said is: 'If I can't completely control everything, and if I can't have what I want, then it's all worthless.'

HOPE AND FANTASY

Hope is an emotion which is bound up with imagination. We imagine a situation which somehow solves the problems that we are experiencing in the present. Perhaps you are not getting on very well with your boss at work. He is being very critical of your efforts and this is making you nervous and accident-prone. If you find this situation stressful, you may start to run a fantasy. It might go like this.

The boss is replaced, sacked or made redundant. You are asked to take over his role. You do it superbly and gain the praise of everyone around. You feel competent and confident as well as popular. Insidiously you start to hope that this situation will come about in reality. When you have a bad day with the boss, you may find yourself entering the hopeful fantasy and embellishing it. The problem is because what you hope for is out of your power to control it, it disables you from taking positive action. You build an imaginary future around a set of circumstances over which you have no control.

Sometimes it can be good to give ourselves some time to fantasise. Reality can be pretty tough and as long as the fantasy has limits, it may not be a bad thing from time to time. In Anna's case the fantasy stops her from seeing the situation as it really is and she is not able to put limits on it. Until she does see the situation and face the despair, fantasising will be a disabling activity for her.

FINDING OUR TRUE HOPES

The roots of hope lie in our deciding at some level that a particular thing, event or person is necessary to make us feel the way we want. Hope always comes out of a dissatisfaction with some aspect of the present and a belief that the future can be better. It's really important to discover *why* we want a particular thing. It often seems obvious to us but underneath the hope is a wish not just for the thing but for the way that having the thing will make us feel.

In other words, we may hope for a tangible thing but what we really want is the feeling it will bring. Here is a way of finding out what that is. Ask a friend to ask you two questions: What do you hope for? What would that bring you? Repeat the second question as many times as necessary. It might go something like this:

What do you hope for?
I'm hoping to make a lot of money out of an idea I have for a business venture.
What would that bring you?
I'd be rich and I'd have the freedom to go wherever I liked.

What would that bring you?
The freedom? Well I wouldn't have to feel subservient to my boss at work.
What would that bring you?
I'd be more powerful, more in charge of my own destiny. I could express what I feel about the way he treats me. And I could help other people, too. I wouldn't use the money just for myself.
What would that bring you?
I suppose a sense that I was a good person.
What would having that bring you?
I'd like to feel that because it would make sense of my life – I'd feel I was here for a purpose. And I'd feel I could choose what I did and when and how. And that would be nice. I think that's really why I want the money.

It's interesting to see how quickly the hope mutates into two feelings: the desire for freedom and the need for personal meaning. There's a further question to ask – are there any other ways in which you could start to feel freer and that your life is meaningful. In your current situation what could you do to make this come about?

It might be that to take half an hour a day to meditate or read or just think would increase your feeling of personal freedom. You might not have the economic power to fly to the other side of the world at will but you could still make a personal space in your life. You may be able to take all sorts of imaginative journeys in that daily half-hour. You have to recognise that this may be smaller and humbler than the grandeur of your hope. But it could still be very valid and bring considerable emotional satisfaction.

Sometimes we're lucky and we get the specific hope we long for. But sometimes we're disappointed. And then we have to look creatively at other ways we could fulfil our longings.

Inner Work

Go back to the list you made earlier of your five top hopes. (The reason for making the list earlier is that the act of making it can cause a change in our thinking. As we allow the passage of time and think about something else our unconscious mind starts working on it. You may find that something has shifted and it's worth noticing that change.)

Now review your hopes and see whether they are in the right order. Now take the top two and start the process described above of asking yourself the two questions: *What do you hope for? What would that bring you? (Repeated as many times as necessary.)* You can do this with a friend or by yourself.

When you have found the feelings that underlie the hope, think about them carefully. Are there other ways you could achieve these feelings? Start to brainstorm alternatives. Make a huge list of everything you can think of. A lot of them will be wild and wildly impractical but don't censor the list. Just write it down. The best thing now is to put the list in a safe place and if possible sleep on it. The next morning, see what emerges from the list as being things you could and would like to do. See if you can bring some of them into your present life.

Now look at the column you wrote earlier about what you feared would happen if your hope was disappointed. Are there any changes? Do the fears seem smaller?

If you start to bring some of these alternatives into your everyday life you may find that you are less fearful of what will happen if your specific hope is not realised. And keep on hoping!

Creative Task

In many parts of the world people tie their hopes, wishes and prayers onto a Wish-granting Tree. The pieces of paper and cloth flutter beautifully in the breeze, a testimony to hope that makes the world more beautiful. There are many ways to make your own tree. You could go for a walk and find a beautiful branch or interestingly shaped stick. Or a piece of driftwood. Perhaps you could draw or paint your tree? Or cut it out of paper? Or maybe stencil it onto your wall? Now write down your hopes on pieces of paper and attach them to the tree.

The point of this exercise is a symbolic act. By putting your hopes to the tree you are letting go of them. After a couple of months, have a look at your hopes and see how they are being fulfilled.

TRANSFORMING HOPE

Hope shows us what we really want to feel. If we understand this and remember to think each time we hope what it is we want, we will find our lives transformed.

Karen says now she realised that what really drove her hope to walk again (which she still and always will have) was the fear of being alone. She thought if she could walk she would always be able to meet new people and make friends. Fortunately she has excellent physical support and is able to get around very successfully. Even more important though, her attitude makes her very attractive to many people and they are drawn to her. Because she rejoices in small things and has developed the attitude of hope, people want to be around her. She brings inspiration to many.

Anna's story is still ongoing. There are many possible reasons why she is involved with a man who is ambivalent and who says one thing but does another. It may indicate that she is afraid of commitment herself because she doesn't put herself to the test. Or it may be that she is playing out deep family patterns. Maybe her own father was away a lot when she was growing up and she missed him but daydreamed that one day he would return. Sometimes our lovers do repeat patterns we have inherited but this is not always the case. Like Karen, she is afraid of being alone, but if you probed deeper you might find that she is afraid of being with someone, too. You can't hurry this realisation. If you are in Anna's shoes, wait patiently for something to change. One day you will wake up and a door will open which makes change possible. You can't make that door open but if you wait for it, you won't miss it.

18

Loneliness

'We need types of leisure which allow for contemplation and meditation. To this end people need the courage to be lonely.'

Viktor Frankl

WHAT IS LONELINESS?

The first thing to grasp about loneliness is that it is a common, perhaps universal, human feeling. The awful trick of this emotion is that if you're lonely, you just can't believe that other people are feeling lonely, too. You think that you're the only person in the world who is feeling this. It's so important to grasp this one truth – *you are not alone in your loneliness*. Many others are feeling it or have felt it, too.

Loneliness can strike us at any time in our lives. It can be triggered by a range of things from simple physical exhaustion to major loss. It can vary from a feeling of sadness at a loved one's absence, a feeling of being excluded from an important social event, to a heart-breaking, all-encompassing feeling of desolation and loss. It can be experienced by anyone: married or single, rich or poor, young or old. Marriage is not a cure for it but an understanding of the roots and triggers of loneliness can help many marriages.

You may be reading this section because you have identified that you are feeling lonely. The first thing to say is that you are to be warmly congratulated for your courage and insight in recognising this. Many people never get to this stage and deny their loneliness in a number of ways. In some sense, our consumer culture is built on a collective denial of the value and reality of this emotion. Buying things can temporarily assuage the feelings of emptiness and rejection that the experience of loneliness brings.

As one person put it, 'To say that you're lonely feels like admitting to a twentieth-century version of leprosy.' This is the pity of it – many people deny it but most people have felt it to some degree at some time in their lives. If we acknowledge our own and other people's loneliness, some of the power goes out of the emotion. We realise we are no longer alone.

In fact, when one woman feels lonely now, she uses it as a prompt to ask herself who in her circle of friends may be feeling lonely, too. She then intuitively selects a name – and usually when she contacts that person, her call is very welcome. In this way, she breaks the isolation of loneliness and makes new connections. Making connections is crucial to being able to move through the emotion of loneliness to the next state.

WHAT DOES LONELINESS FEEL LIKE?

People experience it different ways but it may include the following:

- feeling that you are utterly alone
- feeling that you have been abandoned
- sensation of inner emptiness
- believing that you are cut off from other people (who are having a good time)
- not wanting to communicate with others
- being convinced that others are shunning you

Associated emotions may well be:

- despair
- grief
- fear

- meaninglessness
- envy
- shame

Loneliness in its extreme form is about as painful as any emotion can get. It can be accompanied by feelings of blackest depression, and sometimes thoughts of suicide. Usually suicidal thoughts are a way of expressing our need for a profound change of state. If, however, you have persistent thoughts of suicide, or are making any plans, please turn to the section on suicide in the chapter on Depression (page 120).

You may like to take a moment and evaluate your loneliness at this moment on a scale of 1 – 10. It might be a mild feeling of loneliness and 10 would be your personal worst. Make a note of it and then re-evaluate yourself when you have finished reading the rest of this chapter, and have done the exercises.

How to find a way through his losses – John's story

John, who is in his mid-fifties, has recently been made redundant from the job that he'd had for thirty years. He is married and last year he lost his elder brother whom he was very close to. Work had provided him with companionship and a sense of purpose. The loss of it has triggered the buried emotional pain attached to his brother's death.

He says: 'I feel so lonely and I am without hope of ever feeling whole again. I am too old to find another job, and anyway, even if I did it wouldn't make up for the long-term friendship and comradeship that the old one had. I've tried meeting my former colleagues for a drink but that doesn't work. They don't want to know me.'

John and his wife Denise have been married for thirty years. Now that their children have grown up and left home they find they have nothing to say to each other. Despite Denise's physical presence, John feels totally alone.

John doesn't realise that his loneliness has other emotions attached to it. He is envious of other people who he thinks have fulfilling lives. He is ashamed of his loneliness and shuns people. He rationalises this by saying that they don't want to know him. The reverse is true, he doesn't want to know them, because they are reminders of a world that he has lost.

A life crammed full – Julia's story

Julia is thirty-two and works in a job connected with PR. She is blonde, bright and breezy. She presents herself attractively and, as a result, her credit cards are usually charged up to their limits. Her diary is crammed full of events and she says she never has a minute. Her work requires her to entertain clients frequently and she has a large crowd of acquaintances whom she calls 'the gang'. She never spends an evening or a weekend alone. She has had several affairs with married men.

When Julia is asked if she's lonely she says briskly, 'I just haven't the time to be lonely.' That's the truth. By giving herself no time to feel the emotion, she almost avoids feeling it. But the reality is that she is lonely and only in the depths of a night alone will she admit it. She fills her time with ceaseless activity so that she doesn't have to acknowledge the truth to herself.

Ten years ago she fell in love with Terry and, after a time of going out, he dropped her. Julia had lost her mother as a little girl. Her subsequent step-mother was a cold and hostile woman. As a result Julia had little belief in her capacity to be loved. When she met Terry, she gave her all to make the relationship work and was devastated when it ended. She decided that she could never again allow herself to be vulnerable. Now she has lego-like relationships: if a piece drops out, it can easily be replaced.

Beneath her attractive and competent exterior, Julia is suffering. Her pride will not allow her to admit it. When a crisis forces her to give up her busy life, she has to start acknowledging her loneliness. This, although very painful, is the first step in beginning to move through it.

These two accounts of loneliness are worlds apart but both John and Julia have something in common. They have both suffered major loss and have reacted to it by closing down their capacity for intimate connections so that they wouldn't be hurt again. Without a capacity for making connections we are lonely. Connections don't have to be with people. They can be with animals, hobbies or even the earth itself. They can be with yourself and the purpose of your life, with the work you do or the service you give your local community.

WHY DO WE FEEL LONELY?

Loneliness has both triggers and root causes. The triggers are the present-day events which make us feel lonely. They have their power because they touch on earlier experiences which have made us sensitive to feeling lonely in a particular way.

It's a bit like having an allergy – if you come into contact with pollen you will get hay fever although otherwise you may feel fine. Triggers are the pollen, the root causes are the fact that we are allergic to something. Julia's trigger for realising her loneliness was being forced to give up the frantic life that she'd led. John's was his redundancy.

It's important to understand triggers because each person is individual and unique in what triggers loneliness for them. Don't expect a friend to necessarily understand *why* you feel lonely – their triggers may be completely different.

THE ROOTS OF LONELINESS

The roots of loneliness lie in our deep psychological patterns and early life experiences. In the story of the fall in the Bible, Adam and Eve are cast out of the Garden of Eden. Before that they were in paradise – totally connected to each other and to the divine figure who had created them. Afterwards, they had to make their own way and suffer the loneliness of exclusion and exile. This myth (and there are many others like it in the folklore of the world) has been interpreted as a symbolic way of describing the pain a new-born baby feels when it grasps that it is no longer attached to its mother. In the womb, the baby's every need was attended to and it was never alone. Now it may have to wait to be cuddled, fed and changed. Even a short wait may feel like an abandonment. The baby realises that it is no longer part of another human being but is alone. This is the beginning of our existential loneliness and it is the price we pay for being separate and unique individuals.

In a sense, we need myths to understand this time as it happens before we can consciously remember anything. Although we can't remember these events, we are unknowingly shaped by them.

THE DEVELOPMENT OF THE INNER NURTURING PARENT

As time goes by, the baby develops the capacity to imagine the presence of its nurturing parent – which may be its actual mother or a care-giver. When this nurturing parent is not physically present and the baby is alone, it starts to believe that he or she will return. As we develop and grow up this image becomes our inner nurturing parent. This figure becomes the part of us which can take care of us and is one of the major bulwarks against loneliness. Sometimes you may find that you are thinking to yourself something like: 'It isn't that bad really', or 'I'll just have a comforting cup of tea and a hot bath and an early night.' This is the voice of the inner nurturing parent – it comforts us and provides warmth and companionship.

However, because the parenting that most of us received wasn't perfect, the image of the nurturing parent isn't perfect, either. Sometimes we believe he or she will return and sometimes we don't. Sometimes our experience of aloneness is bearable and sometimes it isn't. If we do some work on strengthening this inner nurturing parent, this usually increases our capacity to be alone and happy with ourselves.

Julia had lost her mother early and had not had the chance to develop a warm relationship with another adult. This left her very vulnerable. When she fell in love with Terry she looked to him to provide a mother's, rather than a lover's, type of caring. When he wasn't able to provide this and he left, she felt literally broken-hearted. She didn't realise (because nobody helped her through this time) that much of the pain was magnified by the anguish of the earlier loss. When this pattern was explained to her, she felt relieved and was able to start grieving for her mother properly. She could then understand that no lover could ever be a substitute for her mother, but that they could be important and valuable in their own right.

Although John's mother had survived into his adulthood, she had not been a strong influence on her children's life. John's parents had been refugees and although they had tried to provide good parenting, they were suffering from their own experiences of having to leave their native land. When his brother died, John felt that he had lost the last link with his original family. He was then deprived of his substitute family, which was his colleagues at work. During the course of his inner work, he came to understand that his redundancy had only been the trigger for his loneliness.

THE TRIGGERS OF LONELINESS

The emotion of loneliness is a cyclical experience which starts with a trigger. This can be almost anything. It may be the ending of a relationship or a job or the loss of a friendship or important possession. Triggers don't have to be major events. Sometimes we feel lonely after an intense effort which has drained us of all our energy. Sometimes a bout of illness or spell in bed can trigger the emotion.

The trigger is about loss: of a loved one, a job, the routine and supports of daily life. This loss makes us feel rejected, which, in its turn, can lead to our rejection of others around us. Then we get into the existential state of loss, which reactivates our root loneliness and loss of the perfect love. We withdraw and lose connection with the rest of the world, believing that we are alone and isolated, and we make our worst fears come true.

It's vital to break the cycle at this stage. The way to do it is to make a new connection with something else. It doesn't have to be a person. It could be a pet, or an activity such as a hobby. If we don't break the cycle, it goes on because fresh triggers are always coming our way.

Sometimes we attempt to 'buy' our way out of the feeling instead of genuinely working through it. We can do this literally by going on a spending spree. Or we can do this with drink or drugs or overeating or indulging in any activity which will change our mood for us. This strategy won't work because once the effect of the wine has worn off or once you've got the clothes home, the feeling of loneliness will return. Other disguises of loneliness include aggressive behaviour, overwork, in fact anything which numbs and deadens.

THE CYCLE OF LONELINESS

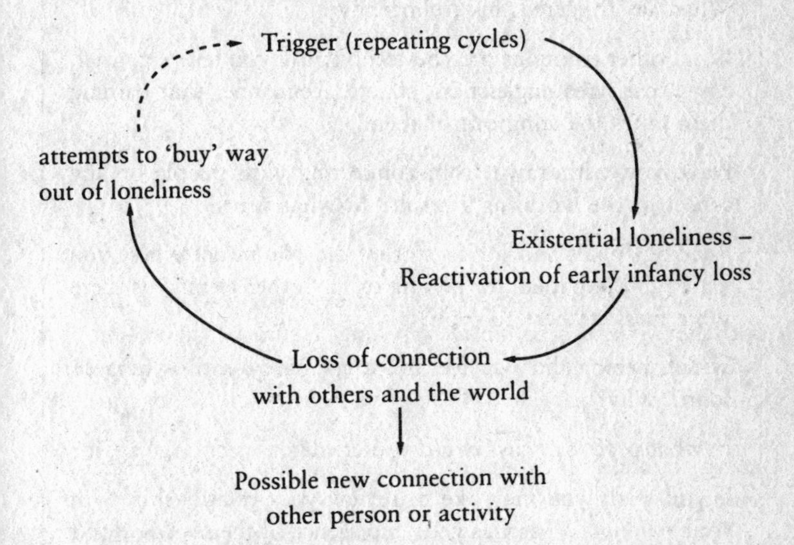

In many ways it's easier to work with the triggers of loneliness than the roots. None of us have had perfect parents – but for some the experiences have been more painful than others. If you find that much pain is coming up for you as you think of these things you may wish to find someone else to work with. This could be a therapist or a co-counsellor or a sympathetic friend. These feelings can be very hard to face – but the important thing to grasp is that, whatever your actual experience was, you can still create a wonderful inner nurturing parent. It's an exercise in imagination and courage, not in finding someone to blame.

You may find you wish just to deal with the triggers in a practical way e.g. like making sure that you have a good night's rest, a party to go to, a friend to visit or whatever would be good for you. That's a good approach, because by caring for yourself, you are in fact being your own nurturing parent.

Inner Work

What are you feeling at this moment? Take some time to describe your feelings. Remember that your journal is private and that it's your companion.

What has triggered this feeling now?

What other emotions are you feeling/have you felt? e.g. grief, envy, fear, meaninglessness, shame. Remember that naming them takes the sting out of them.

Have you withdrawn from connecting with people or any aspect of the world as a result? In what ways?

Reading Julia's and John's stories, did you notice where you felt angry, impatient, or pitying or any other feeling? Is there some message here for you?

Which person did you feel more sympathy with – Julia or John? Why?

In what practical ways could you create connection(s) again?

If you wish, you may like to review your relationship with your parents. What was your experience of them? You don't have to do this exercise, it may just be enough to recognise that your parents were human and not perfect.

CREATING CONNECTION, INTIMACY AND SOLITUDE

When you have done these exercises, give yourself a good treat. A good parent will give a child something nice when she or he has finished a task. As your own nurturing parent, you can put this into practice straight away. During the next few days, practise being a wonderful parent to yourself. If you enjoy the feeling of warmth and security, you have my permission to do this for the rest of your life!

The strange thing is that as you connect with the inner nurturing parent and develop more intimate connections with friends, partners or lovers, you find that your loneliness turns into a joyful sense of solitude. Because you feel the sense of inner support, you no longer feel lonely – even when you're physically alone.

When Julia acknowledged her loneliness, she felt a huge sense of relief. She was lying in a hospital bed and for the first time in years had nothing to do. She was fortunate that someone suggested that she start to work on this and, feeling very lonely, she agreed to do so. This person was able to offer her support and companionship during this time. Through Julia's inner work she came to terms with the pain of losing her mother. She started to see the connection between that and her subsequent relationship with Terry and realise why that relationship wouldn't work.

She found she was able to be alone for the first time in her life and could use the time to get to know herself better. Julia noticed that she had been intimate with nobody. One of the first tasks was to create some space where she could share with trusted friends some of the things that were really important to her. She also realised that the men she had been seeing, although perfectly nice in themselves, were not in a position to give her the sort of relationship she now wanted and felt she could have. She felt she could wait for a man who was also looking for a committed relationship.

Apart from developing a nurturing parent, the inner figure that was most useful to Julia was the inner child. She found herself thinking about herself as a child and realised that before the loss of her mother she had been a hopeful little girl. She found photographs of herself at around that age and made a collage of them with her own drawings. She said: 'I have pasted this up on the wall of my bedroom as a reminder of my good feelings at this time. Funnily enough I've started to notice little girls in the street and to smile at them and usually they smile back to me.' She decided that one day, when the time was right, she would like to have a daughter of her own.

When John started his inner work, he made several interesting discoveries. He realised that his elder brother had been able to give him more love than his actual parents had. Because his brother had become, in some senses, a substitute parent, his death hit John harder than one would expect.

He also realised that his marriage had only been concerned with mortgages, children and practicalities. Though these things were essential, he realised that he didn't know very much about the woman he had lived with for so many years. He and Denise had lived a conventional life, never really looking at what was below the surface. He did his inner work and suggested to her that they did some together. She enjoyed it very much and they started to talk to each other about the things that really mattered to them.

Recognising that all his emotional needs couldn't be met by one person, John started to go out and meet people and found, to his surprise, that they enjoyed his company. He started to fill his days more and volunteered with a local charity. His professional knowledge was of great use to the charity and, apart from the new friends he made, he enjoyed making a contribution to the wider world. All these things helped him to feel a sense of connection.

Creative Task

Write a letter to your inner nurturing parent. Explain how you have felt abandoned and ask for their help. It may be a mother or a father figure – or even a non-gender specific one – whatever feels most natural for you. You may need to write several letters. Put them in a drawer and look at them in six months' time. You may be surprised at the changes that have taken place within you.

TRANSFORMING LONELINESS

The experience of loneliness offers us the chance for personal development and growth. If we move through the emotion, we may find that we are enriched and transformed by it. We can move from a state of where we are living on the surface of life to one where we can connect deeply to people and events around us. The gifts of this work on the personal level are the opportunity for genuine intimacy and a delight in solitude.

Both John and Julia are bigger and more open-hearted people than they were before. As John said: 'It was as if I lived on a small island, not realising there was a world within me.' Being able to acknowledge our loneliness can open us up to vaster and more profound destinies than we had imagined. Instead of looking back to our lost paradise, we start to make connections with the world and to act creatively in and with it. When loneliness returns, as it will from time to time, however painful the feeling is, it is an invitation to new experiences and greater horizons.

19

Love

'Lovers and madmen have such seething brains, such shaping fantasies, that apprehend more than cool reason ever comprehends.'

William Shakespeare

WHAT IS LOVE?

The question of what is love has exercised the imagination of the greatest poets and philosophers for the last two and a half thousand years. So this small chapter cannot attempt any definitive answers to one of the greatest mysteries of human life. Love is fundamentally unknowable. It's like a craggy mountain shrouded in swirling mists which occasionally part to permit a glimpse of the fantastic rock shapes and trees hanging precipitously over chasms. Then the mists close in and the mountain can only be sensed in terms of its massive form. We stand at the base of it and it has the potential to link us to heaven but if love is misunderstood or becomes perverted, out of shape in some way, it thrusts us back into hell.

Love is the motivating force which runs under most of our emotional states. In all of them there is an underground longing for absolute love. Loneliness is an obvious expression of the need for love, as is rejection the expression of blighted love. Fear dreads the loss of love, hate is the other side of the coin, and both depression and boredom long for the passion of love. Grief mourns the loss of love, aggression tries fruitlessly to chase it, and anger is in a rage because it appears that it's nowhere to be found. Pride wants love but is too proud to allow it to break down defensive walls, hope longs for it and anxiety is in a state because love seems ambivalent or absent. So love is literally at the heart of the matter.

There are many different types of love but they all have in common one thing. That is when love is truly engaged, the two (or more) people experiencing it enter into a relationship which is reciprocal. The essence of love is to cease to see the other person as a solution to your own problem, as a bit player in the drama of your own life. It is to respect and value the loved one as a unique individual and to create a space between you that is a relationship. Love consists of allowing this space to take whatever form it does and whatever risk is necessary. This looks like madness to our rational minds so we often try to limit love's power and control for our conscious ends. If we relate to someone with less than our whole being, then we start to bargain for some return, and we become greedy and needy. As we shall see this leads to no end of trouble and the pain of the more negative emotional states. Of course, love in its purest state is rarely experienced but that is no reason not to turn to its potential greatness whenever we can. Love is the essence of transformation because it moves us from the narrow confines of our ego into the broader more generous realms of relationship. To learn to love well is truly as demanding an achievement as mastering a musical instrument to concert-level performance. Very few will be internationally famous. But even if we are only amateurs in love, we may still be able to make a pleasing sound.

This chapter focuses on the emotion of romantic love and you may be reading it because you have just fallen in love and are feeling bewildered and exhilarated. Or you may have lost a love and wonder what went wrong and if you ever dare to try again. This chapter will give you some ideas on how romantic love links with the other forms of love and how to view it with emotional intelligence.

THE DIFFERENT TYPES OF LOVE

Different relationships engender different types of love but at heart they are all connected. Our capacity for romantic love builds on our experience of parental love, our understanding of fraternal love and our commitment to self-love. These are not fixed things within us, they tend to vary like tidal forces. Our ability to love fluctuates between opposite polarities: positive and negative. For example, if things are going well, we may feel very positive about loving ourselves, but if we have a week of disasters, we may feel very negative. A lot of affirmations are based on reinforcing the positive message. If we want emotional literacy, however, it's important not to disregard the feedback from the more negative days. If you can start to know why you're feeling more negative then you can adjust and wait for better days.

Parental love

The first love we experience is that of our parents towards us. As helpless infants, we are given (if we are fortunate) an experience of unconditional love. Our bodily needs are taken care of and we are loved not for any action on our part but simply because we exist. But our needs go beyond the mere physical, we ideally need to have instilled within us a sense that it is good to be alive and a love of life itself.

As Erich Fromm has commented, we need not only milk, which is food and affirmation, but also honey, which represents a taste of the sweetness and bounty of human existence. However, only parents who really believe this in their innermost selves are capable of giving this to their children. Most of us struggle with a bit of the vinegar of our parents' despair as well.

The two polarities which we move between are:

Positive pole: 'Life supports me and everything is fundamentally loving.'

Negative pole: 'Life is a dangerous business and love is very hard to come by.'

Fraternal love

Parental love is based on inequality but fraternal love is essentially love between equals. It is similarly unconditional and depends on finding the other, whether they be a pauper or a prince, to be a brother or sister under the skin, a fellow traveller on the human journey. The essence of fraternal love is the acknowledgement of difference. We don't love someone because they are the same as us but because they exist and we have met them. In its pure form fraternal love is very warm and is characterised by spontaneous affection and generosity of spirit.

The roots of fraternal love lie in the difficulties of sibling rivalry. Almost nobody is pleased with their birth order. Older children frequently envy younger children their carefree freedom and the fact that they are often favoured and 'mother's pets'. Younger children envy their older siblings their privileges and their frequently favoured status. Nobody who has had brothers and sisters has had an experience of equality because families are not equal. But with any luck, enough affection can exist between siblings to make a mature experience of fraternal love possible.

The two polarities which we move between are:

Positive pole: 'This is my brother/sister and I love him/her and find all human beings brothers/sisters.'

Negative pole: 'Brothers/sisters must be guarded against because they take all your goodness away from you.'

Romantic love

Romantic love is different from the other two forms of love discussed because it is focused exclusively on one person. It aims for fusion with another and is the obvious antidote to loneliness. This fusion recalls the paradisal time when we were totally unified with our mother in her womb. Falling in love is frequently accompanied by the urge to merge, which is demonstrated physically by the act of sexual intercourse, but which expresses a far deeper emotional longing for union. Often sex is seen as the exclusive bridge to this union which means that it bears a far heavier load in terms of the relationship than it was designed to do.

When we fall in love, we project *a part of ourselves that we haven't yet recognised* onto the other person. Falling in love is a means, therefore, of seeing ourselves more fully. Mature love requires that ultimately we withdraw the projections from the other person and take them back into ourselves. Then we can love the other person as they really are. When people have repeated patterns of falling in love and then out of it again, it usually means that they cannot love beyond themselves, or, in other words that they cannot really love at all.

The two polarities which we move between are:

Positive pole: 'I love this person despite their many failings (and mine) because I see a part of the spark of humanity reflected in them.'

Negative pole: 'I love this person because they meet my needs.'

Self-love

If we love ourselves enough, we won't be selfish. This paradox goes against most of the wisdom with which we are brought up. We are told to put others first but the real truth is that we can only meet other people's needs if we have taken sufficient care of our own. Love of oneself is not self-indulgence; it does not involve an endless succession of treats and gratifications. It is rather a loving attitude to our self-development that is called for. If we love ourselves we will forgive ourselves, mentor ourselves and push ourselves on when we need to. As a teacher will set harder and harder tasks to stretch a pupil, so we must lovingly do that for ourselves. Only people who truly love themselves reach their full potential. Love of self underscores the successful negotiation of romantic love, and the ability to give both parental and fraternal love.

The two polarities which we move between are:

Positive pole: 'I love and care for myself in order that I may more effectively love and care for others.'

Negative pole: 'I am not really lovable until somebody else loves me.'

HOW DOES IT FEEL?

The feelings of romantic love are usually expressed strongly in the body. People who are in love often sleep lightly and frequently forget to eat. They can seem distracted, almost taken over. There is a desperate and yet wonderful quality to these feelings. Hormones are strenuously pumping around the body and there can be a sense of extreme elation. Some cultures recognise that lovers are unable to concentrate on the simplest of tasks and so do not require them to work at anything sensible until the madness passes. As one man put it, 'This is a crazy state, it's madly inconvenient and I haven't got time for it. And yet, I wouldn't be without it because this experience makes life worth living.'

Associated emotions include:

- fear: 'I hope he or she hasn't realised how much I care for them' or 'I am so afraid of losing her now she's come to mean so much to me.'
- hope: 'I hope this relationship will come to something . . . I hope the other person loves me back or it will be pretty bleak.'
- anxiety: 'Does he or she love me?'
- pride: 'I must be careful not to show how much I love this person or I will be humiliated if I am refused.'
- guilt: 'How can I be falling in love when I am supposed to be married?'

It's the real thing (until the next time) – Bill's story

Bill is a self-confessed romantic. He's thirty-six and has been married, briefly, once. He says: 'I want to be married again and I'm looking for the perfect girl this time.' This quest leads to a pattern of short-term and very intense romances. Although Bill is not classically good-looking, his approach to love sweeps most women off their feet. He enjoys the chase of love, wooing his latest conquest with flowers and exotic adventures. More importantly, he has developed the ability to really talk to a woman. 'He's very empathetic,' said one of his former girlfriends. 'He wants to know all about you but he tells you very little about himself.'

After a few weeks he cools off and the women are surprised and angry to find that their phone calls are not returned. By then he has found another person to pursue. Usually the discarded woman just fades out of the picture thinking that she is at fault in some way. If she seeks him out and challenges him, he reacts by being very nasty to her. Just as nasty as he was previously wonderful.

In fact the real Bill is nowhere to be found. He is hiding behind a smokescreen of being a romantic lover when he is really nothing of the sort. In fact he is merely projecting himself onto each woman he meets. Falling in love replaces the missing piece in his life and he moves on when the piece doesn't work its magic. He cannot move the romance on to finding a form of fraternal love with the woman. This would enable him to appreciate the differences between them and start to see her as a real person. This pattern has worked quite well for him up to now but is essentially unfulfilling. Perhaps he would like to change his pattern?

Caught in an emotional dilemma – Sally's story

Sally is in her mid-fifties although she looks years younger. She has an interesting job and has been married for twenty-seven years. Her husband is now retired and her children have left home to start their own lives. She is looking forward to becoming a grandmother in a few years' time. She thinks her life is comfortably settled and secure. She is amazed, therefore, to find herself passionately in love with a man who's twenty years younger than herself.

They met through their work and have many mutual interests. Sally speaks of the relationship saying: 'Nat and I are soulmates. But this is crazy. The strange thing is that I love my husband, too. Should I leave him for Nat? But then Nat will probably leave me in a few years because I am so much older and he will want a family of his own. But I can't think like that! A few hours or days with Nat is what I want and I will pay any price for it . . . Or will I?'

Sally is caught in an emotional dilemma. Should she be true to her marriage or true to the overwhelming intensity of romantic love? Her love for her husband has become a fraternal love, the love of two people who have walked along the same path together for many years. Her love for Nat appears to touch her soul in a new way. And what are the practicalities of the situation? She could be left alone through either choice, either through death or abandonment.

There are no guarantees for Sally. She has to decide what to do.

THE ROOTS OF LOVE

The one certain thing about love is that it is uncertain. We don't know if our loved one will love us back, or, even if they do whether their life will outlast ours. So the need to accept potential loss is inextricably linked with the emotion of love. Anyone who craves absolute security might as well not bother about love as they will be profoundly disappointed. Love, in the early stages, appears to almost guarantee the opposite, however. It seems to promise the delight of union and fusion which will end our isolation and loneliness.

The first stage of falling in love is rooted in an earlier pattern, that of parental love. We seek the safety of fusion that we once had with a good parent. If you watch lovers at this stage in a restaurant you will notice that they mirror each other like a mother with her infant. One smiles and the other smiles back. One person's body language will reflect the other's. Tellingly people often use baby talk at this stage. All sorts of coincidences and congruities are discovered. 'It seems like fate,' people say and 'This must be meant to be.' The other person just seems to fit like a missing piece of the jigsaw in our life. We say things like, 'Where have you been all my life?'

This seemingly blessed state both looks back and looks forward. It looks back to our earliest time but it also anticipates a potential state where human isolation will be ended. Deep within our psyches is an archetypal longing for the bliss of true human communion without boundaries. It is expressed in the Christian hope of heaven, the Buddhist notion of nirvana, the communist ideal of human equality, and the dreams of utopians and social reformers. This longing has never been realised in human society except in the imagination but it is a powerful motivating force for human development. So romantic love contains the seeds of both a regressive pull backwards but also a progressive push onwards.

But the maintenance of this stage of romantic love is dependent on an illusion. The passion is triggered by the sight and presence of another person but the excitement is really to do with projection. But sooner or later the reality of the other person's true nature is bound to come through. Faced with either a crisis or perhaps the tedium of daily life, they start to show their true colours. Then we say, 'You're not at all what I thought you were.' What we thought previously was beautiful, or noble, or brave, may appear quite the reverse. They, of course, are usually feeling the same way about us.

Sometimes, though, one partner in a relationship will cling to the illusion stage when the other wants to move on. This is understandable because when the projections start to come off, the relationship faces its greatest test. Sometimes the projections wear off in a matter of weeks, in other cases, they may take years. Faced with the other person's difference, we may want to run away and look for another person to project upon. This means that we will reject the first lover. But if we decide, in some way, to stay with it, then fraternal love can come into play. We can see the other person no longer as an extension of us but a fellow human being. Their faults, failings and general disappointments may, with practice, be seen in the light of human forgiveness. If we have overcome our innate sibling rivalry and envy, we may be able to negotiate this stage of love.

When the projections come off our partner, we have to take them back into ourselves. This includes the bad as well as the good. So, instead of telling the other person they are wonderful or hateful, we must own that ourselves. Projections are simply the unseen parts of ourselves. For example, a man may project his weakness or his fragility onto a woman, a woman may project her aggression and anger onto him. This is the time when self-love really comes into play. Although we are deeply concerned about our partner at this stage, we are really engaged on our own self-development work. We may need to take stock of ourselves. We may do this work all the more keenly because we really care for our lover and want to be the best partner possible for them.

Probably we never get to the stage of completely withdrawing all our projections; to have a few illusions is comforting. But in the main, we will be able to see the other person for who they are. This is where the eros of true relationship comes into the situation. Because of our personal work, we no longer see the other person as an answer to our needs, but as a human being in their own right. We may become passionately interested in their self-fulfilment. At this stage, we can take risks with the relationship because the truth of the relationship is more important than having our needs met.

THE CYCLE OF LOVE

In reality these stages don't necessarily follow each other so neatly as is suggested in the diagram below. Aspects of ourselves jump ahead and some things get left behind. In general, though, these are the stages through which romantic love passes.

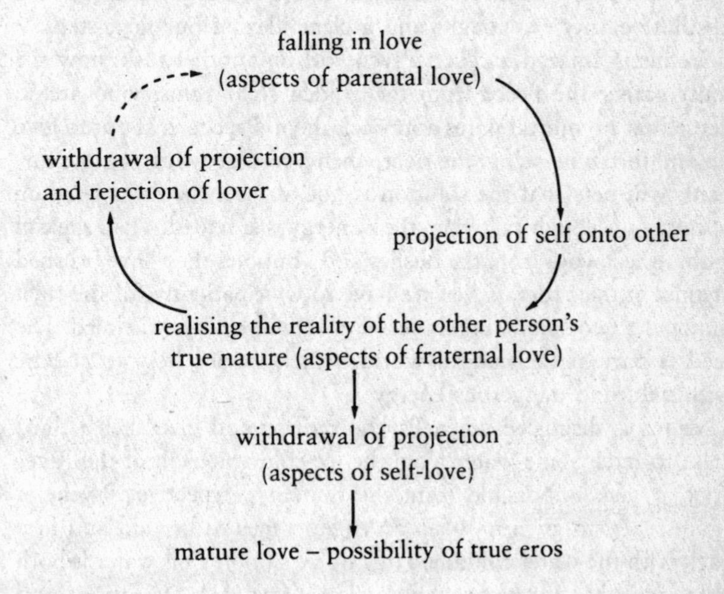

THE DEVELOPMENT OF MATURE LOVE: THE STORY OF PSYCHE AND EROS (II)

In the chapter on envy, we looked at the first part of a classical myth, the story of Psyche and Eros. In the story Psyche is married to the unseen and unknown god, Eros. She lives in a situation of passionate bliss until the envy of her sisters prompts her to find the true identity of her husband. This has been forbidden to her and when she sees him face to face, he runs away in fury and disgust. In order to win Eros back, Psyche has to undergo four tasks which all seem overwhelming to her. The tasks are set by Venus, the goddess of love, who treats Psyche with contempt, ordering her servants, Sorrow and Sadness, to torture her.

The first is to sort out a huge quantity of different seeds before the next morning. This task is impossible for Psyche, but at her moment of despair, ants come and help her. The task of any lover is to sort out what is hers and what is the other person's. The ants symbolise the instinctive power of the unconscious to do this work. All we need to do is to allow the process to take place. The next morning, everything is piled up neatly. We sometimes have this experience, when we wake, after a good night's sleep, with absolute clarity of thought and a clear idea of our next steps.

Venus is amazed and sets Psyche off on another task: now she must gather the fleece from the golden solar rams, who are so fierce that no mortal dares approach them. Psyche is about to give up and throw herself in the river when a reed growing on a nearby bank whispers that the solution is not to meet the rams head on but wait until nightfall when their energy is subdued. Then she can gather their wool from the bushes and brambles they have brushed against in their fury. Often we have to wait patiently for the right moment to do something, otherwise we will be overwhelmed. The reed is part of the natural world, which knows how to coexist with wild and dangerous energy.

Venus is disgusted when Psyche returns and gives her a third task: to fetch some water from the ice-cold waterfall of the River Styx, a task impossible from the human perspective. Psyche is again ready to give up when an eagle comes to her aid and flies back with the water contained in a horse's hoof. This water is both tremendously destructive, but also life-giving. Creation and destruction are two sides of the same coin. We cannot get this water by ordinary means but it can be brought to us by an eagle, who is the king of the birds, and symbolises the royal powers within the psyche.

The fourth and final task is imposed on Psyche: to journey to the underworld and obtain a box containing beauty ointment from Persephone. Interestingly, Psyche fails at this task because she is tempted to open this box before she gives it Venus. She is driven partly by curiosity and partly by the desire to be beautiful in her lover's eyes. The beauty ointment overwhelms her and she falls into a deathly sleep. Eros, who has been sulking all along, then sees her and comes to her rescue. Just when we think that things are going really against us, sometimes they are, in fact, in our favour. There is a danger in this, because if we decide to become helpless, we may think the other person will then rescue us. Psyche doesn't plot or plan this, it just happens.

The drama of Eros and Psyche is not about a woman winning the love of her man. It is rather about the soul having the courage to find true relationship, which is what eros really is. When Psyche and Eros are reunited, they give birth to a daughter, who is Joy. All of us have aspects of Psyche and Eros within us. The point of the tasks is to show us what a wealth of resources we are able to draw upon from the inner world.

Inner Work

Look at the questions posed in the sections on types of love. They are polar opposites that we move between. Make a chart with each of those questions on it and answer them on a scale of 1–10. For example:

Do you feel that:	Or do you feel that:
'I am not really lovable until somebody else loves me.'	'I love and care for myself in order that I may more effectively love others.'

1 2 3 4 5 6 7 8 9 10

1 represents a total belief in the first statement, 10 a total belief in the second, 2 to 9 are the points in between.

Repeat this exercise from time to time and see how your viewpoint changes from day to day, and sometimes from hour to hour.

Look at a past relationship you have had. What qualities did it have? Why did it end? What did you project onto the other person (and they onto you)? What can you learn from it?

Looking at Bill's and Sally's stories, did you find any resonances with your own life? What were they?

Review your relationships with your parent(s). What did you learn in terms of romantic love?

Review your relationship with your sibling(s). (If you were an only child, think who was closest to you when you were growing up, perhaps a cousin, or close friend.) What did you learn in terms of romantic love?

Thinking of the story Psyche and Eros, what could you learn?

What do you want out of your current (or future) relationship that you haven't had in the past? How will you go about getting it?

TRANSFORMING LOVE

When Bill started to look at his pattern of falling in love for a few weeks and then leaving the woman and finding another, he was horrified with himself. He realised that it was a very cold way to live and that the women who fell in love with him found his behaviour very cruel. When he started to review his relationship with his parents, he realised that his mother had been very cold to him. She had been very beautiful and her nickname was 'the ice-queen'. She would sweep into a room and charm everybody present but there was no real warmth about her. Sometimes she wouldn't speak to Bill for days while she punished him for some imagined misdemeanour. Her self-absorption meant that she had almost no empathy or indeed interest in anyone else's feelings. Bill had not been mirrored sufficiently when he was young and so he looked everywhere for this experience of fusion and intimacy. When his romantic relationships failed him by becoming more than mere echoes of a parental love, then he panicked and ran away.

Bill's mother had died a long time ago and so he could not talk to her about it. Instead, he had to talk to his inner mother and explain to her that she had hurt him deeply. He realised that no woman in the world could make up for the loss of a mother's warmth, and that the perfect girl was not going to rescue him. Like Psyche, however, he came to understand that there were many inner resources that he had never even recognised. Human warmth, from a variety of sources, old, young, male, female, became more important to him than the pursuit of endless romantic love. The interesting paradox is that the moment when he gives up the desire for romance is also the moment when he becomes able to really love.

Sally's task is different. She had successfully negotiated the transformation of love in her marriage from a passionate romance, to a fraternal (and sexual) relationship. Her new lover, Nat, showed her aspects of herself that she hadn't previously seen. She didn't need the mirroring part of the romantic relationship in the way that Bill did. She needed to understand that the energy and wonder she saw in Nat were part of herself. Even his very maleness, gentle and strong, were things she could start to recognise as her own. Sally is in a stretch of land where there are no roads to tell her where to go. Should she leave her marriage and live with Nat or should she let Nat go and concentrate on her marriage? A third course exists: to stay married but to see Nat. For the time being, she is adopting that course but she knows that at some stage, in order to be truthful to both the relationships, she must make a choice. Sally's dilemma is essentially one of self-love. Does self-love mean fidelity to a person, or a marriage, or to one's own development? Is there a conflict and how can we resolve it? Each person's answer will be individual and unique.

Love is unknowable and mysterious. All that we can really work for is relationship. As Bill put it: 'In the past I used to relate to women in an I-It mode. They were the object, the missing piece of me. I want now to know the other person to be able relate to them in an I-You way. You will be different from me and will not fit my jigsaw but I want to know you for who you are. Then I can love you.'

20

Pride

'Pride can also come after a fall – it makes the fall's message less life-changing.
Diogenes Small

WHAT IS PRIDE?

Pride has both a positive and a negative face. On the one hand, it can reflect a delight in a particular accomplishment and an enhancement of our self-esteem, but on the other, it can reveal a deadeningly egotistic arrogance and conceit. The former connects us to our achievements and those of people close to us, the other cuts us from other people, locking us away in a sterile and rigid world. Pride is traditionally one of the seven deadly sins and yet imagine a life where we didn't take pride in ourselves and others. It all depends on our attitude to it.

If we totally identify with the emotion then we'll believe that we ourselves have created the thing of which we're proud. The effect of this will make us hang onto our feelings of pride, long after we should. The other way to see pride is as a messenger which has come to bring us the positive news that we, or people we are close to, are on the right track. Then we will see that pride is, at best, temporary encouragement to further action, rather than a state in itself. As one man described it: 'Pride cannot be one of those tenants who gradually takes over the entire house, finally winning squatter's rights. Pride must be a delightful visitor who comes now and again – often at totally unexpected moments.' In other words, we need to process pride fairly quickly before it goes sour and ruins everything.

Many lives have been blighted by the mortifying rigidity of pride. It has kept lovers from declaring their love and being together, it has prevented painful breeches between old friends being repaired, it has halted careers and self-development of all kinds. Despite the best of intentions, the pride of medical staff has probably killed people in hospitals. The collective pride of us all has almost certainly contributed to wars and bloody conflicts of all kinds, the outcomes of which live on until the present day. Much of what has been written about pride is negative which is understandable because of the long shadow which it has cast.

The ancient Greeks called pride *hubris*, and the great tragic plays show how *hubris* contributes to human downfall. The essence of tragedy is that the hero is too proud to recognise his weakness and his ignorance. He arrogantly takes it upon himself to decide things when he should have a more humble attitude to life. If we are caught up with *hubris* we will overreach ourselves and start to act like gods. The action of the tragedy, with its often terrible results, is to correct this basic fault in the character of the hero. Sometimes wars, blindings and dismemberments are the only things which bring us back to the level of humility which is the opposite to *hubris*. The classical tragedies are warnings of the dangers of unprocessed and unrecognised pride.

On a more human level you may be reading this because you feel proud at the moment, and you may be feeling uncomfortable about your pride. People may be saying things like, 'You have a swelled head', and warning you that 'pride goes before a fall'. The very fact that you are aware of it is an excellent sign which will mitigate much of the harm that pride may do. But, on the other hand, you may be reading this because you would like a little more pride and self-respect in your life. As with all emotions, pride points to what we need to do, to the attitudes which need to be repaired and replaced. The following chapter is an attempt to look at the complexities of pride and to provide some sort of route map of its terrain.

HOW DOES IT FEEL?

Pride usually involves feeling 'puffed up'. Some people report that they actually feel physically larger or taller when they're feeling proud. With some, the feeling is more cerebral. But most of us will feel better in some way. Our self-esteem will be raised and there can be agreeable sensations of self-satisfaction. It is almost as though things did not really touch us, that the human concerns of the 'little people' were no longer of any interest to us. If we have had a hard time in life, with a lot of knocks and set-backs, the physical feelings of pride can be addictively pleasant. If, on the other hand, we have inherited our pride, perhaps through our family name or wealth, there may also be an underground feeling that we personally don't quite measure up to all this.

Emotions associated with pride include:

- loneliness: 'I am right and everyone else is wrong.'
- fear: 'I may be proud of this at the moment but I am also afraid of losing it.'
- boredom: 'Now I've got it all – what next?'

Although we said that pride can usually makes us feel better, it can also play a large role in making us feel cut off and lonely. Another negative feeling associated with pride is boredom. A person can feel that he has reached the top of the mountain and that there's nothing left to do.

Pride cuts him off from the things he really wants – George's story

George is now in his mid-forties and somewhat of a loner since his marriage ended some years ago. On the surface he appears cold and reserved and somewhat shy. Underneath he is fiercely proud. He says, 'I would like to meet someone and have a relationship but I am too proud to be dumped – so I always get in first if I am in any doubt about the other person's feelings for me.'

When his marriage was going through difficulties, he had an affair with another woman. This didn't work out and he thought of returning to his marriage but his wife said that she thought that they hadn't been terribly happy for a long while. She suggested going to some form of marriage guidance or relationship counselling. He was too proud to submit himself to what he saw as the judgement of a third party so he declined the offer. Later, he regretted it but by then it was too late as his wife had found another partner.

This pattern of aloofness and pride is apparent through the rest of George's life. At work, he is too proud to ask either for information or help. He is afraid the people will think that he's ignorant or that he's incompetent. This is disabling as it means he spends much of his time hiding his true level of knowledge. Also he can't delegate work because he is too proud to ask for help. Needless to say, this doen't help his career or inspire confidence in his colleagues. But more seriously, George can't find the personal or professional fulfilment he would like.

Recently he has come to see that pride is a hindrance rather than a help. He said, 'I thought pride protected me from making stupid blunders but now I'm coming to see that it stops me from having what I want.'

Is she who she says she is? – Jo's story

Jo presents herself as a well-dressed and attractive person from a certain sort of background. She dresses in a rather whimsical way and has a slightly fey manner. Without being so vulgar as to state the fact, she implies that she comes from an English aristocratic country-house setting. She will give the merest verbal snapshot of her home, 'Well, of course, the drive is very long.' Or, perhaps, she will say, 'The roses are so beautiful at my parents' place at this time of the year. I do wish you could see them.' She shies away from giving precise details, which could be verified, contenting herself with vaguely hinting that the house is somewhere in the West Country.

Most people believe Jo because she's very plausible. By withholding detail, she makes the person she's talking to imagine the details for themselves. They create the fantasy that she implies. In fact, Jo's real background is middle class and suburban. She has created a fake family of origin because she doesn't feel proud of her real one. She expresses great pride in the created family and people feel very in awe of her.

Jo's tactic has been successful in the short term. It has enabled her to escape the trap of shame and to win admiration and respect from people she wants to impress. But the more they are impressed, the more Jo falls into the jaws of negative pride. The more they like her for being what she isn't, the less, she fears, they would like her if they knew her true origins. Her strategy cuts her off from true intimacy, because she cannot show her real self.

THE TWO ROOTS OF PRIDE

As we have seen, pride has two sides, negative and positive. One appears to boost self-esteem, the other really does so. But because negative pride is based on false foundations, it gradually undermines self-esteem. Shame and lack of self-worth underpin negative pride. By contrast, genuine self-esteem, based on true values, underpin positive pride. In order to be emotionally intelligent it is vital to distinguish from which root your pride is derived.

Negative pride and shame

Understanding the negative aspect of pride involves one of pride's seeming opposites, shame. Sometimes pride is used as a cover-up for a shame so deep that it can no longer be felt. Shame says: *You're not good enough, you're ugly, stupid, a loser*. Perhaps each of us has felt this voice whispering in our ear at some time. If we turn to this voice and say something like: *It's interesting to hear what you have to say, perhaps you could tell me why?* or *I'm not sure I agree with you – could you say more?* then we will not be ensnared by shame. Usually the end result of this kind of dialogue is that shame gives up trying to shame us because by consciously facing it we are enabled to see through it. In the end this voice will usually collapse or go away.

As adults we can practise this form of dialogue and start to disperse shame. But the roots of shame frequently start early in life – perhaps even before language is developed. If we are told as tiny children that we are not as intelligent or beautiful or indeed even the sex that our parents had hoped for, then this can give us a most fundamental sense of shame in the core of our being. As no-one has been the perfect child, all of us have some shame in us, at some level. Mostly it can be managed and may even be constructive in spurring us on to improve ourselves. But if shame has entered into us too deeply, then we have no core of true identity that we can build on. If our mother thinks we are profoundly ugly or our father was deeply disappointed by our gender and wished for the opposite, we will not have any pride in ourselves. The negative criticism of the parents becomes an internal voice which can be heard long after the person has left home or after the actual parents have died. This negativity is added to over the years with feedback from teachers, bosses and other people in positions of power and authority. In the end, we may filter out good messages, and only hear the criticisms, as we have become so used to them.

So shame starts with an absence in pride and self-esteem. But because we need pride to function adequately in the world, we will usually try to find it from another source. There are several strategies for this:

- **identification with something that is admired**
  If, for example, the parents longed for a baby boy and a girl was born, then she may try to adopt the characteristics of masculinity as far as possible. The girl's pride will then be centred on the degree to which she can successfully cross the gender divide and not on her own femininity.
- **forming an alliance with a larger, stronger thing**
  If a boy is born weak and puny, and physical strength was admired in his family, he may decide to join a strong group. This could be a political party or movement of some kind. The effect of this will be to encourage his dependence on the group for his self-worth and to diminish his personal self-esteem.
- **creation of a false identity**
  Some people's sense of shame is so great that they create a completely false identity for themselves. This may involve

moving to another country, or denying their social or racial origins. Their pride is then centred on their assumed, or adopted, self and their real self becomes increasingly fragile.

To some extent, we use all these strategies in everyday life. They only become a problem when we lose our sense of our true self and focus our pride in something which isn't really our own. This kind of pride often has a brittle sense to it. This is the link with the Greek *hubris*, where the hero in a classical tragedy becomes inflated with power. Because the hero feels weak, he forms an alliance with a larger and stronger thing. This is usually with a godlike power which is beyond a human level. This forms a massive, but false, pride, which usually leads to a huge downfall. Arrogance gets its strength from an assumed self. The corrective to it is not shame but a revaluation of our real abilities and the discovery of our true self.

Positive pride and self-esteem

This form of pride is deeply rooted both in our self-image and also our values. We can only be proud of those things that we value. If I say I am proud of my physical fitness, then this means that either I set great store in being fit and admire that or that I am proud of the effort that went into achieving that fitness level (which may not be very great). So pride can either reflect an outcome or an activity. People who have a problem with their self-esteem generally focus too much on the outcome and don't give themselves enough credit for their activities and personal qualities. For example, if a very bright person gets good exam results, that is, perhaps, only to be expected of them, but if a person with learning difficulties wins a place at a university, that shows far more than mere academic ability. It demonstrates courage, vision, determination and self-belief. He or she might actually get fewer marks than the academically gifted person, but their achievement will be far greater.

In our capitalist culture, results and outcomes are generally regarded as more important than the process we go through to get to them. This is a pity and denies many of us legitimate pride in our efforts. You might like to spend a few minutes now and think of something you've achieved or attempted of which you feel proud. What personal qualities did it require to acheive it? Focus on the journey there rather than the result.

Here are some suggestions:

courage wisdom grit insight bloody-mindedness
tact patience humility clear-headedness cleverness
ability to make contacts/network creativity compassion
emotional integrity moral fibre imagination shrewdness
teamwork kindliness independence of judgement

You may want to add additional qualities to this list.

Even if the project didn't have quite the outcome you wanted or planned, remember that these are the qualities that you showed nonetheless. Be very creative in the way you interpret this exercise. If you feel proud of something you have inherited rather than created yourself, ask yourself whether you have added anything personal to this inheritance. A man who had inherited a large country estate once told me that he had felt that he had no pride in himself. He felt he had done nothing towards this vast patrimony. But then over the years he realised that he had been a good steward, carefully maintaining the house and the land. The outcome was that he would be able to pass it onto his children, and in a wider sense, to all of us, as part of the national heritage. This was something in which he could feel legitimate pride.

So positive pride will always focus on the whole picture and pay attention to the personal qualities and values that have contributed to the outcome. Positive pride will not be deterred by failure but will see it for what it is and will use its feedback to try more effectively the next time. Finding positive pride is the way out of negative pride.

THE CYCLE OF PRIDE

As we have noted, all of us start with some degree of shame and usually cover this up with something else, which could include identification with a stronger or more desired thing or the creation of a false identity. This leads to a negative form of pride which eats away at the core of our self-esteem as we are proud then of something which is not us. The way through this dilemma is to find our true values and our self-esteem in our qualities. Then we will discover positive pride.

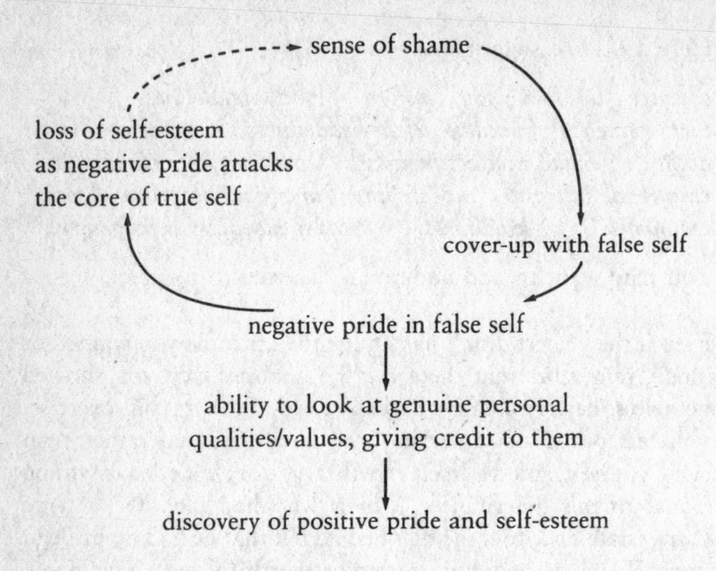

PRIDE AND PREJUDICE

More than most emotions, pride evokes a reaction both within us and within others, which may be extremely counterproductive. Jane Austen's novel *Pride and Prejudice* describes this in depth. At the opening of the novel, Mr Darcy is so arrogant that he dismisses most of the people around him with lofty disdain. Instead of seeing the heroine, Elizabeth Bennett, for the beautiful and unique person she is, he dismisses her as 'merely tolerable'. His haughtiness brings out her prejudice, which was perhaps not very far below the surface, and she sees him only one-dimensionally as a very proud man. Any of his other characteristics are blotted out for her. The resolution of the novel is a marriage between a pride, which has become tempered by humility, and a prejudice, which has seen through its one-sidednesses.

Rejection and suffering bring Mr Darcy to a point where he can drop his attitude of proud conceit. Empathy and self-confidence bring Elizabeth to the point where she can see the human being beneath the mask. Interestingly, some of her early prejudice is founded on the shame she feels about the vulgarity of some of her relations, particularly her mother. As the novel progresses, some other relations, the more educated and elegant Gardiners, of whom she can be proud, take her for a holiday during which they encounter Mr Darcy in his true setting. Jane Austen is perhaps hinting here that, as we realise things about ourselves that make us genuinely proud, we start to be able to drop our prejudices.

The novel makes a point that can be carried far beyond man–woman relationships. If we take *Pride and Prejudice* as an inner drama, we may start to see that prejudice leads to pride and pride often employs prejudice to buttress its position. Prejudice really means to pre-judge a situation and there is nothing more proud and arrogant than that. Judgement is a tricky thing, even when we are in full possession of the facts, but to judge something when we have only half the story is risky indeed. We should start to catch ourselves whenever we hear ourselves say, 'He'll never get married', 'She'll never get to university', or 'I'll never get a job I really want'. They are examples of an attitude which has arrogantly decided the shape of the future. Whether or not these things actually come to pass is irrelevant, we have allowed our pride to poison the marvellous possibilities of the present moment.

Inner Work

Does pride cut you off from possibilies in your life? What are they? What would you gain from letting some of your pride go?

Is your pride more towards the positive or the negative end of the spectrum? (Remember that most of us have both to some degree.)

What do you take pride in? Can you list the personal qualities that have enabled you to achieve this?

Are there attributes which you possess but which have (as yet) no obvious outcome? Could you be proud of them?

Did you feel sympathy or anger for either George or Jo? Is there something here for you?

Are pride and prejudice linked for you?

Do you hide something about yourself that you don't like under a veneer of pride? How could you come to terms with whatever it is?

FAMILY ROMANCE

When Jo created a different background for herself, it is because she was ashamed of her true identity. It would be useless to tell her that her family are perfectly fine perople and she should be proud of them. She isn't proud of them but it is not a simple matter of wishing she came from a seemingly more desirable social class. She has invented her family because she felt that she didn't fit into her family of origin. They were practical, down-to-earth people who dressed sensibly and who called a spade a spade. Her father would say, 'Get down to brass tacks for goodness' sakes, Jo. You're such a dreamer with your head always in the clouds.' Her father and mother would shout and be rude to each other but meant no harm by it. Jo was always a very sensitive child who couldn't bear this way of behaving. She even looked more delicate and aristocratic than the rest of her family.

If we feel deep shame about our family background, we may invent a story of belonging to a completely different family. This is called a family romance and has echoes in the many fairy stories where a king's son or daughter is lost and brought up by fishermen or shepherds. With the dawning of consciousness, usually symbolised by young adulthood, they become aware of their royal blood. Then there is a need for them to return to the court and take up their destiny as a prince or princess. Probably all of us have had this fantasy once upon a time as a passing thing. The person who creates a family romance is making this fantasy literal when it should be kept in the imagination. This is because they feel different. Physically and biologically they are part of their family but psychologically they feel different. Another twist is that they can feel guilty at feeling different because it is a form of rejecting their parents and other siblings.

Jo created a family romance as a means of expressing her difference. It needed more and more people to believe in it in order to sustain it. She felt that she could never let go of her pride sufficiently to tell people that it wasn't true and lived in constant fear of exposure. She felt she would be humiliated beyond words if the truth ever came out. For Jo, the dynamic is between pride and humiliation. The more she fears humiliation, the prouder she becomes. The resolution of her pride will probably only come through one of two events. The first could be that she is publicly discovered and shamed by the truth coming out. Then she would have no fantasy to retreat to. The second, and more positive, would be that she comes to develop a real relationship with herself and enhances her self-esteem. When she has come to see herself for the unique and inwardly royal person she is, she will find no need for a borrowed grand family. Which way will it go? There is no way of telling but it is worth remembering that if we do not do our inner work then sometimes outer life makes us do it by means of a shocking crisis.

THE TRANSFORMATION OF PRIDE

George is at a different stage of life from Jo and more ready to begin his inner work. He has realised that his tyrannical pride is based on lack of self-esteem. The exercise to find out his real qualities and values was a revelation to him. He said: 'I had no idea that I had so many good qualities inside me.' He has come to see that real esteem is so confident that mistakes can be made, learnt from and, ultimately, laughed at. For many people, pride is like an iron band which they think is a support and a defence but instead is a lonely prison.

Recognising the link between pride and prejudice was especially meaningful for George. He said, 'I had decided the future in my own head and as it didn't turn out exactly as I had decided I thought that other people were in the wrong. I became pernickety over the minutest, least important detail because I had pre-judged the situation and had an idea in my head of how things should be. No wonder I was impossible to live with or to work with!'

The emotion of pride points to a psychological attitude which needs to be healed. The true opposite of pride is not shame but humility. Humility is the opposite of judgement, it is patient, grounded and flexible. Humility and positive pride can then walk hand in hand, each reflecting a different aspect of the same truth.

As George said, 'I chose pride because I feared humiliation but the wrong sort of pride leads to endless secret shame. A humble attitude may not seem very glamorous but it leads in the end to the ability to feel real pride.'

21

Rejection

'We are never so defenceless against suffering as when we love, never so unhelplessly unhappy as when we have lost our loved object or its love.'
Sigmund Freud

WHAT IS REJECTION?

The very worst thing has just happened – you've been rejected. You've just had the letter, or e-mail, or fax. Maybe it was written out in black and white or maybe, even more catastrophically, it was hinted at during a telephone conversation. The agony seeped in slowly as you began to realise that you were being rejected. Perhaps it was a job you especially wanted, a course you desperately wanted to do, a house you set your heart on, or a lover you were deeply in love with. Or maybe a long-standing friend turned her back on your friendship and dropped you. You're washed up, dumped, on the shelf, beached, out of the game. You feel a total failure, an utter loser. Rejection has been the trigger for many suicides and descents into the depths of despair. It feels like the most dreadful moment in your life. Perhaps it is, but paradoxically it is also a moment of supreme potential. The ending of a particular dream or the termination of a passion has great power and energy.

This is hard to realise as our belief system tells us that rejection is painful. But in fact the new situation which is opened up contains a myriad of new possibilities. The reason we see the pain and not the power is that we see it as a loss of control. If we believe that it's important to be in control of our life, then we will have serious pain in rejection. But if, by contrast, we have an attitude of surrender to life, then rejection will seem like the opening of a new door in the excitement of our life's journey. The choice is ours, but, of course, it isn't that simple. Rejection contains all the ghosts of our past rejections. In order to move forward into this new state, we must also understand how those past rejections colour and affect our present-day beliefs.

Perhaps you're reading this now because you've just been rejected, or possibly you have been the one rejecting someone or something? Both are two sides of the same coin and so, either way, this chapter will give you some guidelines as to how to look at rejection in new ways. These include an understanding of the way we reject ourselves and the way we set up rejection repetition patterns. You will learn how to re-programme your belief system to see the best in rejection, not to be paralysed by it and to move forward into the next phase.

Rejection is based on decision and if we believe in the importance of allowing ourselves and others to make decisions, we are forced to believe in the possibility of rejection. Both the parties in the rejection event make a choice. The person who is actually doing the rejecting appears to be in control but there are many decisions which the person being rejected has made and can make. The first was to put his love and his energy into someone else's power. If we haven't chosen someone and allowed ourselves to become vulnerable to them then we can't be rejected by them. The second major decision is the choice of how we see it. Some personality types which tend to see the glass as half full rather than half empty will be at an advantage here. But it's an ability that can be developed even if it's not an innate attribute. The third choice will be whether or not ultimately to see rejection as shameful and humiliating. This takes practice but ultimately it is our choice as to whether or not we're humiliated by being rejected.

It takes two to humiliate: one to do the humiliation and one to accept it. As a man put it: 'It was incredibly painful when my girlfriend left me, but when I got over the shock and the pain of the loss, I was glad. I want to spend my life with someone who really values me – as much as I'm starting to value myself. Obviously she wasn't the right person and it's good to know it now. It opens the way for a better person to come into my life.'

HOW DOES IT FEEL?

It can feel physically awful but the mental pain is usually worse. There can be overwhelming waves of disappointment and rage. If we haven't anticipated it, then the shock of it may be very great. People describe it as 'feeling gutted', 'devastated', 'annihilated'. We may feel as if our world has been shattered and everything about us takes on an unpleasant and distressing hue. In the state of acute rejection, we may find everything rejecting us – even buses and trains seem to leave without us. If there's a queue, we will be served last. It isn't quite like that, of course, the trauma of rejection just feels like a global and total emotion. We may cry a lot or not be able to cry at all. If we have been rejected many times already in life then rejection will come as a familiar pain all the worst for being familiar. As a person said: 'Here I go again – when will this cycle of endless rejection ever finish?'

Emotions that are associated with rejection include:

- rage – 'How could they do this to me?'
- grief – 'Now I've lost this irreplaceable thing life will never be the same.'
- depression – 'I remember this awful feeling, perhaps it's better not to hope for anything ever again and to fall into despair.'
- hate – 'I hate them for doing this to me' or alternatively, 'I hate myself because this always happens to me.'
- fear – 'What will become of me now?'

FORMS THAT REJECTION CAN TAKE

Rejection can be very obvious or so subtle that it doesn't look like rejection. The obvious forms have already been mentioned: love, friendships, jobs, opportunities of all kinds. If we are rejecting someone or something, it may be because we feel rejected ourselves. So the power may appear to be in our hands when in fact, it's not.

There is another important category of rejection – and this is self-rejection. All self-rejection stems from an initial feeling of having been rejected at some early stage in our development. This could have been literally by our parents, who may have abandoned us or given us away. In some countries, extreme poverty may lead some people to sell their children. Or we may have been adopted by another family (perhaps with the best of intentions). Or the rejection wound may be less easy to spot. We may have had a depressed mother who couldn't emotionally relate to us because of her own pain and illness. Or our father may have been alcoholic and not emotionally present for us although he was physically there. Or we may have had the misfortune to lose someone through suicide which is a major rejection of those close by. The degree of insecurity we feel in later life about these early rejections will depend on the level of support we received afterwards. Almost all of them can be mitigated by the presence of a loving other person although the early pain usually cannot be entirely taken away.

But if we didn't have the benefit of an alternative source of love, then we are likely to grow up rejecting ourselves. There are several ways this can manifest itself. It may take the form of the repetition compulsion (described below) or may take the form of self-abusive behaviour or deliberate creation of ugliness. Both of these emotional strategies drive other people away. It is almost impossible to love someone who is abusing themselves through drink, drugs, or excessive sex. Their addiction almost cuts out the possibility of real relationship. Addictions are more complex than merely self-rejection but the emotion of rejection will probably be a major causative factor in them.

Another way self-rejection can be expressed is through the way we present and take care of our bodies. Sometimes we are confronted by a person who seems to have deliberately made themselves ugly. Fashions change and this is a difficult area to be definitive about. It is not a question of basic attractiveness or lack of personal beauty. We all start out in different respects here. A person, whatever their original attractiveness inheritance quotient, who has taken some trouble with their appearance, and who has clean clothes and freshly washed hair gladdens the heart of any spectator. By contrast, someone who has neglected basic hygiene or who has chosen unflattering and unaesthetic clothes may be expressing a form of self-rejection. When we meet such a person, we may be tempted to reject them also.

THE REPETITION COMPULSION

A perfectly secure person who has absolute self-confidence, believes that she is fulfilling her destiny and that her life, while sometimes difficult, is profoundly part of a greater plan, will not feel pain upon any rejection. There may be such people in the world but they must be pretty rare. Perhaps some of the great spiritual masters and saints come close but, for most of us, rejection means pain. The degree of the pain, however, will be lessened if we understand the repetition compulsion. When we have an experience which we can't make any sense of, and so cannot come to terms with, we tend to seek a repetition of it. It's called a compulsion because we are not fully aware of what we're doing. Like many things, this is a good idea, but turns out badly in practice unless we manage to become conscious of what we are doing. So, if at some stage we feel we have been rejected but don't have the ability to integrate it, we set up a pattern of rejection. This pattern can be broken. It's worth noting, here, that the repetition compulsion doesn't only operate with rejection situations. Many other traumatic events can be recreated, such as emotional or sexual abuse.

A classic example of the repetition compulsion is the woman whose father left home when she was seven. Although he didn't mean to abandon his little daughter, his work took him to another country and he found the effort to keep in touch too difficult. He probably had a new relationship and his second wife may have been very envious of the first marriage. When the girl grows up she may unconsciously seek out men who abandon her. First one, then another, and then a third. When she tells you the story, you think – *how unlucky this woman has been! All these men let her down. How cruel life is.*

The truth is that the woman never understood or came to terms with the first rejection she ever suffered – the one she experienced from her father. Because neither of her parents could explain the complexity of that emotional situation to her, she is, quite understandably, in the dark about it. She may say she never thinks about it and she may rationalise it away but in fact, beneath her no-nonsense manner, she is still puzzling and in pain about it. So, without realising it, in adult life, she has set up a pattern of men rejecting her. The rejection may come about because she has chosen men who can't love her because of their own problems or conflicts. Or it may come about because her behaviour drives them away. She may actually behave in such a way that it makes it impossible for him to stay. (His side of the story may be that he felt himself rejected by her sexually or emotionally and felt he had no option but to leave.) It doesn't really matter how the rejection comes about. This looks like self-defeating behaviour but in fact it's an attempt to come to terms with the first loss. We can change this losing pattern into an intelligent emotional response if we realise we're doing it. It's not just a blind compulsive re-enactment, it's a genuine attempt to learn.

A repetition pattern is not the same as a run of bad luck, which anyone can have. It is not always easy to distinguish between the two but if you have a persistent feeling of *here we go again*, it's probably worth investigating a little further. There are many patterns which we can set up. The repetition compulsion doesn't only operate with love relationships. Anything which is important to us can be repeated negatively. This can include gaining a good job, winning a place to study on a course we want, getting a house-share or a house. The list is endless. In fact anything where there's an element of a competition which we can lose can be drawn into this repeating pattern. This can also be linked to anything where there is anxiety concerning the outcome. In fact anything which we can't control. We may repeat the rejection in one sphere and allow ourselves success in another or the unconscious compulsion may be so profound that we deny ourselves any success at all. When we speak of someone who is one of life's losers, we are speaking about the crippling effects of the repetition compulsion.

The way to understand and break the repetition compulsion involves the following steps:

- a recognition of the repetition pattern. This means we say,

'Yes, I am trapped in this pattern. Although I may have had bad luck, some of this is down to my choice.'

- a wish to get out of it. This is harder than it looks because the pattern has kept going because we are unconscious about it. It is both a source of great pain, but also, in a curious way, a form of comfort.
- an acknowledgement that we are creating the pattern because we are in deep pain about the loss we have suffered and of which we may only be partially aware.
- a preparedness to come to terms with the original rejection (if we can discover it) or at any rate to accept that the rejection we fear so desperately has already happened. As it's already happened and we have survived it, we can survive the next one.
- letting go of the need for control and certainty in life and allowing ourselves to not know the outcome of a situation. Giving ourselves permission to compete with others and to fail if that happens.
- rejecting rejection and accepting reality.

THE CYCLE OF REJECTION

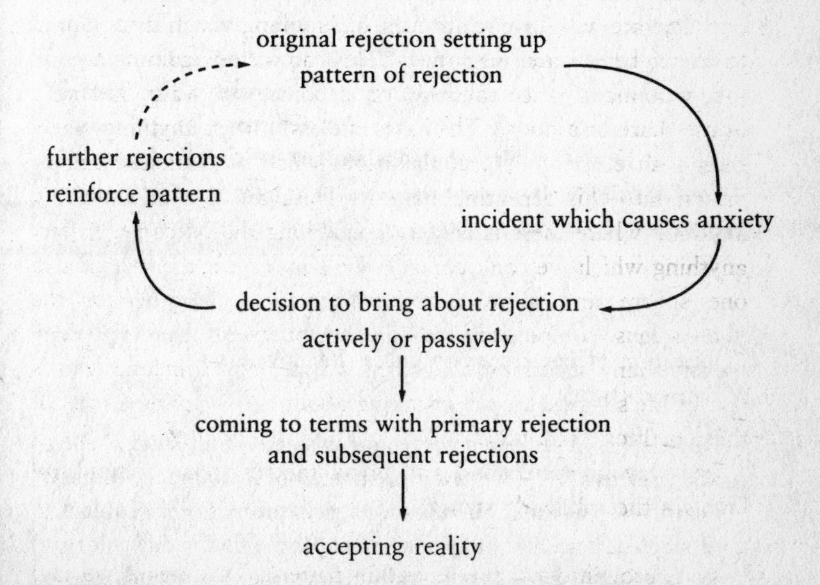

Too ugly to be loved – Peter's story

Peter is twenty-eight. He has a long scar down the side of his face that he received in a car crash when he was a young teenager. Although this disfigurement is not life-threatening or in any way physically painful, Peter feels that his life has been ruined.

He still lives at home and he has never had the courage to start an independent life separately from his parents. He is gay and has had a pattern of relationships in which men he loves reject him. He says, 'In the gay scene, looks are important, if you haven't got the looks, well, too bad.' He thinks that his lovers have taken up with him out of pity and leave him because they find him too repulsive to be with. Partly this is true but it is not really the scar that they find a problem. It is rather more the case that his scarred personality destroys, time and time again, the possibility of happiness in a partnership.

In a way, Peter's scar has come to stand for all that he rejects and hates in himself. He does not fully accept that he's gay. He says, 'It's another cross to bear, being different and society really makes you feel it.' He feels that he has no choice but to be gay. Although his parents accept his sexual orientation, Peter does not. Deep down he believes that homosexuality is somehow inferior to heterosexuality. This is very understandable given the long history of prejudice against homosexuality that has existed in Western cultures. But, in order to overcome the self-defeating pattern of endless rejection, Peter has to come to accept the reality of who he is.

Rejection of her creativity makes her loveless – Patricia's story

Patricia has just turned forty and is single. 'Still single,' she adds defensively. 'I feel deeply ashamed of it, so much so that I can't sleep at night.' In a way, Patricia presents her problem of singleness so forcefully that most people find it difficult to see beyond that to what is really happening. She spends ages with her women friends agonising over the latest man she's met and then tearing his character to shreds. A relationship may begin but either she will find out something really impossible about the man or he will drop her. As she says, 'None of my relationships last very long, I'm afraid. Perhaps that's for the best. I mean if something's not going to work out then it's best to know sooner than later.'

But Patricia's real problem is nothing to do with romantic rejection or the inability to find a partner in life. It is more profound than that. It is that she has rejected a part of herself – her own creativity. Patricia was a talented potter when she was young. She could create fantastic designs from her head which resonated with the poetry of her own interior life. One day she stopped doing this, because she thought that her major life task was to look for a husband. 'Once I've got that sorted out then I can go back to my creativity. But I need the security of love.'

Unfortunately life isn't so simple. Patricia's creativity stemmed from the depths of her nature. It needed to be expressed and if it wasn't, then she somehow expected the man in her life to bring her this level of fulfilment. This was too much for the relationship to bear as the man had his own work to do as well. Either he rejected her because she was too demanding or she rejected him because he didn't give her the internal feeling of satisfaction and pleasure that making a truly beautiful and unique piece of pottery did.

TRUST AND CONTROL

The essence of dealing with rejection is an acceptance of reality. Where we start from influences our possibility of reaching the destination. The Irish joke 'If I wanted to go to Dublin, I wouldn't be starting from here' contains this wisdom. Nested within the ability to start from the basis of reality is a decision to trust life. If we do not trust life, we will never be able to accept reality. As a human being grows and matures, there are basic choices to be made. In order to get to the next level, as it were, we have to decide one way or the other. One of the most crucial choices is that between trust and distrust. We can either trust life blindly with all its peculiar ups and downs or we can doubt that we should be on this planet. We can shrink away from life into an autistic, closed-in response and not relate to our fellow human beings at all.

Very few of us fall definitively into either camp. Most of us have had good experiences of love and joy, which have reinforced our ability to trust, as well as bad experiences of distress and loss, which have strengthened our capacity for distrust. So we end up somewhere along the spectrum of trust and distrust, sometimes at one end of it, sometimes going closer to the other. If we want to be able to accept the rejection and see the reality of it – as a temporary set-back, as a course correction, as a blessing in disguise – we have to be able to move towards the trust end of the spectrum.

As we move in this ambivalent grey area, it's always worth noting where, on a given day, you fall on the spectrum of trust and distrust. A further difficulty with distrust is that it leads us to try to control a situation. We cannot tolerate not knowing so we rather reject someone than risk having them reject us later.

Spectrum of trust and distrust

Basic trust – 'Life is good and there is destiny for me'	**Basic distrust –** 'Life is bad and I must continually watch my back'
← **Ambivalent area** →	
Rejection is positive 'It shows me my true path'	**Rejection is awful** 'It confirms what I know'
Freedom to allow	**Need to control**

The painful paradox is that the more awful we find rejection, the more likely we are to keep repeating it. Peter's pattern was to repeat the experience of rejection by falling in love over and over again. Falling in love opens up the possibility of rejection in a way that nothing else does. People who have difficulty with rejection either fall in love too easily or not at all. Instead of waiting and seeing if this new person will be right for them, there is a tendency to jump right in and make their demands known very early and very forcefully.

Peter always insisted that his lovers accept his scar. If they so much as looked at another man, he would fall into jealous sulks. Instead of seeing that his behaviour might be more the problem than his appearance, he blamed every rejection on his disfigurement. As we have already seen, Peter's own rejection of his sexuality plays an important role here. Peter's work is to first of all accept himself. Only when he does that will his self-defeating pattern of behaviour change.

A NEW LOOK AT ENDING

The last twist in the story of rejection concerns our attitude to the necessity of ending. Endings are part of life yet they bring such loss that most of us are in at least partial denial about them. The final ending is death and endings all along the way can seem like little deaths. Rejection is fundamentally the ending of a relationship, a dream, or a hope. In Nick Hornby's novel, *High Fidelity*, the central character is rejected by his long-term girlfriend, Laura. As he reflects on the past romantic rejections he has suffered and dealt out in his thirty-six years, he comes to see that his inability to make an authentic commitment to Laura stems from his fear of death. A commitment, and possibly children, would set him on the inescapable path of life – the ending of which is certainly the grave. Instead he prefers the abortive pattern of finding a new woman to fall in love with, so that he doesn't have to face the prospect of dying.

In a way, Patricia's problem is a bit like this. By refusing to do her creative work, she is refusing her uniqueness and denying her adulthood. Her underlying fear is – *when I have made the best pot I can, what will happen then?* She thinks that she can put off growing up, getting old and dying, by staying at an early stage of her life, the courtship phase. The phrase she uses to describe her search for a mate, security, is very telling in this context. She wants the security of control and won't give this up to trust in life. It is, in fact, very likely that when she does accept the person she is, she will either find the right man for her or perhaps find her fulfilment through her creative work.

Inner Work

What do you feel about rejection? Is it an opportunity for change or devastating defeat?

Do you accept yourself? What things do you reject in yourself and why?

Do you find yourself repeating patterns of rejection and failure?

Where do you find yourself on the spectrum of trust and distrust?

Did you find yourself becoming angry with or sympathetic towards Peter or Patricia? Is there a message here for you?

What do you feel about endings? Do you try to avoid major ones by starting new and repetitive cycles?

THE TRANSFORMATION OF REJECTION INTO ACCEPTANCE

The ability to say yes to life, with all its pain and heartaches, banishes the agony of rejection. It also removes the need for excuses. As Peter worked through the truth of his situation he was able to say, 'I see now that the scar's pretty unimportant in the scheme of things.' He allowed the genuine attractiveness of self-acceptance to shine through and found that he was no longer rejected in the same way. This didn't mean that no rejection came his way, of course it did, but it felt far less devastating. Much of his work was around understanding the collective views on homosexuality and having the courage to follow his own path.

Patricia took a long time realise what was happening to her. She resisted the truth for some months. Part of this was the fear that, if she changed course, she would have to come to terms with the wasted life that she had already lived. Little by little the thought of wasting her future life seemed worse than the realisation that she had wasted some of her past and so she took up her creative work again. Ultimately she may come to realise that none of her experience was wasted. All of it got her to the reality of the present moment and all was valuable.

Accepting rejection, and seeing it for what it is, opens the door to true freedom and a passionate involvement in life that can come from no other source.

Epilogue

The Cultivation of Joy

> 'I cannot hope from outward forms to win
> The passion and the life whose fountains are within.'
>
> Coleridge

THE SECRET AGENDA OF HAPPINESS

Joy and happiness are not the same thing but they are often confused. Joy is a form of grace which comes upon us when we are engaged in something. It can come in the most ghastly or depressing of outward circumstances. Happiness, on the other hand, is an emotion which is triggered by a favourable outward state of affairs. Joy is inner-directed and independent, happiness is outer-directed and dependent. We need both. Joy shows us our creative and transformative potential while happiness connects us in relationships to people and things in the world. All our goals, whether they be business or career related, or aimed at bringing about relationships, power, beauty, health, wealth, or personal development, have a secret agenda. We believe that when we attain them, we will be happy. This belief gives us the energy to pursue them.

By contrast, joy seems to strike us when we are in the process of an activity. It is related to the here-and-now whereas happiness is concerned with the future. Joy comes and goes and we cannot control it. All we can do is to open our hearts and our minds to its possibility. We will never stop longing for people and things to make us happy. That is part of the human condition but the cultivation of joy makes the quest for happiness more fun and more light-hearted. We can become less attached to our goals because we are enjoying the path to them more. Happiness is an all-or-nothing thing and can so easily be marred by one thing going wrong. If we are attuned to joy rather than happiness, then we won't regard things going wrong destructively. Instead, we'll see their potential for growth and change. We will no longer be ruled by the iron bands of our secret agenda but instead we will feel like flexible pieces of bamboo moving softly in the breeze of our life.

There is no direct route to either joy or happiness except through our attitudes. This is what the work of the previous chapters has been about. Through accepting our painful emotions and working creatively to transform them while at the same time allowing them to transform us, we may get many spontaneous experiences of joy. Although we can never control its occurrence, we can maximise our chances of joy by understanding more about how it occurs.

FLOW STATES

There are many words for the extreme forms of joy. In the Buddhist tradition, it is called bliss and is considered to be a natural state arising from non-attachment and compassion. Meditation is a way of attaining it. When a person is no longer bound by his desires or emotional needs, then life can be experienced as bliss. Many other religious practices bring about ecstasy, literally standing outside oneself. In ecstasy, we transcend time and space. The mundane everyday world with its pains, disappointments and difficulties drops away. People report that they feel connected with God, or with nature, or indeed with the whole cosmos. In these moments, an individual person senses they are an indissoluble part of a much greater whole.

Another route to ecstasy is orgasm and yet another way is to induce it through drugs. It's interesting that the major illegal 'social' drug of the nineties is called Ecstasy. The problem with drugs as a route to joy is that it creates an increasing dependence on the drug to produce the desired state. The essence of joy is that it is independent and free. If we don't get there under our steam, as it were, then we may have the experience but it will probably be accompanied by an anxious need to recreate it. We then start to plan to have this experience again rather than regarding it as a blessing. This is not true joy and does not ultimately liberate us.

Yet another term for extreme joy is flow state and much research, particularly in America, has been done on it. Flow states are characterised by an intense concentration, a loss of self-consciousness and an altered perception of the passage of time. Body chemistry appears to change and our immunological systems perform better. Athletes experience them, as do artists, and in fact almost all activities which are perceived as meaningful can yield flow experiences. Even people in positions of poverty, social deprivation or disability can experience flow. A blind telephonist could speak of her disability as a blessing as it had brought her to the work which for her was joy. Many highly skilled people report flow, such as pilots and surgeons. Flow requires the learning of skills, the setting of goals, the acceptance of parameters and boundaries. Chaos cannot bring about flow, there has to be an acceptance of order.

Between boredom and anxiety there is a channel in which flow can exist if we recognise it. When we are able to do a thing easily, it doesn't challenge us and we run the risk of becoming bored. On the other hand, when our skills fall too far short of the task, our anxiety is very high. Flow occurs at that moment when we can just about do something but it is still a challenge. The important thing to understand about flow is that it is not concerned with any hidden pay-offs or ultimate agendas; it is simply that the experience itself is the goal. Although sports, the arts, work and family life are all potential carriers of flow, so, too, is the practice of emotional intelligence.

WHAT STOPS US?

Flow is a delightful blessing which turns mere events into meaningful experiences. But many of us refuse it, denying that it exists. If we see no space between anxiety and boredom, then we will tend to close off the flow channel.

Letting go of our demands is another way to open the channel of flow. Marion Milner, in *A Life of One's Own*, reports an experience of flow when she was lying in bed, feeling ill and fretful. Looking vacantly at a faded cyclamen, she said to herself, 'I want nothing.' She writes of the experience that, 'Immediately I was so flooded with the crimson of the petals that I thought I had never known before what colour was.' The stimulus was faded and she was jaded but flow occurred when she gave up her expectation of what should be and allowed in what might be. Many people report that just saying the three words, 'I want nothing', to themselves can have a huge effect.

The following are the major blocks to flow:

- *Seeking for pleasure*

When we chase a specific pleasure, we focus on the outcome of the experience rather than its process. We demand that the experience yield us what we want rather than allow it to simply be. Hunting pleasure arouses both envy and greed, as well as fear and anxiety. As we start to want more, we notice less. Joy, which comes as the by-product of an activity, is ultimately more fulfilling.

- *Expecting permanence*

The essence of flow and joy is their transience. As we relinquish control, so we do not attempt to keep these visitors with us by force. As with human relationships, the more you let loved ones go, the more they seek you out. The paradox is that as we give up the idea of permanence, we tend to get the feeling of joy more and more. As Blake noted, 'He who kisses a joy as it flies, lives in eternity's sunrise.'

- *Refusal to accept reality*

Sometimes when a person has suffered greatly, they will refuse joy. By denying their current reality they are also denying the reality of a painful past. Disappointment can stunt our acceptance of the generosity of flow. The work of emotional intelligence can overcome this understandable pain. Reality also implies certain unalterable givens, such as gender, genetic inheritance, age etc. By accepting the things we cannot alter, we make possible the changes that we can bring about.

• *Fantasies*

Some of us decide what we want and then demand of life that it brings joy to us in the form we fantasise. We construct all sorts of fantasies and then feel very frustrated when they don't come about. We need to develop a critical and creative attitude to fantasy so that we can understand the emotional desire it masks. When we understand why we are fantasising a particular thing then we can start to focus on the emotional feeling we're seeking rather than on the specific outcome.

• *Social conditioning*

All societies have expectations about what their members should enjoy and strive for. These may be of a spiritual, material, educational or recreational nature. We may need to examine the beneath the surface assumptions of the society we live in and ask ourselves whether we agree with them. If we do not agree with them, then they will never satisfy us.

• *Inability to attend*

Flow is primarily to do with attention – the stretching forth of ourselves to something else. A lazy and passive attitude will not bring about flow but similarly neither will a desperate over-concentration. Flow seems to happen when we focus very hard on mastering something and then allow a creative pause as if we were waiting for an answer. Attention ensures that we will hear the answer – in whatever form it comes.

ATTENDING TO THE IMAGINATION

We cannot make flow and joy happen but we can provide the interior situations where they are most likely. As we have noted, there are attitudinal blocks which have to be overcome, or at least worked with, to facilitate the process. Beyond this, it's also worth looking at the nature of our attention. Attention is a harsh-sounding word, which many of us have heard as a command from our school days. But the root of the word deserves examination. It is derived from the same root as tend. So giving attention to something really means giving it our love and our care. Attention is like a lens: it can be tightly focused or more widely open and we need to become aware of what state our attention is in.

When attention is focused narrowly it is highly selective. We have decided what we want, e.g. food, shelter, employment or a mate, and we are looking specifically for it. Anything which falls outside the parameters we have set is discarded. It is obviously useful in terms of biology because this form of attention ensures our physical survival. In focused attention, the ego decides what is important and excludes the rest. It's a bit like a dog who is determined to follow one scent alone.

When our attention is more widely open, it is perceptive and tends to give everything it encounters equal value. We don't discriminate between one thing and another, there is no need to select an image or a sound or a smell. We allow ourselves to be flooded with whatever comes to us. Art is a very good training for this sort of attention because there are always surprises in a great work. In a painting for example, you may look and look and then suddenly notice a small cat. It has been 'hiding' in the shadow cast by the voluminous folds of a brocade curtain. Seeing the cat brings a shock of pleasure which upsets our ordered notions of the world. The ego has decided what the subject of the painting is – but suddenly it has changed. So the ego has to accept that although it is a leader, it does not dominate. In this form of attention, the ego becomes muted and the figures in the psyche can speak. This form of attention makes possible the work of the imagination. Imagination is simply the allowing of the glorious, terrifying and extraordinary possibilities of the current moment. At its height, the moment becomes linked with eternity.

The work of emotional intelligence demands both forms of attention. Many of the exercises in the chapters on emotions have required a focused attention. But to complete the work fully, we also need to let go this focus and allow our imagination to finish the work. Emotional intelligence is not an exact science and is perhaps not a science at all. It is rather a way of being which broadens and deepens our experience of life. Joy is truly an imaginary condition.

I would like to end this book by saying thank you to all of you who have read thus far. Imagining your participation in this work gave me the strength to write it. You may have gone through it with a fine-tooth comb and done all the exercises, or you may have dipped in here and there but, whatever you have done, it is a contribution towards world-wide emotional intelligence. If enough people do this work, a critical mass will be reached, and everyone will receive a benefit from it. As we approach the millennium, it may be your contribution or mine that tips the scale in favour of sanity, insight and joy.

Bibliography

This book is presented without footnotes and other academic paraphernalia, in order not to burden the reader with overmuch detail. But the ideas discussed here come from a wide range of sources. Suggestions for further reading as well as the debts owed to other writers and thinkers are listed below.

Beebe, John. *Integrity in Depth*, Fromm International Publishing, New York, 1995

Buber, Martin. *I and Thou*, T. and T. Clark, Edinburgh, 1958

Cameron, Julia. *The Artist's Way*, Pan, London, 1994

Cooper, Robert and Ayman, Sawaf. *Executive EQ: Emotional Intelligence in Business*, Orion Business Books, London, 1997

Cozens, Jenny. *OK2 Talk Feelings*, BBC Books, London, 1991

Csikszentmihalyi, Mihaly. *Flow – the Psychology of Happiness*, Routledge, London, 1992

Dowrick, Stephanie. *The Intimacy and Solitude Self-Therapy Book*, The Women's Press, London, 1993

Goleman, Daniel. *Emotional Intelligence*, Bloomsbury, London, 1996

Goleman, Daniel (edit). *Healing Emotions: Conversations with the Dalai Lama on Mindfulness, Emotions and Health*, Shambala, Boston and London, 1997

Gottman, John. *The Heart of Parenting*, Bloomsbury, London, 1997

Hillman, James. *Emotion*, Northwestern University Press, Evanston, Illinois, 1960
Hillman, James. *The Soul's Code*, Random House, New York, 1996
Hollis, James. *Swamplands of the Soul: New Life in Dismal Places*, Inner City Books, Toronto, Canada, 1996
Holmes, Ros and Jeremy. *The Good Mood Guide*, Orion Books, London, 1993
Johnson, Robert. *Owing your own Shadow*, Harper San Francisco, USA, 1991
Kast, Verena. *A Time to Mourn*, Daimon Verlag, Einsiedeln, Switzerland, 1993
Kast, Verena. *Joy, Inspiration and Hope*, Forum International Publishing, New York, 1991
Klein, Melanie. *Envy and Gratitude*, Vintage, London, 1997
LeDoux, Joseph. *The Emotional Brain*, Weidenfeld and Nicolson, London, 1998
Leonard, Linda Schierse. *On the Way to the Wedding*, Shambala, Boston and London, 1986
Lewis, C. S. *A Grief Observed*, Faber, London, 1961
Luke, Helen. *Dark Wood to White Rose: Journey and Transformation in Dante's* Divine Comedy, Parabola Books, New York, 1989
May, Rollo. *Freedom and Destiny*, Delta, New York, 1981
May, Rollo. *Love and Will*, Delta, New York, 1989
Milner, Marion. *A life of One's Own*, Virago, London, 1986
Milner, Marion. *Eternity's Sunrise: A Way of Keeping a Diary*, Virago, London, 1987
Perera, Sylvia. *The Scapegoat Complex: Toward a Mythology of Shadow and Guilt*, Inner City Books, Toronto, Canada, 1986
Person, Ethel. *The Force of Fantasy*, HarperCollins, London, 1997
Pert, Candace. *Molecules of Emotion: Why You Feel the Way You Feel*, Simon and Schuster, London, 1998
Rilke, Rainer Maria. *Selected Poetry*, Picador Classics, London, 1987
Rosen, David. *Transforming Depression*, Penguin Arkana, London, 1993
Rowe, Dorothy. *Beyond Fear*, HarperCollins, London, 1994
Rumi. *Daylight*, Threshold Books, Putney, Vermont, 1994

Steiner, Claude. *Achieving Emotional Literacy*, Bloomsbury, London, 1997

Storr, Anthony. *Human Aggression*, Penguin, London, 1968

Storr, Anthony. *Solitude*, Penguin, London, 1988

Tannen, Deborah. *You just don't understand: Men and Women in Conversation*, Virago, London, 1990

Tarnas, Richard. *The Passion of the Western Mind*, Pimlico, London, 1991

Von Franz, Marie-Louise. *Archetypal Patterns in Fairy Tales*, Inner City Books, Toronto, Canada, 1997

Von Franz, Marie-Louise. *The Golden Ass of Apuleius; the Liberation of the Feminine in Man*, Shambala, Boston and London, 1970

Yalom, Irvin. *Existential Psychotherapy*, Basic Books, USA, 1980

References for Chapter Quotations

William Blake in *The Complete Writings of William Blake* edited by G. Keynes (Random House)
Rainer Maria Rilke in *Letters to a Young Poet* (New World Library)
E. M. Forster in *Howards End* (Penguin)
Rumi in *Love is a Stranger* (Threshold Books)
Martin Luther King in *The Oxford Dictionary of Modern Quotations* (Oxford University Press)
Aristotle in *Living a Good Life: Advice on Virtue Love and Action from the Ancient Greek Masters* translated by Thomas Cleary (Shambala)
James Hollis in *Swamplands of the Soul: New Life in Dismal Places* (Inner City Books)
James Hillman in A *Blue Fire: the Essential James Hillman* edited by Thomas Moore (Routledge)
John Berryman in *The Oxford Dictionary of Modern Quotations* (Oxford University Press)
Chaucer in *Swamplands of the Soul: New Life in Dismal Places* by James Hollis (Inner City Books)
Eleanor Roosevelt in *The Oxford Dictionary of Modern Quotations* (Oxford University Press)
C. S. Lewis in *A Grief Observed* (Faber)

Doris Lessing in *The Grass is Singing* (Flamingo)
Hermann Hesse in *The Oxford Dictionary of Modern Quotations* (Oxford University Press)
Charles Revson in *The Oxford Dictionary of Modern Quotations* (Oxford University Press)
Viktor Frankl in *The Doctor and the Soul* (Vintage)
William Shakespeare in *Shakespeare's Guide to Life* (HarperCollins)
Sigmund Freud in *Civilisation and Its Discontents* (The Hogarth Press)
Samuel Taylor Coleridge in *Collected Poems* (Everyman)

BRITAIN ON THE COUCH

Oliver James

'Vital questions are explored in this stimulating tract for our times, which deserves to be widely read, especially by those who govern us' Anthony Storr

Why are we unhappier compared with 1950, despite being richer? Oliver James proves that we are and offers an original explanation of why, modern life does not meet our primeval needs. It makes us feel like losers, even if we are winners.

Oliver James shows that the way we live now, rather than genes, induces in our bodies low levels of the 'happiness brain chemical', serotonin. Depressed, violent and compulsive people all have low levels and he suggests that we can correct the chemical imbalance by psychotherapy as well as by taking pills, but that only changes in the way we are organised as a society will address the fundamental problem.

'Well worth reading… the author has recognised important social phenomena which have escaped less astute or honest observers.' *Sunday Telegraph*

'A fascinating book' Simon Jenkins, *Sunday Times*

'A number of compelling arguments' Tim Lott, *The Times*

'Oliver James offers a visionary overview of how the structure of our societies affect our minds and brains. He puts capitalism, with its polarising winner-loser psychology, in the dock as never before, finding that while it may be good for business it is bad for mental health. He presents a detailed map of the pathways to recovery from low serotonin for the individual and the community.' Paul Gilbert, Professor of Evolutionary Psychology, author of *Depression: the Evolution of Powerlessness*

THE ROAD LESS TRAVELLED

M. Scott Peck

A new psychology of love, traditional values and spiritual growth.

Confronting and solving problems is a painful process which most of us attempt to avoid. And the very avoidance results in greater pain and an inability to grow both mentally and spiritually. Drawing heavily on his own professional experience, Dr M. Scott Peck, a practising psychiatrist, suggests ways in which facing our difficulties – and suffering through the changes – can enable us to reach a higher level of self-understanding. He discusses the nature of loving relationships: how to recognize true compatability; how to distinguish dependecy from love: how to become one's own person and how to be a more sensitive parent.

This book is a phenomenon. Continuously on the US bestseller list for five years, it will change your life.

'Magnificent ... This is not just a book, but a spontaneous act of generosity written by an author who leans towards the reader for the purpose of sharing something larger than himself' – *Washington Post*

I'M OK – YOU'RE OK

Thomas A. Harris M. D.

I'm OK – You're OK
I'm not OK – You're not OK
I'm OK – You're not OK
I'm OK – You're OK

This practical guide to Transactional Analysis is a unique approach to your problems.

Hundreds of thousands of people have found this phenomenal breakthrough in psychotherapy a turning point in their lives.

In sensible non-technical language, Thomas Harris explains how to gain control of yourself, your relationships and your future – no matter what has happened in the past.